BANQ...
BLACK WIDOWERS

"*Banquets of the Black Widowers* is Asimov at his finest.... Asimov's humor, wisdom and puzzle-making (and solving) gives plenty of food for thought. It's a lot of fun."

The Chattanooga Times

"A delightful, amusing, intriguing group of stories."

Charleston Evening Post

"Asimov deftly blends P.G. Wodehouse bonhomie with Ellery Queen—type complexity in these generally nonviolent but engaging mysteries.

Booklist

BANQUETS OF THE BLACK WIDOWERS

Isaac Asimov

FAWCETT CREST • NEW YORK

A Fawcett Crest Book
Published by Ballantine Books
Copyright © 1984 by Nightfall, Inc.

Library of Congress Catalog Card Number: 84-1592

ISBN 0-449-20980-6

This edition published by arrangement with Doubleday and Company, Inc.

Printed in Canada

First Ballantine Books Edition: June 1986

To the memory of
Gilbert Cant
(1911–1982),
who was the inspiration
for Thomas Trumbull,
and
to the memory of.
Frederic Dannay
(1905–1982),
without whom it is unlikely
the Black Widowers stories
would ever have been written.

Contents

Introduction

This is the fourth book of the Black Widowers series and it comes after somewhat of a hiatus. The third book, *Casebook of the Black Widowers,* was published in 1980, so you can see it took me four years to write the dozen stories included herein.

This is rather more than it usually takes me to write a dozen stories if I set my mind to it, and there is an explanation. About four years ago, a magazine asked me to write a mystery for each of its issues, which meant twelve a year. They were to be only two thousand words long or so, and there was no question but that I could manage it—it amounted to only half a day a month—and it was the sort of challenge I rather liked.

So I did it and kept it going for over three years.

But there was a catch. Although the writing task was trivial, I did have to make up a gimmick a month. The stories were supposed to be puzzles with all the clues laid out for the readers, and you'd be surprised how much time it can take to invent a clever little twist. You might want to hang a story on the fact that a character is color-blind, but what can you do with that that hasn't already been done?

Well, I managed. I figured out ways to hide a package that was six feet tall and one inch thick so that it couldn't be found; and ways to tell whether a writer was really a writer just from the furnishings of his workroom; and so on.

And that meant I had trouble with my Black Widowers. Every time I wanted to think up an interesting plot for one of their banquets, I found that the twist I was going to use had to be used instead for one of my monthly yarns. The inexorable deadline was coming up and there was nothing I could do about it.

For a couple of years, therefore, I wrote hardly any Black Widowers stories. The result was that I began to get complaining letters from my readers who wanted to know what had gone wrong. That was gratifying, of course, because I couldn't help but be pleased by the numbers who insisted they couldn't live without them; but it also activated my feelings of guilt.

I did what I could. I took thirty of my small monthly stories and put them together in a book called *The Union Club Mysteries,* which Doubleday published in 1983, and of course it did well enough—but it wasn't quite the same thing.

And then, with no encouragement on my part, the magazine that printed my monthly stories changed its executive staff and I was told that I could stop writing them. I was rather relieved.

I instantly returned to my Black Widowers and now we have *Banquets of the Black Widowers* as a result. And I assure you I will keep on while life and health allow.

And for that matter, I won't cease my short Union Club mysteries either. I will write them, too, as the spirit moves me; and, in fact, I have sold four of them to *Ellery Queen's Mystery Magazine* so far. But now I don't have to write them every month, and I don't have to use up my entire supply of gimmickry on them.

Sixty Million Trillion Combinations

Since it was Thomas Trumbull who was going to act as host for the Black Widowers that month, he did not, as was his wont, arrive at the last minute, gasping for his preprandial drink.

There he was, having arrived in early dignity, conferring with Henry, that peerless waiter, on the details of the menu for the evening, and greeting each of the others as he arrived.

Mario Gonzalo, who arrived last, took off his light overcoat with care, shook it gently, as though to remove the dust of the taxicab, and hung it up in the cloakroom. He came back, rubbing his hands, and said, "There's an autumn chill in the air. I think summer's over."

"Good riddance," called out Emmanuel Rubin, from where he stood conversing with Geoffrey Avalon and James Drake.

"I'm not complaining," called back Gonzalo. Then, to Trumbull, "Hasn't your guest arrived yet?"

Trumbull said distinctly, as though tired of explaining, "I have not brought a guest."

"Oh?" said Gonzalo, blankly. There was nothing absolutely irregular about that. The rules of the Black Widowers did not require a guest, although not to have one was most unusual. "Well, I guess that's all right."

"It's more than all right," said Geoffrey Avalon, who had just drifted in their direction, gazing down from his straight-backed height of seventy-four inches. His thick graying eyebrows hunched over his eyes and he said, "At least that

1

guarantees us one meeting in which we can talk aimlessly and relax."

Gonzalo said, "I don't know about that. I'm used to the problems that come up. I don't think any of us will feel comfortable without one. Besides, what about Henry?"

He looked at Henry as he spoke and Henry allowed a discreet smile to cross his unlined, sixtyish face. "Please don't be concerned, Mr. Gonzalo. It will be my pleasure to serve the meal and attend the conversation even if there is nothing of moment to puzzle us."

"Well," said Trumbull, scowling, his crisply waved hair startlingly white over his tanned face, "you won't have that pleasure, Henry. I'm the one with the problem and I hope someone can solve it: *you* at least, Henry."

Avalon's lips tightened, "Now by Beelzebub's brazen bottom, Tom, you might have given us *one* old-fashioned—"

Trumbell shrugged and turned away, and Roger Halsted said to Avalon in his soft voice, "What's that Beelzebub bit? Where'd you pick that up?"

Avalon looked pleased. "Oh, well, Manny is writing some sort of adventure yarn set in Elizabeth's England— Elizabeth I of course—and it seems—"

Rubin, having heard the magic sound of his name, approached and said, "It's a sea story."

Halsted said, "Are you tired of mysteries?"

"It's a mystery also," said Rubin, his eyes flashing behind the thick lenses of his glasses. "What makes you think you can't have a mystery angle to *any* kind of story?"

"In any case," said Avalon, "Manny has one character forever swearing alliteratively and never the same twice and he needs a few more resounding oaths. Beelzebub's brazen bottom is good, I think."

"Or Mammon's munificent mammaries," said Halsted.

Trumbull said, violently, "There you are! If you don't come up with some problem that will occupy us in worthwhile fashion and engage our Henry's superlative mind, the whole evening would degenerate into stupid triplets—by Tutankhamen's tin trumpet.''

"It gets you after a while," grinned Rubin, unabashed.

"Well, get off it," said Trumbull. "Is dinner ready, Henry?"

"Yes it is, Mr. Trumbull."

"All right, then. If you idiots keep this alliteration up for more than two minutes, I'm walking out, host or no host."

The table seemed empty with only six about it, and conversation seemed a bit subdued with no guest to sparkle before.

Gonzalo, who sat next to Trumbull, said, "I ought to draw a cartoon of you for our collection since you're your own guest, so to speak." He looked up complacently at the long list of guest-caricatures that lined the wall in rank and file. "We're going to run out of space in a couple of years."

"Then don't bother with me," said Trumbull, sourly, "and we can always make space by burning those foolish scrawls."

"Scrawls!" Gonzalo seemed to debate within himself briefly concerning the possibility of taking offense. Then he compromised by saying, "You seem to be in a foul mood, Tom."

"I seem so because I am. I'm in the situation of the Chaldean wise men facing Nebuchadnezzar."

Avalon leaned over from across the table. "Are you talking about the Book of Daniel, Tom?"

"That's where it is, isn't it?"

Gonzalo said, "Pardon me, but I didn't have my Bible lesson yesterday. What are these wise men?"

"Tell him, Jeff," said Trumbull. "Pontificating is your job."

Avalon said, "It's not pontificating to tell a simple tale. If you would rather—"

Gonzalo said, "I'd rather you did, Jeff. You do it much more authoritatively."

"Well," said Avalon, "it's Rubin, not I, who was once a

boy preacher, but I'll do my poor best.—The second chapter of the Book of Daniel tells that Nebuchadnezzar was once troubled by a bad dream and he sent for his Chaldean wise men for an interpretation. The wise men offered to do so at once as soon as they heard the dream but Nebuchadnezzar couldn't remember the dream, only that he had been disturbed by it. He reasoned, however, that if wise men could interpret a dream, they could work out the dream, too, so he ordered them to tell him both the dream *and* the interpretation. When they couldn't do this, he very reasonably—by the standards of Oriental potentates—ordered them all killed. Fortunately for them Daniel, a captive Jew in Babylon, could do the job."

Gonzalo said, "And that's your situation, too, Tom?"

"In a way. I have a problem that involves a cryptogram—but I don't have the cryptogram. I have to work out the cryptogram."

"Or you'll be killed?" asked Rubin.

"No. If I fail, I won't be killed, but it won't do me any good, either."

Gonzalo said, "No wonder you didn't feel it necessary to bring a guest. Tell us about it."

"Before the brandy?" said Avalon, scandalized.

"Tom's host," said Gonzalo, defensively. "If he wants to tell us now—"

"I don't," said Trumbull. "We'll wait for the brandy as we always do, and I'll be my own griller, if you don't mind."

When Henry was pouring the brandy, Trumbull rang his spoon against his water glass and said, "Gentlemen, I will dispense with the opening question by admitting openly that I cannot justify my existence. Without pretending to go on by question-and-answer, I will simply state the problem. You are free to ask questions, but for God's sake, don't get me off on any wild-goose chases. This is serious."

Avalon said, "Go ahead, Tom. We will do our best to listen."

Trumbull said, with a certain weariness, "It involves a fellow named Pochik. I've got to tell you a little about him in order to let you understand the problem but, as is usual in these cases, I hope you don't mind if I tell you nothing that isn't relevant.

"In the first place he's from Eastern Europe, from someplace in Slovenia, I think, and he came here at about fourteen. He taught himself English, went to night school and to University Extension, working every step of the way. He worked as a waiter for ten years, while he was taking his various courses, and you know what that means.—Sorry, Henry."

Henry said, tranquilly, "It is not necessarily a pleasant occupation. Not everyone waits on the Black Widowers, Mr. Trumbull."

"Thank you, Henry. That's very diplomatic of you.—However, he wouldn't have made it, if it weren't plain from the start that he was a mathematical wizard. He was the kind of young man that no mathematics professor in his right mind wouldn't have moved heaven and earth to keep in school. He was their claim to a mark in the history books—that they had taught Pochik. Do you understand?"

Avalon said, "We understand, Tom."

Trumbull said, "At least, that's what they tell me. He's working for the government now, which is where I come in. They tell me he's something else. They tell me he's in a class by himself. They tell me he can do things no one else can. They tell me they've got to have him. I don't even know what he's working on, but they've got to have him."

Rubin said, "Well, they've got him, haven't they? He hasn't been kidnapped and hijacked back across the Iron Curtain, has he?"

"No, no," said Trumbull, "nothing like that. It's a lot more irritating. Look, apparently a great mathematician can be an idiot in every other respect."

"Literally an idiot?" asked Avalon. "Usually idiots savants have remarkable memories and can play remarkable tricks in computation, but that is far from being any kind of mathematician, let alone a great one."

"No, nothing like that, either." Trumbull was perspiring and paused to mop at his forehead. "I mean he's childish. He's not really learned in anything but mathematics and that's all right. Mathematics is what we want out of him. The trouble is that he feels backward; he feels stupid. Damn it, he feels inferior, and when he feels *too* inferior, he stops working and hides in his room."

Gonzalo said, "So what's the problem? Everyone just has to keep telling him how great he is all the time."

"He's dealing with other mathematicians and they're almost as crazy as he is. One of them, Sandino, hates being second best and every once in a while he gets Pochik into a screaming fit. He's got a sense of humor, this Sandino, and he likes to call out to Pochik, 'Hey, waiter, bring the check.' Pochik can't ever learn to take it."

Drake said, "Read this Sandino the riot act. Tell him you'll dismember him if he tries anything like that again."

"They did," said Trumbull, "or at least as far as they quite dared to. They don't want to lose Sandino either. In any case, the horseplay stopped but something much worse happened.—You see there's something called, if I've got it right, 'Goldbach's conjecture.'"

Roger Halsted galvanized into a position of sharp interest at once. "Sure," he said. "Very famous."

"You know about it?" said Trumbull.

Halsted stiffened. "I may just teach algebra to junior high school students, but yes, I know about Goldbach's conjecture. Teaching a junior high school student doesn't *make* me a junior—"

"All right. I apologize. It was stupid of me," said Trumbull. "And since you're a mathematician, you can be temperamental too. Anyway, can you explain Goldbach's conjecture?—Because I'm not sure I can."

"Actually," said Halsted, "it's very simple. Back in 1742, I think, a Russian mathematician, Christian Goldbach, stated that he believed every even number greater than 2 could be written as the sum of two primes, where a prime is any number that can't be divided evenly by any other number but itself and 1. For instance, $4 = 2 + 2$; $6 = 3 + 3$; $8 = 3 + 5$; $10 = 3 + 7$; $12 = 5 + 7$; and so on, as far as you want to go."

Gonzalo said, "So what's the big deal?"

"Goldbach wasn't able to prove it. And in the two hundred and something years since his time, neither has anyone else. The greatest mathematicians haven't been able to show that it's true."

Gonzalo said, "So?"

Halsted said patiently, "Every even number that has ever been checked always works out to be the sum of two primes. They've gone awfully high and mathematicians are convinced the conjecture is true—but no one can *prove* it."

Gonzalo said, "If they can't find any exceptions, doesn't *that* prove it?"

"No, because there are always numbers higher than the highest we've checked, and besides we don't know all the prime numbers and can't, and the higher we go, then the harder it is to tell whether a particular number is prime or not. What is needed is a *general* proof that tells us we don't have to look for exceptions because there just aren't any. It bothers mathematicians that a problem can be stated so simply and seems to work out, too, and yet that it can't be proved."

Trumbull had been nodding his head. "All right, Roger, all right. We get it. But tell me, does it *matter*? Does it really matter to anyone who isn't a mathematician whether Goldbach's conjecture is true or not; whether there are any exceptions or not?"

"No," said Halsted. "Not to anyone who isn't a mathematician; but to anyone who is and who manages either to prove or disprove Goldbach's conjecture, there is an immediate and permanent niche in the mathematical hall of fame."

Trumbull shrugged. "There you are. What Pochik's really doing is of great importance. I'm not sure whether it's for the Department of Defense, the Department of Energy, NASA, or what, but it's vital. What *he's* interested in, however, is Goldbach's conjecture, and for that he's been using a computer."

"To try higher numbers?" asked Gonzalo.

Halsted said promptly, "No, that would do no good. These days, though, you can use computers on some pretty recalcitrant problems. It doesn't yield an elegant solution, but it is a solution. If you can reduce a problem to a finite number of possible situations—say, a million—you can program a computer to try every one of them. If every one of them checks out as it's supposed to, then you have your proof. They recently solved the four-color mapping problem that way; a problem as well known and as recalcitrant as Goldbach's conjecture."

"Good," said Trumbull, "then that's what Pochik's been doing. Apparently, he had worked out the solution to a particular lemma. Now what's a lemma?"

Halsted said, "It's a partway solution. If you're climbing a mountain peak and you set up stations at various levels, the lemmas are analogous to those stations and the solution to the mountain peak."

"If he solves the lemma, will he solve the conjecture?"

"Not necessarily," said Halsted, "any more than you'll climb the mountain if you reach a particular station on the slopes. But if you *don't* solve the lemma, you're not likely to solve the problem, at least not from that direction."

"All right, then," said Trumbull, sitting back. "Well, Sandino came up with the lemma first and sent it in for publication."

Drake was bent over the table, listening closely. He said, "Tough luck for Pochik."

Trumbull said, "Except that Pochik says it wasn't luck. He claims Sandino doesn't have the brains for it and couldn't have taken the steps he did independently; that it is asking too much of coincidence."

Drake said, "That's a serious charge. Has Pochik got any evidence?"

"No, of course not. The only way that Sandino could have stolen it from Pochik would have been to tap the computer for Pochik's data and Pochik himself says Sandino couldn't have done that."

"Why not?" said Avalon.

"Because," said Trumbull, "Pochik used a code word. The code word has to be used to alert the computer to a particular person's questioning. Without that code word, everything that went in *with* the code is safely locked away."

Avalon said, "It could be that Sandino learned the code word."

"Pochik says that is impossible," said Trumbull. "He was afraid of theft, particularly with respect to Sandino, and he never wrote down the code word, never used it except when he was alone in the room. What's more, he used one that was fourteen letters long, he says. Millions of trillions of possibilities, he says. No one could have guessed it, he says."

Rubin said, "What does Sandino say?"

"He says he worked it out himself. He rejects the claim of theft as the ravings of a madman. Frankly, one could argue that he's right."

Drake said, "Well, let's consider. Sandino is a good mathematician and he's innocent till proven guilty. Pochik has nothing to support his claim and Pochik actually denies that Sandino could possibly have gotten the code word, which is the only way the theft could possibly have taken place. I think Pochik has to be wrong and Sandino right."

Trumbull said, "I *said* one could argue that Sandino's right, but the point is that Pochik won't work. He's sulking in his room and reading poetry and he says he will never work again. He says Sandino has robbed him of his immortality and life means nothing to him without it."

Gonzalo said, "If you need this guy so badly can you talk Sandino into letting him have his lemma?"

"Sandino won't make the sacrifice and we can't make him unless we have reason to think that fraud was involved.

If we get any evidence to that effect we can lean on him hard enough to squash him flat.—But now listen, I think it's possible Sandino *did* steal it."

Avalon said, "How?"

"By getting the code word. If I knew what the code word was, I'm sure I could figure out a logical way in which Sandino could have found it out or guessed it. Pochik, however simply won't let me have the code word. He shrieked at me when I asked. I explained why, but he said it was impossible. He said Sandino did it some other way— but there is no other way."

Avalon said, "Pochik wants an interpretation but he won't tell you the dream, and you have to figure out the dream first and then get the interpretation."

"Exactly! Like the Chaldean wise men."

"What are you going to do?"

"I'm going to try to do what Sandino must have done. I'm going to try to figure out what the fourteen-letter code word was and present it to Pochik. If I'm right, then it will be clear that what I could do, Sandino could do, and that the lemma was very likely stolen."

There was a silence around the table and then Gonzalo said, "Do you think you can do it, Tom?"

"I don't think so. That's why I've brought the problem here. I want us all to try. I told Pochik I would call him before 10:30 P.M. tonight"—Trumbull looked at his watch—"with the code word just to show him it *could* be broken. I presume he's waiting at the phone."

Avalon said, "And if we don't get it?"

"Then we have no reasonable way of supposing the lemma was stolen and no really ethical way of trying to force it away from Sandino. But at least we'll be no worse off."

Avalon said, "Then you go first. You've clearly been thinking about it longer than we have, and it's your line of work."

Trumbull cleared his throat. "All right. My reasoning is that if Pochik doesn't write the thing down, then he's got to remember it. There are some people with trick memories and such a talent is fairly common among mathematicians. However, even great mathematicians don't always have the ability to remember long strings of disjointed symbols and, upon questioning of his coworkers, it would seem quite certain that Pochik's memory is an ordinary one. He can't rely on being able to remember the code unless it's easy to remember.

"That would limit it to some common phrase or some regular progression that you couldn't possibly forget. Suppose it were ALBERT EINSTEIN, for instance. That's fourteen letters and there would be no fear of forgetting it. Or SIR ISAAC NEWTON, or ABCDEFGHIJKLMN, or, for that matter, NMLKJIHGFEDCBA. If Pochik tried something like this, it could be that Sandino tried various obvious combinations and one of them worked."

Drake said, "If that's true, then we haven't a prayer of solving the problem. Sandino might have tried any number of different possibilities over a period of months. One of them finally worked. If he got it by hit-and-miss over a long time, we have no chance in getting the right one in an hour and a half, without even trying any of them on the computer."

"There's that, of course," said Trumbull, "and it may well be that Sandino had been working on the problem for months. Sandino pulled the waiter routine on Pochik last June, and Pochik, out of his mind, screamed at him that he would show him when his proof was ready. Sandino may have put this together with Pochik's frequent use of the computer and gotten to work. He may have had months, at that."

"Did Pochik say something on that occasion that gave the code word away?" asked Avalon.

"Pochik swears all he said was 'I'll show you when the proof is ready,' but who knows? Would Pochik remember his own exact words when he was beside himself?"

Halsted said, "I'm surprised that Pochik didn't try to beat up this Sandino."

Trumbull said, "You wouldn't be surprised if you knew them. Sandino is built like a football player and Pochik weighs 110 pounds with his clothes on."

Gonzalo said, suddenly, "What's this guy's first name?"

Trumbull said, "Vladimir."

Gonzalo paused a while, with all eyes upon him, and then he said, "I knew it. VLADIMIR POCHIK has fourteen letters. He used his own name."

Rubin said, "Ridiculous. It would be the first combination anyone would try."

"Sure, the purloined letter bit. It would be so obvious that no one would think to use it. Ask him."

Trumbull shook his head. "No. I can't believe he'd use that."

Rubin said, thoughtfully, "Did you say he was sitting in his room reading poetry?"

"Yes."

"Is that a passion of his? Poetry? I thought you said that outside mathematics he was not particularly educated."

Trumbull said, sarcastically, "You don't have to be a Ph.D. to read poetry."

Avalon said, mournfully, "You would have to be an idiot to read modern poetry."

"That's a point," said Rubin. "Does Pochik read contemporary poetry?"

Trumbull said, "It never occurred to me to ask. When I visited him, he was reading from a book of Wordsworth's poetry, but that's all I can say."

"That's enough," said Rubin. "If he likes Wordsworth then he doesn't like contemporary poetry. No one can read that fuddy-duddy for fun and like the stuff they turn out these days."

"So? What difference does it make?" asked Trumbull.

"The older poetry with its rhyme and rhythm is easy to remember and it could make for code words. The code word could be a fourteen-letter passage from one of Wordsworth's poems, possibly a common one: LONELY AS A CLOUD has fourteen letters. Or any fourteen-letter combinations from such lines as 'The child is father of the man' or 'trailing clouds of glory' or 'Milton! thou shouldst be living at this hour.'—Or maybe from some other poet of the type."

Avalon said, "Even if we restrict ourselves to passages from the classic and romantic poets, that's a huge field to guess from."

Drake said, "I repeat. It's an impossible task. We don't have the time to try them all. And we can't tell one from another without trying."

Halsted said, "It's even more impossible than you think, Jim. I don't think the code word was in English words."

Trumbull said, frowning, "You mean he used his native language?"

"No, I mean he used a random collection of letters. You say that Pochik said the code word was unbreakable because there were millions of trillions of possibilities in a fourteen-letter combination. Well, suppose that the first letter could be any of the twenty-six, and the second letter could be any of the twenty-six, and the third letter, and so on. In that case the total number of combinations would be $26 \times 26 \times 26$, and so on. You would have to get the product of fourteen 26's multiplied together and the result would be"—he took out his pocket calculator and manipulated it for a while— "about 64 million trillion different possibilities.

"Now, if you used an English phrase or a phrase in any reasonable European language, most of the letter combinations simply don't occur. You're not going to have an HGF or a QXZ or an LLLLC. If we include only *possible* letter combinations in words then we might have trillions of possibilities, probably less, but certainly not millions of trillions. Pochik, being a mathematician, wouldn't say millions of trillions unless he meant exactly that, so I expect the code word is a random set of letters."

Trumbull said, "He doesn't have the kind of memory—"

Halsted said, "Even a normal memory will handle fourteen random letters if you stick to it long enough."

Gonzalo said, "Wait awhile. If there are only so many

combinations, you could use a computer. The computer could try every possible combination and stop at the one that unlocks it."

Halsted said, "You don't realize how big a number like 64 million trillion really is, Mario. Suppose you arranged to have the computer test a billion different combinations every second. It would take two thousand solid years of work, day and night, to test all the possible combinations."

Gonzalo said, "But you wouldn't have to test them all. The right one might come up in the first two hours. Maybe the code was AAAAAAAAAAAAAA and it happened to be the first one the computer tried."

"Very unlikely," said Halsted. "He wouldn't use a solid-A code any more than he would use his own name. Besides Sandino is enough of a mathematician not to start a computer attempt he would know could take a hundred lifetimes."

Rubin said, thoughtfully, "If he did use a random code I bet it wasn't truly random."

Avalon said, "How do you mean, Manny?"

"I mean if he doesn't have a superlative memory and he didn't write it down, how could he go over and over it in his mind in order to memorize it? Just repeat fourteen random letters to yourself and see if you can be confident of repeating them again in the exact order immediately afterward. And even if he *had* worked out a random collection of letters and managed to memorize it, it's clear he had very little self-confidence in anything except mathematical reasoning. Could he face the possibility of not being able to retrieve his own information because he had forgotten the code?"

"He could start all over," said Trumbull.

"With a new random code? And forget that, too?" said Rubin. "No. Even if the code word seems random, I'll bet Pochik has some foolproof way of remembering it, and if we can figure out the foolproof way, we'd have the answer. In fact, if Pochik would give us the code word, we'd see how he memorized it and see how Sandino broke the code."

Trumbull said, "And if Nebuchadnezzar would only have remembered the dream, the wise men could have interpreted it. Pochik won't give us the code word, and if we work it with hindsight, we'll never be sufficiently sure Sandino cracked it without hindsight.—All right, we'll have to give it up."

"It may not be necessary to give it up," said Henry, suddenly. "I think—"

All turned to Henry, expectantly. "Yes, Henry," said Avalon.

"I have a wild guess. It may be all wrong. Perhaps it might be possible to call up Mr. Pochik, Mr. Trumbull, and ask him if the code word is WEALTMDITEBIAT," said Henry.

Trumbull said, *"What?"*

Halsted said, his eyebrows high, "That's some wild guess, all right. Why that?"

Gonzalo said, "It makes no sense."

No one could recall ever having seen Henry blush, but he was distinctly red now. He said, "If I may be excused. I don't wish to explain my reasoning until the combination is tried. If I am wrong, I would appear too foolish.—And, on second thought, I don't urge it be tried."

Trumbull said, "No, we have nothing to lose. Could you write down that letter combination, Henry?"

"I have already done so, sir."

Trumbull looked at it, walked over to the phone in the corner of the room, and dialled. He waited for four rings, which could be clearly heard in the breath-holding silence of the room. There was then a click, and a sharp, high-pitched "Hello?"

Trumbull said, "Dr. Pochik? Listen. I'm going to read some letters to you—No, Dr. Pochik, I'm not saying I've worked out the code. This is an exper— It's an experiment sir. We may be wrong—No, I can't say how—Listen, W, E, A, L— Oh, good God." He placed his hand over the mouthpiece. "The man is having a fit."

"Because it's right or because it's wrong?" asked Rubin.

"I don't know." Trumbull put the phone back to his ear. "Dr. Pochik, are you there?—Dr. Pochik?—The rest is"— he consulted the paper—"T, M, D, I, T, E, B, I, A, T." He listened. "Yes, sir, I think Sandino cracked it, too, the same way we did. We'll have a meeting with you and Dr. Sandino, and we'll settle everything. Yes—please, Dr. Pochik, we will do our best."

Trumbull hung up, heaved an enormous sigh, then said, "Sandino is going to think Jupiter fell on him.—All right, Henry, but if you don't tell us how you got that, you won't have to wait for Jupiter. I will kill you personally."

"No need, Mr. Trumbull," said Henry. "I will tell you at once. I merely listened to all of you. Mr. Halsted pointed out it would have to be some random collection of letters. Mr. Rubin said, backing my own feeling in the matter, that there had to be some system of remembering in that case. Mr. Avalon, early in the evening, was playing the game of alliterative oaths, which pointed up the importance of initial letters. You yourself mentioned Mr. Pochik's liking for old-fashioned poetry like that of Wordsworth.

"It occurred to me then that fourteen was the number of lines in a sonnet, and if we took the initial letters of each line of some sonnet we would have an apparently random collection of fourteen letters that could not be forgotten as long as the sonnet was memorized or could, at worst, be looked up.

"The question was: which sonnet? It was very likely to be a well-known one, and Wordsworth had written some that were. In fact, Mr. Rubin mentioned the first line of one of them: 'Milton! thou shouldst be living at this hour.' That made me think of Milton, and it came to me that it *had* to be his sonnet 'On His Blindness' which as it happens, *I* know by heart. Please note the first letters of the successive lines. It goes:

"When I consider how my light is spent
Ere half my days, in this dark world and wide,
And that one talent which is death to hide,

Lodged with me useless, though my soul more bent
To serve therewith my Maker, and present
My true account, lest he returning chide;
'Doth God exact day-labor, light denied?'
I fondly ask; But Patience, to prevent
That murmur, soon replies, 'God doth not need
Either man's work or his own gifts; who best
Bear his mild yoke, they serve him best. His state
Is kingly. Thousands at his bidding speed
And post o'er land and ocean without rest: . . . .'"

Henry paused and said softly, "I think it is the most beautiful sonnet in the language, Shakespeare's not excepted, but that was not the reason I felt it must hold the answer. It was that Dr. Pochik had been a waiter and was conscious of it, and I am one, which is why I have memorized the sonnet. A foolish fancy, no doubt, but the last line, which I have not quoted, and which is perhaps among the most famous lines Milton ever constructed—"

"Go ahead, Henry," said Rubin. "Say it!"

"Thank you, sir," said Henry, and then he said, solemnly,

" 'They also serve who only stand and wait.' "

Afterword

I have a feeling that titles are an important part of a story and I take considerable care in choosing one. In fact, I cannot start a story until I have chosen a title.

However, I don't follow certain clever rules in making the choice. I don't really know what makes a title good—or the reverse. It's just a gut feeling with me. I pick one that seems to suit the story, and even add to it.

And often Fred Dannay, the editor of *EQMM*, would disagree with me—and I would then disagree with him and restore my own title when I put the story into a collection.

On the other hand, sometimes Fred would choose a title that is an improvement (or so it would seem to me) and, since I am not a willfully stubborn man, I would go along with him.

For instance, I called the story you have just finished "Fourteen Letters" which is, after all, what it's about; but Fred, when it appeared in the May 5, 1980, issue of *EQMM*, called it "Sixty Million Trillion Combinations," which is also what it's about; and Fred's is infinitely more dramatic so I accepted it—with my usual annoyance at myself for not having thought of it to begin with.

The Woman in the Bar

The hits and outs of baseball did not, as a rule, disturb the equanimity (or lack of it) of a Black Widowers banquet. None of the Black Widowers were sportsmen in the ordinary sense of the word, although Mario Gonzalo was known to bet on the horses on occasion.

Over the rack of lamb, however, Thomas Trumbull brushed at his crisply waved white hair, looked stuffily discontented, and said, "I've lost all interest in baseball. Once they started shifting franchises, they broke up the kind of loyalties you inherited from your father. I was a New Yorks Giants fan when I was a young man, as was my father before me. The San Francisco Giants were strangers to me and as for the Mets, well, they're just not the same."

"There are still the New York Yankees," said Geoffrey Avalon, deftly cutting meat away from bone and bending his dark eyebrows in concentration on the task, "and in my own town, we still have the Phillies, though we lost the Athletics."

"Chicago still has both its teams," said Mario Gonzalo, "and there are still the Cleveland Indians, the Cincinnati Reds, the St. Louis—"

"It's not the same," said Trumbull, violently. "Even if I were to switch to the Yankees, half the teams they play are teams Lou Gehrig and Bill Dickey never heard of. And now you have each league in two divisions, with playoffs before the World Series, which becomes almost anticlimactic, and a batting average of .290 marks a slugger. Hell, I remember when you needed .350 if you were to stand a chance at cleanup position."

Emmanuel Rubin listened with the quiet dignity he considered suitable to his position as host—at least until his guest turned to him and said, "Is Trumbull a baseball buff, Manny?"

At that, Rubin reverted to his natural role and snorted loudly. His sparse beard bristled. "Who, Tom? He may have watched a baseball game on TV, but that's about it. He thinks a double is two jiggers of Scotch."

Gonzalo said, "Come on, Manny, you think a pitcher holds milk."

Rubin stared at him fixedly through his thick-lensed spectacles, and then said, "It so happens I played a season of semi-pro baseball as shortstop in the late 1930s."

"And a shorter stop—" began Gonzalo and then stopped and reddened.

Rubin's guest grinned. Though Rubin was only five inches above the five-foot mark, the guest fell three inches short of that. He said, "I'd be a shorter stop if I played."

Gonzalo, with a visible attempt to regain his poise, said, "You're harder to pitch to when you're less than average height, Mr. Just. There's that."

"You're heavily underestimated in other ways, too, which is convenient at times," agreed Just. "And, as a matter of fact, I'm not much of a baseball buff myself. I doubt if I could tell a baseball from a golf ball in a dim light."

Darius Just looked up sharply at this point. "Waiter," he said, "if you don't mind, I'll have milk rather than coffee."

James Drake, waiting expectantly for his own coffee, said, "Is that just a momentary aberration, Mr. Just, or don't you drink coffee?"

"Don't drink it," said Just. "Or smoke, or drink alcohol. My mother explained it all to me very carefully. If I drank my milk and avoided bad habits, I would grow to be big and strong; so I did—and I didn't. At least, not big. I'm strong enough. It's all very un-American, I suppose, like not liking baseball. At least you can fake liking baseball, though that can get you in trouble, too.—Here's the milk. How did that get there?"

Gonzalo smiled. "That's our Henry. Noiseless and efficient."

Just sipped his milk contentedly. His facial features were small but alive and his eyes seemed restlessly aware of everything in the room. His shoulders were broad, as though they had been made for a taller man, and he carried himself like an athlete.

Drake sat over his coffee, quiet and thoughtful, but when Rubin clattered his water glass with his spoon, the quiet ended. Drake's hand was raised and he said, "Manny, may I do the honors?"

"If you wish." Rubin turned to his guest. "Jim is one of the more reserved Black Widowers, Darius, so you can't expect his grilling to be a searching one. In fact, the only reason he's volunteering is that he's written a book himself and he wants to rub shoulders with other writers."

Just's eyes twinkled with interest. "What kind of a book, Mr. Drake?"

"Pop science," said Drake, "but the questions go the other way.—Henry, since Mr. Just doesn't drink, could you substitute ginger ale for the brandy. I don't want him to be at a disadvantage."

"Certainly, Mr. Drake," murmured Henry, that miracle of waiters, "if Mr. Just would like that. With all due respect, however, it does not seem to me that Mr. Just is easily placed at a disadvantage."

"We'll see," said Drake, darkly. "Mr. Just, how do you justify your existence?"

Just laughed. "It justifies itself to me now and then when it fills me with gladness. As far as justification to the rest of the world is concerned, that can go hang.—With all due respect, as Henry would say."

"Perhaps," said Drake, "the world will go hang even without your permission. For the duration of this evening, however, you must justify your existence to *us* by answering our questions. Now I have been involved with the Black Widowers for more than half of a reasonably lengthy existence and I can smell out remarks that are worth elaboration. You said that you could get in trouble if you faked the liking of baseball. I suspect you did once, and I would like to hear about it."

Just looked surprised, and Rubin said, staring at his brandy, "I warned you, Darius."

"You know the story, do you, Manny?" said Drake.

"I know there is one but I don't know the details," said Rubin. "I warned Darius we'd have it out of him."

Just picked up the caricature Mario Gonzalo had drawn of him. There was a face-splitting grin on it and arms with prodigious biceps were lifting weights.

"I'm not a weight lifter," he said.

"It doesn't matter," said Gonzalo. "That is how I see you."

"Weight lifting," said Just, "slows you. The successful attack depends entirely on speed."

"You're not being speedy answering my request," said Drake, lighting a cigarette.

"There *is* a story," said Just.

"Good," said Drake.

"But it's an unsatisfactory one. I can't supply any rationale, any explanation—"

"Better and better. Please begin."

"Very well," said Just—

"I like to walk. It's an excellent way of keeping in condition and one night I had made my goal the new apartment of a friend I hadn't seen in a while. I was to be there at 9 P.M., and it was a moderately long walk by night, but I don't much fear the hazards of city streets in the dark though I admit I do not seek out particularly dangerous neighborhoods.

"However, I was early and a few blocks from my destination, I stopped at a bar. As I said, I don't drink, but

I'm not an absolute fanatic about it and I will, on rare occasions, drink a Bloody Mary.

"There was a baseball game on the TV when I entered, but the sound was turned low, which suited me. There weren't many people present, which also suited me. There were two men at a table against the wall, and a woman on a stool at the bar itself.

"I took the stool next but one to the woman, and glanced at her briefly after I ordered my drink. She was reasonably pretty, reasonably shapely, and entirely interesting. Pretty and shapely is all right—what's not to like—but interesting goes beyond that and it can't be described easily. It's different for each person, and she was interesting in my frame of reference.

"Among my abstentions, women are not included. I even speculated briefly if it were absolutely necessary that I keep my appointment with my friend, who suffered under the disadvantage, under the circumstances, of being male.

"I caught her eye just long enough before looking away. Timing is everything and I am not without experience. Then I looked up at the TV and watched for a while. You don't want to seem too eager.

"She spoke. I was rather surprised. I won't deny I have a way with women, despite my height, but my charm doesn't usually work *that* quickly. She said, 'You seem to understand the game.' It was just make-talk. She couldn't possibly know my relationship with baseball from my glazed-eye stare at the set.

"I turned, smiled, and said, 'Second nature. I live and breathe it.'

"It was a flat lie, but if a woman leads, you go along with the lead.

"She said, rather earnestly, 'You really understand it?' She was looking into my eyes as though she expected to read the answer on my retina.

"I continued to follow and said, 'Dear, there isn't a move in the game I can't read the motivations of. Every toss of the ball, every crack of the bat, every stance of the fielder, is a note in a symphony I can hear in my head.' After all, I'm a writer; I can lay it on.

"She looked puzzled. She looked at me doubtfully; then, briefly, at the men at the table. I glanced in their direction, too. They didn't seem interested—until I noticed their eyes in the wall mirror. They were watching our reflection.

"I looked at her again and it was like a kaleidoscope shifting and suddenly making sense. She wasn't looking for a pickup, she was scared. It was in her breathing rate and in the tension of her hands.

"And she thought I was there to help her. She was expecting someone and she had spoken to me with that in mind. What I answered was close enough—by accident—to make her think I might be the man, but not close enough to make her sure of it.

"I said, 'I'm leaving soon. Do you want to come along?' It sounded like a pickup, but I was offering to protect her if that was what she wanted. What would happen afterward—well, who could tell?

"She looked at me unenthusiastically. I knew the look. It said: 'You're five-foot-two; what can you do for me?'

"It's a chronic underestimate that plays into my hands. Whatever I do do is so much more than they expect that it assumes enormous proportions. I'm the beneficiary of a low baseline.

"I smiled. I looked in the direction of the two men at the table, looked back, let my smile widen and said, 'Don't worry.'

"There were containers of cocktail amenities just behind the bar where she sat. She reached over for the maraschino cherries, took a handful and twisted the stems off; then one by one flicked them broodingly toward me, keeping her eyes fixed on mine.

"I didn't know what her game was. Perhaps she was just considering whether to take a chance on me and this was a nervous habit she always indulged in when at a bar. But I always say: Play along.

"I had caught four and wondered how many she would

flick at me, and when the barman would come over to rescue his supply, when my attention shifted.

"One of the men who had been seated was now between the woman and myself, and was smiling at me without humor. I had been unaware of his coming. I was caught like an amateur, and the kaleidoscope suddenly shifted again. That's the trouble with kaleidoscopes. They keep shifting.

"Sure the woman was afraid. She wasn't afraid of the men at the table. She was afraid of *me*. She didn't think I was a possible rescuer; she thought I was a possible spoiler. So she kept my attention riveted while one of her friends got in under my guard—and I had let it happen.

"I shifted my attention to the man now, minutes after I should have done so. He had a moon face, dull eyes, and a heavy hand. That heavy hand, his right one, rested on my hand on the bar, pinning it down immovably.

"He said, 'I think you're annoying the lady, chum.'

"He underestimated me, too; took me for what I was not.

"You see, I've never been any taller than I am now. When I was young I was, in point of fact, smaller and slighter. When I was nineteen, I would have had to gain five pounds to be a ninety-six-pound weakling.

"The result you can guess. The chivalry and sportsmanship of young people is such that I was regularly beaten up to the cheers of the multitude. I did not find it inspiring.

"From nineteen on, therefore, I was subscribing to build-yourself-up courses. I struggled with chest expanders. I took boxing lessons at the Y. Bit by bit, I've studied every one of the martial arts. It didn't make me any taller, not one inch, but I grew wider and thicker and stronger. Unless I run into a brigade, or a gun, I don't get beaten up.

"So the fact that my left arm was pinned did not bother me. I said, 'Friend, I don't like having a man hold my hand, so I think I will have to ask you to remove it.' I had my own right hand at eye level, palm up, something that might have seemed a gesture of supplication.

"He showed his teeth and said, 'Don't ask anything, pal. *I'll* ask.'

"He had his chance. You must understand that I don't fight to kill, but I do fight to maim. I'm not interested in breaking a hold; I want to be sure there won't be another one.

"My hand flashed across between us. Speed is of the essence, gentlemen, and my nails scraped sideways across his throat en route, as the arc of my hand brought its edge down upon his wrist. *Hard!*

"I doubt that I broke his wrist that time, but it would be days, perhaps weeks, before he would be able to use that hand on someone else as he had on me. My hand was free in a moment. The beauty of the stroke, however, was that he could not concentrate on the smashed wrist. His throat had to be burning and he had to be able to feel the stickiness of blood there. It was just a superficial wound, literally a scratch, but it probably frightened him more than the pain in his wrist did.

"He doubled up, his left hand on his throat, his right arm dangling. He was moaning.

"It was all over quickly, but time was running out. The second man was approaching, so was the bartender, and a newcomer was in the doorway. He was large and wide and I was in no doubt that he was a member of the charming group I had run into.

"The risks were piling up and the fun flattening out, so I walked out rapidly—right past the big fellow, who didn't react quickly enough, but stood there, confused and wondering, for the five seconds I needed to push past and out.

"I didn't think they'd report the incident to the police, somehow. Nor did I think I'd be followed, but I waited for a while to see. I was on a street with row houses, each with its flight of steps leading to the main door well above street level. I stepped into one of the yards and into the shadow near the grillwork door at the basement level of a house that had no lights showing.

"No one came out of the barroom. They weren't after me. They weren't sure who I was and they still couldn't believe that anyone as short as I was could be dangerous. It was the providential underestimate that had done well for me countless times.

"So I moved briskly along on my original errand, listening for the sound of footsteps behind me or the shifting of shadows cast by the streetlights.

"I wasn't early any longer and I arrived on the corner where my friend's apartment house was located without any need for further delay. The green light glimmered and I crossed the street, and then found matters were not as straightforward as I had expected.

"The apartment house was not an only child but was a member of a large family of identical siblings. I had never visited the complex before and I wasn't sure in which particular building I was to find my friend. There seemed no directory, no kiosk with a friendly information guide. There seemed the usual assumption underlying everything in New York that if you weren't born with the knowledge of how to locate your destination, you had no business having one.

"The individual buildings each had their number displayed, but discreetly—in a whisper. Nor were they illuminated by the glint of the streetlights, so finding them was an adventure.

"One tends to wander at random at first, trying to get one's bearings. Eventually, I found a small sign with an arrow directing me into an inner courtyard with the promise that the number I wanted was actually to be found there.

"Another moment and I would have plunged in when I remembered that I was, or just conceivably might be, a marked man. I looked back in the direction from which I had come.

"I was spared the confusion of crowds. Even though it was not long after 9 P.M., the street bore the emptiness characteristic of night in any American city of the Universal Automobile Age. There were automobiles, to be sure, in an unending stream, but up the street I had walked, I could see only three people in the glow of the streetlights, two men and a woman.

"I could not see faces, or details of clothing, for though I have 20/20 vision, I see no better than that. However, one of the men was tall and large and his outline was irresistibly reminiscent of the man in the doorway whom I had dodged past in leaving the bar.

"They had been waiting for him, of course, and now they had emerged. They would probably have come out sooner, I thought, but there had been the necessity of taking care of the one I had damaged and, I supposed, they had left him behind.

"Nor, I gathered, were they coming in search of me. Even from a distance I could tell their attention was not on something external to the group, as though they were searching for someone. Attention was entirely internal. The two men were on either side of the woman and were hurrying her along. It seemed to me that she was reluctant to move, that she held back, that she was being urged forward.

"And once again, the kaleidoscope shifted. She was a woman in distress after all. She had thought I was her rescuer and I had left her cold—and still in distress.

"I ran across the avenue against the lights, dodging cars, and racing toward them. Don't get me wrong. I am not averse to defending myself; I rather enjoy it as anyone would enjoy something he does well. Just the same I am not an unreasoning hero. I do not seek out a battle for no reason. I am all for justice, purity, and righteousness, but who's to say which side, if either, in any quarrel represents those virtues?

"A personal angle is something else, and in this case, I had been asked for help and I had quailed.

"Oh, I quailed. I admit I had honestly decided the woman was not on my side and needed no help, but I didn't really stay to find out. It was that large man I was ducking, and I had to wipe out that disgrace.

"At least that's what I decided in hot blood. If I had had time to think, or to let the spasm of outrage wear off, I might have just visited my friend. Maybe I would have called the police from a street phone without leaving my name and *then* visited my friend.

"But it *was* hot blood, and I ran toward trouble, weighing the odds very skimpily.

"They were no longer on the street, but I had seen which gate they had entered, and they had not gone up the steps. I chased into the front yard after them and seized the grill-work door that led to the basement apartment. It came open but there was a wooden door beyond that did not. The window blinds were down but there was a dim light behind them.

"I banged at the wooden door furiously but there was no answer. If I had to break it down, I would be at a disadvantage. Strength, speed, and skill are not as good at breaking down a door as sheer mass is, and mass I do not have.

"I banged again and then kicked at the knob. If it were the wrong apartment, it was breaking and entry, which it also was if it was the right apartment. The door trembled at my kick, but held. I was about to try again, wondering if some neighbor had decided to get sufficiently involved to call the police—when the door opened. It was the large man—which meant it was the right apartment.

"I backed away. He said, 'You seem uncomfortably anxious to get in, sir.' He had a rather delicate tenor voice and the tone of an educated man.

"I said, 'You have a woman here. I want to see her.'

"'We do not have a woman here. She has us here. This is a woman's apartment and we are here by her invitation.'

"'I want to see her.'

"'Very well, then, come in and meet her.' He stepped back.

"I waited, weighing the risks—or I tried to, at any rate, but an unexpected blow from behind sent me staggering forward. The large man seized my arm and the door closed behind me.

"Clearly, the second man had gone one floor upward, come out the main door, down the stairs and behind me. I should have been aware of him, but I wasn't. I fall short of superman standards frequently.

"The large man led me into a living room. It was dimly lit. He said, 'As you see, sir—our hostess.'

"She was there. It was the woman from the bar but this time the kaleidoscope stayed put. The look she gave me was unmistakable. She saw me as a rescuer who was failing her.

" 'Now,' said the large man, 'we have been polite to you although you treated my friend in the bar cruelly. We have merely asked you in when we might have hurt you. In response, will you tell us who you are and what you are doing here?'

"He was right. The smaller man did not have to push me in. He might easily have knocked me out, or done worse. I presume, though, that they were puzzled by me. They didn't know my part in it and they had to find out.

"I looked about quickly. The smaller man remained behind me, moving as I did. The large man, who must have weighed 250 pounds, with little of it actually fat, remained quietly in front of me. Despite what happened in the bar, they still weren't afraid of me. It was, once again, the advantage of small size.

"I said, 'This young woman and I have a date. We'll leave and you two continue to make yourself at home here.'

"He said, 'That is no answer, sir.'

"He nodded and I saw the smaller man move out of the corner of my eye. I lifted my arms to shoulder level as he seized me about the chest. There was no use allowing my arms to be pinned if I could avoid it. The smaller man held tightly, but it would have taken more strength than he had at his disposal to break my ribs. I waited for the correct positioning and I hoped the large man would give it to me.

"He said, 'I do need an answer, sir, and if I do not get one very quickly, I will have to hurt you.'

"He came closer, one hand raised to slap.

"What followed took less time than it will to explain but it went something like this. My arms went up and back, and around the smaller man's head to make sure I had a firm backing, and then my feet went up.

"My left shoe aimed at the groin of the large gentleman and the man doesn't live who won't flinch from that. The large man's hips jerked backward and his head automatically bent downward and encountered the heel of my right shoe moving upward. It's not an easy maneuver, but I've practiced it enough times.

"As soon as my heel made contact, I tightened my arm grip and tossed my head backward. My head and that of the smaller man made hard contact and I didn't enjoy it at all, but the back of my head was not as sensitive as the nose of the man behind me.

"From the woman's point of view, I imagine, there could be no clear vision of what had happened. One moment, I seemed helplessly immobilized and then, after a flash of movement, I was free, while both of my assailants were howling.

"The smaller man was on the floor with one hand over his face. I stamped on one ankle hard to discourage him from attempting to get up. No, it was not Marquis of Queensberry rules, but there were no referees around.

"I then turned to face the larger man. He brought his hands away from his face. I had caught him on the cheekbone and he was bleeding freely. I was hoping he had no fight left in him, but he did. With one eye rapidly puffing shut, he came screaming toward me in a blind rage.

"I was in no danger from his mad rush as long as I could twist away, but once he got a grip on me in his present mood, I would be in serious trouble. I backed away, twisted. I backed away, twisted again. I waited for a chance to hit him again on the same spot.

"Unfortunately, I was in a strange room. I backed away, twisted, and fell heavily over a hassock. He was on me, his knee on my thighs, his hands on my throat, and there was no way I could weaken that grasp in time.

"I could hear the loud thunk even through the blood roaring in my ears and the large man fell heavily on me—but his grip on my throat had loosened. I wiggled out from below with the greatest difficulty though the woman did her best to lift him.

"She said, 'I had to wait for him to stop moving.' There was a candle holder lying near him, a heavy wrought-iron piece.

"I remained on the floor, trying to catch my breath. I gasped out, 'Have you killed him?'

"'I wouldn't care if I did,' she said, indifferently, 'but he's still breathing.'

"She wasn't exactly your helpless heroine. It was her apartment so she knew where to find the clothesline, and she was tying both of them at the wrists and ankles very efficiently. The smaller man screamed when she tightened the ropes at his ankle, but she didn't turn a hair.

"She said, 'Why the hell did you mess up the response in the bar when I asked you about baseball? And why the hell didn't you bring people with you? I admit you're a pint-sized windmill, but couldn't you have brought *one* backup?'

"Well, I don't really expect gratitude, but—

"I said, 'Lady, I don't know what you're talking about. I don't know about the baseball bit, and I don't go about in squadrons.'

"She looked at me sharply. 'Don't move. I'm making a phone call.'

"'The police?'

"'After a fashion.'

"She went into the other room to call. For privacy, I suppose. She trusted me to stay where I was and do nothing. Or thought me stupid enough to do so. I didn't mind. I wasn't through resting.

"When she came back, she said, 'You're not one of us. What *was* that remark about baseball?'

"I said, 'I don't know who us is, but I'm not one of anybody. My remark about baseball was a remark. What else?'

"She said, 'Then how—Well, you had better leave. There's no need for you to be mixed up in this. I'll take care of everything. Get out and walk some distance before you hail a taxi. If a car pulls up at this building while you're within earshot, don't turn around and for God's sake, don't turn back.'

"She was pushing and I was out in the yard when she said, 'But at least you knew what I was telling you in the bar. I am glad you were here and waiting.'

"'At last! Gratitude! I said, 'Lady, I don't know what—' but the door was closed behind me.

"I made it over very quickly to my friend's apartment. He said nothing about my being an hour late or being a little the worse for wear and I said nothing about what had happened.

"And what did happen was nothing. I never heard a thing. No repercussions. And that's why it's an unsatisfactory story. I don't know who the people were, what they were doing, what it was all about. I don't know whether I was helping the good guys or the bad guys, or whether there were any good guys involved. I may have bumped into two competing bands of terrorists playing with each other.

"But that's the story about my faking a knowledge of baseball."

When Just was done, a flat and rather unpleasant silence hung over the room, a silence that seemed to emphasize that for the first time in living memory a guest had told a rather long story without ever having been interrupted.

Finally, Trumbull heaved a weary sigh and said, "I trust you won't be offended, Mr. Just, if I tell you that I think you are pulling our leg. You've invented a very dramatic story for our benefit, and you've entertained us—me, at least— but I can't accept it."

Just shrugged, and didn't seem offended. "I've embroidered it a little, polished it up a bit—I'm a writer, after all—but it's true enough."

Avalon cleared his throat. "Mr. Just, Tom Trumbull is sometimes hasty in coming to conclusions but in this case I am forced to agree with him. As you say, you're a writer. I'm sorry to say I have read none of your works but I imagine you write what are called tough-guy detective stories."

"As a matter of fact, I don't," said Just, with composure. "I have written four novels that are, I hope, realistic, but are not unduly violent."

"It's a fact, Jeff," said Rubin, grinning.

Gonzalo said, "Do *you* believe him, Manny?"

Rubin shrugged. "I've never found Darius to be a liar, and I know *something* happened, but it's hard for a writer to resist the temptation to fictionalize for effect. Forgive me, Darius, but I wouldn't swear to how much of it was true."

Just sighed. "Well, just for the record, is there anyone here who believes I told you what actually happened?"

The Black Widowers sat in an embarrassed silence, and then there was a soft cough from the direction of the sideboard.

"I hesitate to intrude, gentlemen," said Henry, "but despite the over-romantic nature of the story, it seems to me there is a chance that it is true."

"A chance?" said Just, smiling. "Thank you, waiter."

"Don't underestimate the waiter," said Trumbull, stiffly. "If he thinks there is a chance the story is true, I'm prepared to revise my opinion.—What's your reasoning, Henry?"

"If the story were fiction, Mr. Trumbull, it would be neatly tied. This one has an interesting loose end which, if it makes sense, cannot be accidental.—Mr. Just, just at the end of the story, you told us that the woman remarked at her relief that you knew what she was telling you in the bar. What had she told you?"

Just said, "This *is* a loose end, because she didn't tell me a damn thing. I could easily make something up, if I weren't telling the truth."

"Or you could let it remain loose now," said Halsted, "for the sake of verisimilitude."

Henry said, "And yet if your story is accurate, she may indeed have told you, and the fact that you don't understand that is evidence of its truth."

"You speak in riddles, Henry," said Just.

Henry said, "You did not, in your story, mention precise locations; neither the location of the bar, nor of the apartment complex in which your friend lives. There are a number of such apartment complexes in Manhattan.''

"I know," interposed Rubin, "I live in one of them."

"Yours, Mr. Rubin," said Henry, "is on West End Avenue. I suspect that the apartment complex of Mr. Just's friend is on First Avenue.''

Just looked astonished. "It *is*. Now how did you know that?''

Henry said, "Consider the opening scene of your story. The woman at the bar knew she was in the hands of her enemies and would not be allowed to leave except under escort. The two men in the bar were merely waiting for their large confederate. They would then take her to her apartment for reasons of their own. The woman thought you were one of her group, felt you could do nothing in the bar, but wanted you on the spot, near her apartment, with reinforcements.

"She therefore flicked maraschino cherries at you—an apparently harmless and, possibly, flirtatious gesture, though even that roused the suspicions of the two men in the bar.''

Just said, "What of that?"

Henry said, "She had to work with what she could find. The cherries were small spheres—little balls—and she sent you four, one at a time. You had claimed to be a baseball fanatic. She sent you four balls, and, in baseball parlance— as almost anyone knows—four balls, that is, four pitches outside the strike zone, means the batter may advance to first base. More colloquially, he 'walks to first.' That's what she was telling you and you, quite without understanding this, did indeed walk to First Avenue for reasons of your own.''

Just looked stupefied. "I never thought of that."

"It's because you didn't and yet incorporated the incident into the account," said Henry, "that I think your story is essentially true.''

Afterword

I once wrote a mystery novel entitled *Murder at the ABA* in which my hero was a little guy named Darius Just. I liked the book very much.

(I usually like my own books very much, which is a lucky thing. Can you imagine how miserable my life would be if I disliked my books, considering how many of them I write?)

I particularly liked Darius and I kept planning to write other books in the series, but somehow I never got the chance. In the first place there were *so* many nonfiction books I had to write and then, when the time came when Doubleday grabbed me by the throat and told me I had to write more fiction, they made it plain that by fiction they meant science fiction.

So my hopes for additional Darius Just novels went glimmering—for a while anyway.

But then it occurred to me that there was nothing to prevent me from putting Darius into an occasional short story and I thought up "The Woman in the Bar" specifically for him.

When Fred published the story in the June 30, 1980, issue of *EQMM*, by the way, he called it "The Man Who Pretended to Like Baseball" and that is an example of a title I didn't like. Too long and too off-center in my opinion. So back to "The Woman in the Bar."

The Driver

Roger Halsted looked over his drink and said in his soft voice, "Successful humor has its incongruity. That is why people laugh. The sudden change in point of view does it and the more sudden and extreme the change, the louder the laugh." His voice took on the slight stutter that marked his more earnest moments.

James Drake thought about it. "Well, maybe, Roger. There are lots of theories about humor, but for my money, once you've dissected a joke, you're about where you are when you've dissected a frog. It's dead."

"But you've learned something.—Think of a joke."

Drake said, "I'm trying to."

Mario Gonzalo, resplendent in a turtlenecked shirt in rich purple under a beige jacket, said, "Try Manny Rubin."

Emmanuel Rubin, having glowered at Gonzalo, and turned away with a look of unmistakable pain, said, "I claim no expertise in humor. My writing is invariably serious."

Gonzalo said, "I'm not talking about your writing. I'm talking about *you*."

Rubin said, "I'd answer that, Mario, but dressed as you are, you're taking an unfair advantage. I keep fighting nausea."

The monthly banquet of the Black Widowers was in full swing and Henry, the indispensable waiter at these functions, announced that dinner was served.

"Easy on the food, Manny," said Mario, "it's roast beef

37

and Yorkshire pudding today, Henry tells me, and we don't want trouble with your delicate intestines and gross wit."

"Writing your own material, I see," said Rubin. "Too bad.—Ah, there's Tom."

Tom Trumbull's white thatch of hair showed as he moved hastily up the stairs, followed by the rest of him. "Apologies, gentlemen, minor family crisis, all taken care of and—Thank you, Henry." He seized his Scotch and soda gratefully. "You haven't begun eating yet?"

Geoffrey Avalon said gravely, "Roger is buttering his roll but that's as far as we've gotten."

Drake said, "Tom Trumbull, meet my guest, Kurt Magnus. He's an exobiologist."

Trumbull shook hands. "Pardon me, Mr. Magnus. I didn't quite get Jim's job description."

Magnus was tall and thin, with lank black hair worn at medium length and a boyish face. He spoke quickly, but with intervals of careful enunciation. "Exobiologist, Mr. Trumbull. *E-x-o*, a Greek prefix meaning 'outside.' Personally, I prefer 'xenobiologist,' which sounds as though it starts with a *z*, but is *x-e-n-o* from a Greek word meaning 'stranger.' Either way it's the study of life on other worlds."

"Like Martians," said Trumbull.

"Or Mario in his shirt," said Rubin.

Magnus smiled. "The subject evokes laughter, I admit. There is a certain incongruity in a field of study that includes no known cases and, as Mr. Halsted was saying, incongruity is the very stuff of humor."

"Exactly," said Halsted, swallowing a mouthful of kidney-on-toast. "I'll give you an example.—Jack is sitting glumly in a bar, staring at his beer. Bob walks in, looks at Jack and says, 'What's the matter?' Says Jack, 'My wife ran away with my best friend.' Bob says, 'What are you talking about? I'm your best friend.' And Jack says, 'Not anymore.'"

There was general laughter and even Trumbull condescended to smile.

"You see," said Halsted, "you're allowed to assume that Jack is weighted down with grief until the last three—"

"We got it, Rog," said Rubin. "No need to belabor it."

"Or take the following—"

"Praise the Lord," said Trumbull when Drake rattled his spoon on the water glass. "Henry, make mine a double brandy.—Oh, you have!"

"Yes, sir," said Henry, blandly, "I anticipated the need when Mr. Halsted began to quote limericks."

"I've already remembered you in my will, Henry, and more of these sessions will hasten your role as beneficiary.—What?"

"I said," said Drake, patiently, "that I would like you to do the honors, Tom, and grill our exobiologist."

"My pleasure," said Trumbull, "if I may be allowed one invigorating sip.—Ah. Now, Mr. Magnus, it is usual for us to begin by asking a guest to justify his existence but I will make the question less general.—How does your role as exobiologist justify your existence?"

Magnus smiled. "Would you believe the glory of seeking knowledge?"

"For yourself, certainly, and for me, maybe—but your researches draw heavily on the public purse. How do you justify your existence to the taxpayer?"

"I wish I could, Mr. Trumbull. I wish I could say to him loudly enough to be heard—'Sir, the world pays out 400 billion dollars each year for its various sets of armed forces in order to buy nothing but the increasing certainty of destruction. Let us have one tenth of one percent of that to gain what may be fundamental knowledge concerning the Universe.'"

Avalon shook his head severely and said, "That won't work, Dr. Magnus. The public sees national defense as their security against invasion and oppression by hated foreigners. They may be wrong, but what have you to offer instead? What if you *do* discover life on Mars? Who cares? Why should anyone care?"

Magnus sighed. "Somehow I didn't expect Philistinism here."

Avalon said, "I plead the Philistine case on behalf of my exorbitant tax bill. What is your answer?"

"That your tax bill is exorbitant for reasons that have nothing to do with exobiology or science and a great deal to do with folly and corruption, worldwide. If we did discover life on Mars, which, since the Viking landings, is unlikely, then no matter how simple it is, it will offer us for observation, for the first time, a life structure not in any way related to ourselves.

"All life forms on Earth, plant, animal, bacterial, and viral, are built around the same scheme; all the two million or so species are interconvertible in the sense that any one of them can be part of a food chain that ends in any other. Martian life, however simple it might be, would instantly double the varieties of life we know, with results of possibly incalculable benefits to the biologist and, of course, to all of us. After all, the better we can understand life, the better our chances for such things as disease cure and life extension."

Rubin interposed. "But the fact is that there is probably no life on Mars, however simple."

Magnus said, "The odds now are that there isn't."

"Or anywhere in the Solar System."

"Possibly not."

"And if there were, it might after all be built on the same plan as is Earth life."

"That is conceivable."

"And if it isn't, the difference may not help us understand ourselves at all."

"I would hate to believe that, but I suppose that might be so."

Rubin said, "Then, playing the devil's advocate, wouldn't you say that the odds you offer aren't worth the money you ask?"

Trumbull said, "Manny, it's worse than that. I don't think exobiology concerns itself with the Solar System only.

Aren't there plans for trying to detect radio signals of intelligent origin from other stars?"

"From planets circling other stars, yes," said Magnus.

"And wouldn't that cost millions of dollars?"

"Many millions if done properly."

"And if we locate this life and draw their attention to us, then what? Do they invade us and take us over? Is that what we'll pay those many millions for?"

For the first time, Magnus allowed a look of impatience to cross his face. "In the first place," he said, "we are merely listening. The process is SETI, 'search for extra-terrestrial intelligence.' If we receive signals, we need not try to answer, if we do not wish to. In the second place, the chances are that if we do receive signals, the source will be anywhere from dozens to hundreds of light-years away. That means it will take them decades to centuries to receive any message we send them and with conversations like that danger wouldn't seem to be imminent. In the third place, even if they could move faster than light and wanted to reach us, we have no reason to suppose conquest and destruction are what they have in mind. We think that only because we insist on transferring our own bestiality to them. In the fourth place, we have, in any case, given away our existence. We have been leaking electromagnetic radiation of clearly intelligent origin for eight decades and the leakage has been growing steadily more intense every year. So they'll know we're here if they want to listen. And in the fifth place—" He stopped suddenly.

Trumbull said, "You rattle that off as though you have much occasion to go through the list."

"I do," said Magnus.

"Then why did you stop? Have you forgotten the fifth place?"

"No, it is, in fact, the easiest one to remember. We're not spending millions of dollars, you see, so the taxpayer has no worries for either his bankroll or his life. In point of fact, we're spending almost nothing."

Rubin said, "What about Project Cyclops?—Over a

thousand radio telescopes computerized into unison to listen for signals from any star within a thousand light-years, one by one. Don't tell me that won't cost a fortune."

"Of course it would, and a bargain, too, at almost any price. Even if we pick up no signals of intelligent origin at all, who can tell what bizarre and unexpected discoveries we will make when we probe the Universe with an instrument whole orders of magnitude more refined than anything we use now?"

"Exactly," said Rubin. "Who can tell? No one. For it may come up with nothing."

"Well, no point in arguing," said Magnus. "It's very doubtful we'd ever get the necessary funds voted us by Congress. So far, it's been hard enough to get the money for some of us to attend international conferences on the subject and even that may be phased out, thanks to the damndest set of circumstances." A spasm of unhappiness crossed his face.

There was a short silence and then Avalon, drawing his formidable eyebrows together said, "Would you care to describe the circumstances, Dr. Magnus?"

"There's not much to describe," said Magnus. "There's a dull fog of suspicion that won't lift and that plays right into the hands of the millions-for-defense-but-not-one-cent-for-survival band of fools."

Gonzalo looked delighted. "A dull fog of suspicion is just what we like to hear. Tell us the details."

"It would scarcely be discreet to do so."

Trumbull said at once, "Nothing said here is ever repeated outside. We are all discreet and that includes our esteemed waiter, Henry."

"When I say it would not be discreet to tell you the details," said Magnus, sadly, "I am referring to my own folly. I am afraid it is I who caused the trouble and I find it embarrassing to discuss."

"If that's what's bothering you," said Trumbull, "then please tell us. Confession is good for the soul and even if it weren't, the condition of the dinner, as Jim has no doubt told you, is submission to our grilling."

"He told me," said Magnus. "Very well—"

"Some time ago," said Magnus, "we held an international meeting for those interested in SETI in New Brunswick, in Canada. The Soviets sent a sizable contingent of some of their top-flight astronomers, and, of course, we ourselves were present in force as were Canadians, British, French, Australians, Japanese, and a scattering of others, including a few Eastern Europeans.

"There were also auxiliary personnel—translators, for instance, though most of those attending could speak very good English. Oddly enough, the purest and most smoothly colloquial English came from the sole Bulgarian delegate, who sounded perfectly Ohio at our social gatherings, but insisted on speaking Bulgarian and using an interpreter in the formal sessions, perhaps to show his orthodox side to the Soviets—but that's neither here nor there.

"Included also were, I am quite certain, a few Soviet ringers who were, in actual fact, part of their security apparatus. I am equally certain that American security personnel were also present."

Gonzalo said, "What for, Mr. Magnus? Where's the danger in listening to the stars? Are the Soviets afraid we'll make an alliance with some little green men against them?"

"Or vice versa?" asked Halsted, dryly.

Magnus said, "No, but knowledge is indivisible. Those of us who are experts on radio astronomy know a good deal about such things as reconnaissance satellites and killer satellites, and on handling, misleading, and aborting electronic reconnaissance. Both sides, therefore, would be anxious to prevent their own men from being indiscreet and to trap their opposite numbers into being overtalkative."

Avalon said, "It seems to me that security would be helpless in such matters. Could a CIA operative know when an astronomer was being indiscreet when he probably couldn't understand the subject matter?"

Magnus said, "You underestimate the training special agents undergo. Then, too, actual astronomers on either side might double as security. I name no names."

Trumbull said, "No point in going into that any further. Would you go on, Dr. Magnus?"

"Certainly," said Magnus. "I have stressed the total size of the delegation in order to explain that we could not all be housed in one place. In fact, the New Brunswick site, although suitable as a quasi-neutral spot—an earlier meeting had been held in Finland—and although beautiful and isolated, to say nothing of possessing tennis courts and a swimming pool, did not offer adequate housing. Personnel were rather widely scattered and the Canadian government supplied transportation.

"We had several cars, each with a driver, and these were in constant demand. The Americans used a limousine which could hold six easily, although the driver would readily carry even a single passenger back and fourth. Wasteful of gasoline, but convenient.

"The driver was Alex Jones, an eager young man in his late twenties, who seemed to have the fixed notion that we were all astrologers. He was as ignorant as anyone could be without actually being retarded, but he was fascinated by us. He knew each one of us and called us all by some weird variety of our name.

"I got off rather lightly. He called me Maggins, which is rather close, and once Maggots, which is not so close. I didn't mind and I didn't try to correct him. Alfred Binder of Arizona State was routinely called Bandage, however, and he seethed each time. Sometimes, Binder shouted at the young man in a rather uncalled-for manner."

Avalon said, "May I interrupt, Dr. Magnus? Are you getting off the subject? You sound as though you were reminiscing rather aimlessly."

There was a trace of stiffness in Magnus's response. "I am sorry, Mr. Avalon, but this is all essential to the story. There is little that is aimless about my manner of thought."

Avalon cleared his throat and said in a subdued tone,

"My apologies, sir," then took a rather agitated sip at what was clearly an empty brandy glass. Henry quietly poured him a refill at once.

"No offense, sir," said Magnus. "Alex was not the only driver, of course. There were half a dozen at least, but he was the one who usually serviced the American delegation. Binder I think, occasionally hitched a ride with the Canadians or British just to get away from Alex. I suspect he would have ridden with the Soviets if he had thought he could clear it with security on both sides.

"I must confess that Binder's irritation with Alex amused me. My sense of humor tends to be on the unkind side now and then, and when Binder was in the car I would encourage Alex to ask questions. He would invariably ask what constellations we were studying, for instance, and which constellation was lucky for that day. Once, I even called Binder 'Dr. Bandage' when we were in the car—not really on purpose—and afterward he blew up at me."

Rubin said, "People are generally sensitive about their names."

"Granted," said Magnus, "and, as I said, I'm not really pleased with the direction my sense of humor takes, but when I am caught up in the fury of it, so to speak, I can't resist the joke.

"Of course, you must not suppose that these interludes in the car were nothing but nonsense. In fact, I should say most of the delegates spoke about their work with a feverish intensity, since we were there as our own little clique. Alex listened without understanding a word and to me that was an added incentive, for I loved his off-target remarks. Once when someone mentioned Cygnus X-I—the putative black hole, you know—Alex said, 'We're all sinners but it can't be helped. It's in the stars.' For a minute there, I didn't see what he meant, but he was never completely off-base. It was a matter of 'Cygnus' and 'sinner' and Alex free-associated them.

"But the conference was drawing to its close. We had all given our talks, we had all had our informal discussions over meals and during evening relaxation, and on the last day but one we were having a symposium, including six of the more vociferous attendees, whose attitudes were sufficiently different to promise some exciting give-and-take.

"A group of us were being driven to luncheon, with the symposium slated for the afternoon, and the people in the car were speculating on how hectic the arguments might get. Out of sheer troublemaking I suppose, and in order to bait Binder, I said, 'And what do you think of the people who will be in the symposium, Alex?'

"Alex said, 'Pluhtahn,' in a low voice and I said, 'Pluhtahn? Who's he?'

"That was where Binder overflowed. 'What's the use of asking that idiot? God knows what poor devil he's plastered with that name or what he's talking about. Why in hell do you encourage him?'

"That, in turn, made me stubborn. I said, 'Come on, he may not get the names quite right, but he refers to definite people.'

"Binder said, 'There's no one in our group who has a name anything like Pluhtahn. It's just idiocy.'

" 'He's not an idiot,' I said in a low voice, and anxious to prove that, I said, 'Come on, Alex, which one of us is Pluhtahn? What's he look like?'

"But Alex looked terribly upset. I could see him in profile as I leaned over the back of the front seat. His lips were trembling and he had to swallow before he could say anything. Clearly, Binder's rage had frightened him. He muttered, 'I guess I must have made a mistake, Mr. Maggins.'

"He was silent for the short remainder of the trip and when he piled out, he skipped his customary wave of the hand and his toothy grin. Poor fellow! I called out to him but he didn't answer. I couldn't help but think of Binder as a pompous fool.

"If I had left it at that, all might have been well but, by pure chance, Yuri sat down next to me at lunch.

"Yuri was a member of the Soviet group, of course, a

dumpy man, quite stout, who was bald except for a fringe of dark hair, which he kept quite short. He always wore a gray suit and a maroon tie and, while an excellent radio astronomer, he was given to grumpiness. I never saw him smile and probably that's why I couldn't resist kidding him.—That, and my troublemaking sense of humor.

"I said to him, 'What's this I hear, Yuri, about your driving in our group's limousine?'

"He put down his knife and stared at me indignantly, 'What are you talking about?' He spoke English quite well, as did most of the Soviets—which was humiliating for us, in a way, since none of us could speak more than a few words of Russian.

"You see, Yuri's last name was Platonov, accent on the second syllable, and it just struck me that if Alex had had him in the car, the name Pluhtahn could well have been wished on him. Of course, I knew that Platonov would never have used our car. Of the entire Soviet group, he was the least likely to chance anything unorthodox. He was never friendly and some of us were convinced he was a member of Soviet security.

"Of course, that made my joking seem all the funnier to me. I said, 'Our driver, Alex Jones, mentioned you, Yuri, so I gather you've been driving with him and talking to him. What have you been doing? Trying to get him to defect?'

"Yuri grew furious. He said, 'Is this a joke? I warn you, I shall place a protest. I do not think a sober scientific gathering is the place for tasteless remarks.'

"Well, it *was* tasteless, I suppose, and besides, Yuri had raised his voice and people were looking at us from all parts of the room. So I backed off. I said, 'No offense, Yuri. I just mentioned the symposium to our driver and he mumbled something about Pluhtahn and I thought I would tease you. Our driver always gets names wrong and it doesn't mean anything.'

"Yuri said, grumpily, 'Keep your teasing to yourself.' He settled down to eat and neither looked at me nor talked to me during the remainder of the meal. In fact, he said nothing at all to anybody and seemed rather deep in thought.

"My conscience smote me. He might not be part of Soviet security. He might, in fact, be very vulnerable. If anyone on the Soviet side had heard me, all of Yuri's protestations and all my insistence that I was just making a bad joke might do no good. The unreasoning arrow of suspicion might come to rest on him and, conceivably, his career might be ruined. By the time I reached that stage in my thoughts, I felt pretty sick, and I did *not* enjoy the symposium.

"In fact, the symposium was just a bit of a fizzle. Yuri, who was one of the participants, had been counted on for fireworks and he didn't offer any. He seemed almost absentminded, as though he had something on his mind. I felt terrible and, of course, things got worse—"

At this point, Gonzalo interrupted. "Don't tell me this guy Platonov got in trouble and has been sent to Siberia!"

Magnus said, "No, not as far as I know. What did happen was that that evening, our last at the conference, Alex died."

"The driver?" said Avalon, clearly astonished.

Trumbull said, "How did he die?"

"Well, that's it," said Magnus. "It was not a natural death. Do you remember I mentioned a Bulgarian in the group who spoke excellent English? Well, he was driving one of the smaller cars of those reserved for the Soviet contingent to the village on an errand of some sort and he said that Alex came staggering into the road in front of him and there was no way of avoiding him."

"Did it happen in the village?" asked Rubin.

"No, on the grounds, when the rest of us were gathering for the post-dinner convivial hour, so to speak, and most of us were there when the local police gathered. It was clear that the Bulgarian—his name was Gabrilovich, by the way—expected to be imprisoned and charged with murder, and he feared the excesses of the capitalist-imperialist constabulary, but there was nothing like that, of course. He was an honored foreign guest of the nation and was given the benefit of the doubt. During the night the autopsy was performed and it seemed that Alex had indeed been loaded with alcohol. He was quite drunk enough to have staggered out into the road helplessly.

"We carried on with the final summarizing session the next morning—which Gabrilovich did not attend—and had permission to leave and go about our business after lunch. Gabrilovich himself had to stay an extra day to undergo additional questioning, which must have frightened him badly. Several on the Soviet side kept him company and then they all left, too.

"I called the Canadian police a few days later, but the case was closed. Alex had no relatives and no possessions to speak of. He was buried and that was the end of it."

Halsted said, his high forehead pink with suppressed excitement, "But you think it was no accident. Right?"

Magnus nodded. "Two reasons. First, what was Gabrilovich doing driving to the village alone when the people on the Soviet side, including the Eastern Europeans, *never* went in groups of less than three?"

"Come, come," said Avalon, "that is custom and not cosmic law."

"Custom is sometimes surer," said Magnus, "and a man who could speak English perfectly, but used Bulgarian to parade his loyalty, would not break that custom. Furthermore, he was going into town to buy himself an electric shaver, he said, because he was tired of nicking himself with his Bulgarian straight razor. However, I had never seen nicks on his face and it seemed to me that he would not so parade his infatuation with Western technology."

"Not so," said Avalon. "I imagine that there's nothing wrong with that. The Soviets buy all the effete bourgeois products they can get their hands on. To give them credit, they make no bones about admiring the technology while claiming to despise the economic principles that go along with it."

Magnus shrugged. "Maybe. The second thing that

bothers me is that Alex simply didn't seem like a drinker to me. Drinkers lard their conversation with casual references to drinks, and Alex never did."

"That's even weaker than the first reason," said Avalon. "You can never tell a secret drinker. For all you know Alex was an alcoholic trying to stay off the booze at a conference where it probably drenched the proceedings at all times. On the last evening, he couldn't resist a drink, which led to another and another—No, Dr. Magnus, his death may not have been an accident but what you advance for thinking so would not suffice to make the police act upon it."

Magnus said, "But consider the coincidence. Earlier that day I had joked with Yuri Platonov concerning Alex's use of the name of Pluhtahn. That night he was dead."

Rubin said, skeptically, "Do you think the joke was worth a murder?"

"Suppose," said Magnus, "Yuri *had* been in the automobile which Alex was driving. Suppose he had been talking to some Westerner, receiving information. They might well have disregarded Alex, who was so clearly not mentally equipped to be dangerous. But suppose Alex had heard the Westerner address the other as Platonov and had picked up the name. Who knows what else he would remember? So he was killed to keep from blowing the cover of an important spy in the enemy camp."

Avalon said, "Surely, the chances that an ignorant young man could have heard anything of importance—"

"If he could identify who was with Platonov at that time, and he might, that would be enough.—In any case," Magnus said, broodingly, "I'm not the only one who suspects murder and treason. I strongly suspect that American security has tumbled to the possibility probably because of what I was overheard to say. I've been discreetly questioned about events at the conference, and I gather that a few others have been, too. What's more, there's a certain amount of red tape that is slowing our ability to attend other conferences abroad."

"In other words," said Trumbull, "you think the government suspects that one of the American delegation to the New Brunswick conference is a traitor, but it doesn't know which one."

Magnus nodded wordlessly.

"Do you think it's true?" said Trumbull.

Magnus said, "I don't know. I hate to believe it's true. But it might be. The worst of it is that if it hadn't been for my joking in the car and at the luncheon table, there would be no grounds for supposing Alex's death to be anything but accident.—And maybe it *was* accident."

Gonzalo said suddenly, "No, it wasn't. It was murder."

Rubin looked outraged, "On what grounds, Mario?"

"The best in the world," said Gonzalo. "When Dr. Magnus said Alex had died that night, I happened to have my eye on Henry—and while the rest of you were registering surprise, Henry nodded his head just a little as though he'd been expecting it. Come on, Henry, what do you think of that automobile accident?"

Henry hesitated a moment, then said, "Clearly murder, I should say, Mr. Gonzalo. I feel it to be uncomfortably melodramatic to say so, but I suspect Alex Jones was pumped full of alcohol by persuasion or force, then pushed into the road in front of the car which Gabrilovich was driving for the sole purpose of committing a murder that was to be made to look like an accident."

Everyone stared at Henry in astonishment and Trumbull said, "This time, Henry, you've gone too far. On what can you possibly base that scenario, which you yourself call melodramatic?"

Magnus, who looked rather thunderstruck at the sudden participation of the waiter in the discussion, said, "Yes. Why do you say that?"

"It's simple enough," said Henry. "When you mentioned the symposium, Mr. Magnus, Alex responded with 'Pluhtahn.' As it happens, there is a great literary work known as the *Symposium*. To mention it is bound to give rise, irresistibly, to the name of its author in anyone with a classical education. The author happens to be Plato and

'Plato's *Symposium*' is practically one word; one implies the other.''

Magnus said, "You mean that when I said 'symposium,' Alex couldn't resist saying 'Plato'? Alex? He had no classical education. I doubt if he finished grade school.''

Henry said, "It is easy to pretend to be uneducated and simpleminded. If anything, Alex worked too hard at it. This business of mispronouncing names was rather a case of painting the lily, and in itself it arouses suspicion.''

Magnus said, "You can't have it both ways. If it was 'Plato' he was trying to say, he pronounced it incorrectly, which blows the theory of education sky-high.''

"Ah," said Henry, "but he did *not* mispronounce Plato's name, Dr. Magnus. *We* do. In the original Greek, the name was 'Platon' and was pronounced closer to 'Pluhtahn' than to our own 'Playtoe.' The Russians kept both the spelling and the pronunciation and there was a famous high official of the Russian Church named Platon. I looked him up in the Biographical Dictionary while you were telling your story just to make sure I remembered correctly.''

"You remembered correctly," said Avalon. "Now why on earth didn't I think of that. 'Platon' is the Greek word for 'broad' and Plato received it as a nickname because of his broad shoulders. His real name was Aristocles.''

Magnus said, "But why should Alex use the Russian version of the name?''

Henry said, "I suppose because he was Russian, and when you said 'symposium,' the free association trapped him into the Russian, rather than the English, version of the name. I imagine he was a Soviet agent, planted as a Canadian national, and playing the role of simpleton. His assignment at the time was, undoubtedly, to listen to the conversations in the car.

"However, when he muttered 'Pluhtahn' and you picked that up, Dr. Magnus, the driver realized he might have revealed his identity. You said he seemed stricken. You thought it was by Dr. Binder's rage, but I suspect it was for a more serious reason.

"Then, when you joked about it with Mr. Platonov, *he* had no trouble recognizing the author of *Symposium* and it seemed to him, too, that Alex had given himself away. Even if you did not see it, Dr. Magnus, you might mention it to someone who would. The Soviets might well suppose that Alex would no longer be reliable; that he might be picked up; that he might defect out of the fear of the consequences. And if he had become an embarrassment and danger while alive, he might be better off dead."

Magnus was thoughtful for a moment. "I think I ought to report all this."

Trumbull said, "It would lift some of the undeserved heat from the astronomers at the conference. If you'll give me permission, I will make a phone call that will set the machinery moving."

"Yes, yes, of course," said Magnus. "How strange for Alex to give himself away in such a fashion when he played his part so well."

Avalon said, philosophically, "Oh, well, educated men required to sound silly are under an intolerable strain. Sooner or later, they cannot resist the urge to display their erudition. It *will* burst forth."

"You demonstrate that all the time, Jeff," said Gonzalo.

"I believe," said Avalon, austerely, "that I am not the only one here who is guilty in that respect."

"I myself," said Henry, "fear I am not quite innocent—in that respect."

Afterword

Fred Dannay didn't like this one. At least he sent it back to me.

In a way it was my fault. This was before I had begun my Union Club series, and I was going hot and heavy on the Black Widowers. As it happened, I wrote two of them in succession, "The Driver," and "The Good Samaritan," which follows.

I then, in an attack of hubris, brought them in on the same day and handed them in together.

This is clearly a matter of bad tactics. If an editor reads two of your stories at the same time, he is very likely to like one of the stories better than the other. If he had read the weaker story by itself, suitably isolated from a similar story that came previously, it might seem a little weak even so, but perhaps not too weak to publish. With the direct comparison of the other story, its flaws are magnified, and back it goes.

Fred accepted "The Good Samaritan" and when "The Driver" came back, I reread the two stories and decided that Fred was right and that "The Good Samaritan" was the better of the two.

The lesson I learned, then, was not to tempt an editor by giving him two at once. And (since I'm prejudiced) I don't think that "The Driver" is so weak that it ought to be discarded altogether. It appears here, then, for the first time in print.

The Good Samaritan

The Black Widowers had learned by hard experience that when Mario Gonzalo took his turn as host of the monthly banquet, they had to expect the unusual. They had reached the point where they steeled themselves, quite automatically, for disaster. When his guest arrived there was a lightening of spirit if it turned out he had the usual quota of heads and could speak at least broken English.

When the last of the Black Widowers arrived, therefore, and when Henry's efficient setting of the table was nearly complete, Geoffrey Avalon, standing, as always, straight and tall, sounded almost light-hearted as he said, "I see that your guest has not arrived yet, Mario."

Gonzalo, whose crimson velvet jacket and lightly striped blue pants reduced everything else in the room to monochrome said, "Well—"

Avalon said, "What's more, a quick count of the settings placed at the table by our inestimable Henry shows that six people and no more are to be seated. And since all six of us are here, I can only conclude that you have not brought a guest."

"Thank Anacreon," said Emmanuel Rubin, raising his drink, "or whatever spirit it is that presides over convivial banquets of kindred souls."

Thomas Trumbull scowled and brushed back his crisply waved white hair with one hand. "What are you doing, Mario? Saving money?"

"Well—" said Gonzalo again, staring at his own drink with a totally spurious concentration.

Roger Halsted said, "I don't know that this is so good. I like the grilling sessions."

"It won't hurt us," said Avalon, in his deepest voice, "to have a quiet conversation once in a while. If we can't amuse each other without a guest, then the Black Widowers are not what once they were and we should prepare, sorrowing, for oblivion. Shall we offer Mario a vote of thanks for his unwonted discretion?"

"Well—" said Gonzalo a third time.

James Drake interposed, stubbing out a cigarette and clearing his throat. "It seems to me, gentlemen, that Mario is trying to say something and is amazingly bashful about it. If he has something he hesitates to say, I fear we are not going to like it. May I suggest we all keep quiet and let him talk."

"Well—" said Gonzalo, and stopped. This time, though, there was a prolonged and anxious silence.

"Well—" said Gonzalo again, "I *do* have a guest," and once more he stopped.

Rubin said, "Then where the hell is he?"

"Downstairs in the main dining room—ordering dinner—at my expense, of course."

Gonzalo received five blank stares. Then Trumbull said, "May I ask what dunderheaded reason you can possibly advance for that?"

"Aside," said Rubin, "from being a congenital dunderhead?"

Gonzalo put his drink down, took a deep breath, and said, firmly, "Because I thought she would be more comfortable down there."

Rubin managed to get out an "And why—" before the significance of the pronoun became plain. He seized the lapels of Gonzalo's jacket. "Did you say *'she'*?"

Gonzalo caught at the other's wrists. "Hands off, Manny. If you want to talk, use your lips not your hands. Yes, I said 'she.'"

Henry, his sixtyish, unlined face showing a little concern,

raised his voice a diplomatic notch and said, "Gentlemen! Dinner is served!"

Rubin, having released Gonzalo, waved imperiously at Henry and said, "Sorry, Henry, there may be no banquet.— Mario, you damned jackass, *no woman can attend these meetings."*

There was, in fact, a general uproar. While no one quite achieved the anger and decibels of Rubin, Gonzalo found himself at bay with the five others around him in a semicircle. Their individual comments were lost in the general explosion of anger.

Gonzalo, waving his arms madly, leaped onto a chair and shouted, "Let me speak!" over and over until out of exhaustion, it seemed, the opposition died off into a low growl.

Gonzalo said, "She is not our guest at the banquet. She's just a woman with a problem, an old woman, and it won't do us any harm if we see her *after* dinner."

There was no immediate response and Gonzalo said, "She needn't sit at the table. She can sit in the doorway."

Rubin said, "Mario, if she comes in here, I go, and if I go, damn it, I may not come back ever."

Gonzalo said, "Are you saying you'll break up the Black Widowers rather than listen to an old woman in trouble?"

Rubin said, "I'm saying rules are *rules!"*

Halsted, looking deeply troubled, said, "Listen, Manny, maybe we ought to do this. The rules weren't delivered to us from Mount Sinai."

"You, too?" said Rubin, savagely. "Look, it doesn't matter what any of you say. In a matter as fundamental as this, one blackball is enough, and I cast it. Either she goes or I go and, by God, you'll never see me again. In view of that, is there anyone who wants to waste his breath?"

Henry, who still stood at the head of the table, waiting with markedly less than his usual imperturbability for the company to seat itself, said, "May I have a word, Mr. Rubin?"

Rubin said, "Sorry, Henry, no one sits down till this is settled."

Gonzalo said, "Stay out, Henry. I'll fight my own battles."

It was at this point that Henry departed from his role as the epitome of all Olympian waiters and advanced on the group. His voice was firm as he said, "Mr. Rubin, I wish to take responsibility for this. Several days ago, Mr. Gonzalo phoned me to ask if I would be so kind as to listen to a woman he knew who had the kind of problem he thought I might be helpful with. I asked him if it was something close to his heart. He said that the woman was a relative of someone who was very likely to give him a commission for an important piece of work—"

"Money!" sneered Rubin.

"Professional opportunity," snapped Gonzalo. "If you can understand that. And sympathy for a fellow human being, if you can understand *that*."

Henry held up his hand. *"Please,* gentlemen! I told Mr. Gonzalo I could not help him but urged him, if he had not already arranged a guest, to bring the woman. I suggested that there might be no objection if she did not actually attend the banquet itself."

Rubin said, "And why couldn't you help her otherwise?"

Henry said, "Gentlemen, I lay no claims to superior insight. I do not compare myself, as Mr. Gonzalo occasionally does on my behalf, to Sherlock Holmes. It is only after you gentlemen have discussed a problem and eliminated what is extraneous that I seem to see what remains. Therefore—"

Drake said, "Well, look, Manny, I'm the oldest member here, and the original reason for the prohibition. We might partially waive it just this once."

"No," said Rubin, flatly.

Henry said, "Mr. Rubin, it is often stated at these banquets that I am a member of the Black Widowers. If so, I wish to take the responsibility. I urged Mr. Gonzalo to do this and I spoke to the woman concerned and assured her that she would be welcomed to our deliberations after dinner. It was an impulsive act based on my estimate of the characters of the gentlemen of the club.

"If the woman is now sent away, Mr. Rubin, you understand that my position here will be an impossible one and I will be forced to resign my position as waiter at these banquets. I would have no choice."

Almost imperceptibly the atmosphere had changed while Henry spoke and now it was Rubin who was standing at bay. He stared at the semicircle that now surrounded him and said, rather gratingly, "I appreciate your services to the club, Henry, and I do not wish to place you in a dishonorable position. Therefore, on the stipulation that this is not to set a precedent and reminding you that you must not do this again, I will withdraw my blackball."

The banquet was the least comfortable in the history of the Black Widowers. Conversation was desultory and dull and Rubin maintained a stony silence throughout.

There was no need to clatter the water glass during the serving of the coffee, since there was no babble of conversation to override. Gonzalo simply said, "I'll go down and see if she's ready. Her name, by the way, is Mrs. Barbara Lindemann."

Rubin looked up and said, "Make sure she's had her coffee, or tea, or whatever, downstairs. She can't have anything up here."

Avalon looked disapproving, "The dictates of courtesy, my dear Manny—"

"She'll have all she wants downstairs at Mario's expense. Up here, we'll listen to her. What more can she want?"

Gonzalo brought her up and led her to an armchair that Henry had obtained from the restaurant office and that he had placed well away from the table.

She was a rather thin woman, with blunt good-natured features, well-dressed and with her white hair carefully set. She carried a black purse that looked new and she clutched it tightly. She glanced timidly at the faces of the Black Widowers and said, "Good evening."

There was a low chorused rumble in return and she said, "I apologize for coming here with my ridiculous story. Mr. Gonzalo explained that my appearance here is out of the ordinary and I have thought over my dinner that I should not disturb you. I will go if you like, and thank you for the dinner and for letting me come up here."

She made as though to rise and Avalon, looking remarkably shamefaced, said, "Madame, you are entirely welcome here and we would like very much to hear what you have to say. We cannot promise that we will be able to help you, but we can try. I'm sure that we all feel the same way about this. Don't you agree, Manny?"

Rubin shot a dark look at Avalon through his thick-lensed glasses. His sparse beard bristled and his chin lifted but he said in a remarkably mild tone, "Entirely, ma'am."

There was a short pause, and then Gonzalo said, "It's our custom, Mrs. Lindemann, to question our guests and under the circumstances, I wonder if you would mind having Henry handle that. He is our waiter, but he is a member of our group."

Henry stood motionless for a moment, then said, "I fear, Mr. Gonzalo, that—"

Gonzalo said, "You have yourself claimed the privilege of membership earlier this evening, Henry. Privilege carries with it responsibility. Put down the brandy bottle, Henry, and sit down. Anyone who wants brandy can take his own. Here, Henry, take my seat." Gonzalo rose resolutely and walked to the sideboard.

Henry sat down.

Henry said mildly to Mrs. Lindemann, "Madame, would you be willing to pretend you are on the witness stand?"

The woman looked about and her look of uneasiness dissolved into a little laugh. "I never have been and I'm not sure I know how to behave on one. I hope you won't mind if I'm nervous."

"We won't, but you needn't be. This will be very informal and we are anxious only to help you. The members of the club have a tendency to speak loudly and excitably at times, but if they do, that is merely their way and means nothing.—First, please tell us your name."

She said, with an anxious formality, "My name is Barbara Lindemann. Mrs. Barbara Lindemann."

"And do you have any particular line of work?"

"No, sir, I am retired. I am sixty-seven years old as you can probably tell by looking at me—and a widow. I was once a schoolteacher at a junior high school."

Halsted stirred and said, "That's my profession, Mrs. Lindemann. What subject did you teach?"

"Mostly I taught American history."

Henry said, "Now from what Mr. Gonzalo has told me you suffered an unpleasant experience here in New York and—"

"No, pardon me," interposed Mrs. Lindemann, "it was, on the whole, a very pleasant experience. If that weren't so, I would be only too glad to forget all about it."

"Yes, of course," said Henry, "but I am under the impression that you *have* forgotten some key points and would like to remember them."

"Yes," she said, earnestly. "I am so ashamed at not remembering. It must make me appear senile, but it was a very *unusual* and *frightening* thing in a way—at least parts of it were—and I suppose that's my excuse."

Henry said, "I think it would be best, then, if you tell us what happened to you in as much detail as you can and, if it will not bother you, some of us may ask questions as you go along."

"It won't bother me, I assure you," said Mrs. Lindemann. "I'll welcome it as a sign of interest."

She said, "I arrived in New York City nine days ago. I was going to visit my niece, among other things, but I didn't want to stay with her. That would have been uncomfortable for her and confining for me, so I took a hotel room.

"I got to the hotel at about 6 P.M. on Wednesday and after

a small dinner, which was very pleasant, although the prices were simply awful, I phoned my niece and arranged to see her the next day when her husband would be at work and the children at school. That would give us some time to ourselves and then in the evening we could have a family outing.

"Of course, I didn't intend to hang about their necks the entire two weeks I was to be in New York. I fully intended to do things on my own. In fact, that first evening after dinner, I had nothing particular to do and I certainly didn't want to sit in my room and watch television. So I thought— well, all of Manhattan is just outside, Barbara, and you've read about it all your life and seen it in the movies and now's your chance to see it in real life.

"I thought I'd just step out and wander about on my own and look at the elaborate buildings and the bright lights and the people hurrying past. I just wanted to get a *feel* of the city, before I started taking organized tours. I've done that in other cities in these recent years when I've been travelling and I've always so enjoyed it."

Trumbull said, "You weren't afraid of getting lost, I suppose."

"Oh, *no*," said Mrs. Lindemann, earnestly. "I have an excellent sense of direction and even if I were caught up in my sight-seeing and didn't notice where I had gone, I had a map of Manhattan and the streets are all in a rectangular grid and numbered—not like Boston, London, or Paris, and I was never lost in those cities. Besides, I could always get in a taxi and give the driver the name of my hotel. In fact, I am sure anyone would give me directions if I asked."

Rubin emerged from his slough of despond to deliver himself of a ringing, "In Manhattan? Hah!"

"Why, certainly," said Mrs. Lindemann, with mild reproof. "I've always heard that Manhattanites are un-friendly, but I have not found it so. I have been the recipient of many kindnesses—not the least of which is the manner in which you gentlemen have welcomed me even though I am quite a stranger to you."

Rubin found it necessary to stare intently at his fingernails.

Mrs. Lindemann said, "In any case, I did go off on my little excursion and stayed out much longer than I had planned. Everything was so colorful and busy and the weather was so mild and pleasant. Eventually, I realized I was terribly tired and I had reached a rather quiet street and was ready to go back. I reached in one of the outer pockets of my purse for my map—"

Halsted interrupted. "I take it, Mrs. Lindemann, you were alone on this excursion."

"Oh, yes," said Mrs. Lindemann, "I always travel alone since my husband died. To have a companion means a perpetual state of compromise as to when to arise, what to eat, where to go. No, no, I want to be my own woman."

"I didn't quite mean that, Mrs. Lindemann," said Halsted. "I mean to ask whether you were alone on this particular outing in a strange city—at night—with a purse."

"Yes, sir. I'm afraid so."

Halsted said, "Had no one told you that the streets of New York aren't always safe at night—particularly, excuse me, for older women with purses who look, as you do, gentle and harmless?"

"Oh, dear, of *course* I've been told that. I've been told that of every city I've visited. My own town has districts that aren't safe. I've always felt, though, that all life is a gamble, that a no-risk situation is an impossible dream, and I wasn't going to deprive myself of pleasant experiences because of fear. And I've gone about in all sorts of places without harm."

Trumbull said, "Until that first evening in Manhattan, I take it."

Mrs. Lindemann's lips tightened and she said, "Until then. It was an experience I remember only in flashes, so to speak. I suppose that because I was so tired, and then so frightened, and the surroundings were so new to me, much of what happened somehow didn't register properly. Little things seem to have vanished forever. That's the problem."

She bit her lips and looked as though she was battling to hold back the tears.

Henry said softly, "Could you tell us what you remember?"

"Well," she said, clearing her throat and clutching at her purse, "as I said, the street was a quiet one. There were cars moving past, but no pedestrians, and I wasn't sure where I was. I was reaching for the map and looking about for a street sign when a young man seemed to appear from nowhere and called out, 'Got a dollar lady?' He couldn't have been more than fifteen years old—just a boy.

"Well, I would have been perfectly willing to let him have a dollar if I thought he needed it, but really, he seemed perfectly fit and reasonably prosperous and I didn't think it would be advisable to display my wallet, so I said, 'I'm afraid I don't, young man.'

"Of course, he didn't believe me. He came closer and said, 'Sure you do, lady. Here, let me help you look,' and he reached for my purse. Well, I wasn't going to let him have it, of course—"

Trumbull said, firmly, "No 'of course' about it, Mrs. Lindemann. If it ever happens again, you surrender your purse at once. You can't save it in any case, and the hoodlums will think nothing of using force, and there is nothing in the purse that can possibly be worth your life."

Mrs. Lindemann sighed. "I suppose you're right, but at the time I just wasn't thinking clearly. I held on to my purse as a reflex action, I suppose, and that's when I start failing to remember. I recall engaging in a tug-of-war and I seem to recall other young men approaching. I don't know how many but I seemed surrounded.

"Then I heard a shout and some very bad language and the loud noise of feet. There was nothing more for a while except that my purse was gone. Then there was an anxious voice, low and polite, 'Are you hurt, madam?'

"I said, 'I don't think so, but my purse is gone.' I looked about vaguely. I think I was under the impression it had fallen to the street.

"There was an older young man holding my elbow respectfully. He might have been twenty-five. He said, 'They got that, ma'am, I'd better get you out of here before they come back for some more fun. They'll probably have knives and I don't.'

"He was hurrying me away. I didn't see him clearly in the dark but he was tall and wore a sweater. He said, 'I live close by, ma'am. It's either get to my place or we'll have a battle.' I *think* I was aware of other young men in the distance, but that may have been a delusion.

"I went with the new young man quite docilely. He seemed earnest and polite and I've gotten too old to feel that I am in danger of—uh—*personal* harm. Besides, I was so confused and light-headed that I lacked any will to resist.

"The next thing I remember is being at his apartment door. I remember that it was apartment 4-F. I suppose that remains in my mind because it was such a familiar combinaton during World War II. Then I was inside his apartment and setting in an upholstered armchair. It was a rather run-down apartment, I noticed, but I don't remember getting to it at all.

"The man who had rescued me had put a glass into my hand and I sipped at it. It was some kind of wine, I think. I did not particularly like the taste, but it warmed me and it seemed to make me less dizzy—rather than more dizzy, as one would suppose.

"The man seemed anxious about my possibly being hurt, but I reassured him. I said if he would just help me get a taxi I would get back to my hotel. He said I had better rest a while.

"He offered to call the police to report the incident, but I was adamant against that. That's one of the things I remember *very* clearly. I knew the police could not recover my purse and I did *not* want to become a newspaper item.

"I think I must have explained that I was from out of town because he lectured me, quite gently, on the dangers of walking on the streets of Manhattan.—I've heard so much on the subject in the last week. You should hear my niece go on and on about it.

"I remember other bits of the conversation. He wanted to know whether I'd lost much cash and I said, well, about thirty or forty dollars, but that I had traveller's checks which could, of course, be replaced. I think I had to spend some time reassuring him that I knew how to do that, and that I knew how to report my missing credit card. I had only had one in my purse.

"Finally, I asked him his name so that I could speak to him properly and he laughed and said, 'Oh, first names will do for that.' He told me his and I told him mine. And I said, 'Isn't it astonishing how it all fits together, your name, and your address, and what you said back there.' I explained and he laughed and said he would never have thought of that.—So you see I knew his address.

"Then we went downstairs and it was quite late by then, at least by the clock, though, of course, it wasn't really very late by my insides. He made sure the streets were clear, then made me wait in the vestibule while he went out to get a cab. He told me he had paid the driver to take me wherever I wanted to go and then before I could stop him he put a twenty-dollar bill in my hand because he said I mustn't be left with no money at all.

"I tried to object, but he said he loved New York, and since I had been so mistreated on my first evening there by New Yorkers, it had to be made up for by New Yorkers. So I took it—because I knew I would pay it back.

"The driver took me back to the hotel and he didn't try to collect any money. He even tried to give me change because he said the young man had given him a five-dollar bill but I was pleased with his honesty and I wouldn't take the change.

"So you see although the incident began very painfully, there was the extreme kindness of the Good Samaritan young man and of the taxi driver. It was as though an act of unkindness was introduced into my life in order that I might experience other acts of kindness that would more than redress the balance.—And I *still* experience them; yours, I mean.

"Of course, it was quite obvious that the young man was not well off and I strongly suspected that the twenty-five dollars he had expended on me was far more than he could afford to throw away. Nor did he ask my last name or what my hotel was. It was as though he knew I would pay it back without having to be reminded. Naturally, I would.

"You see, I'm quite well-to-do really, and it's not just a matter of paying it back. The Bible says that if you cast your bread upon the waters it will be returned tenfold, so I think it's only fair that if he put out twenty-five dollars, he ought to get two hundred fifty back and I can afford it.

"I got back to my room and slept so soundly after all that; it was quite refreshing. The next morning, I arranged my affairs with respect to the credit card and the traveller's checks and then I called my niece and spent the day with her.

"I told her what had happened, but just the bare essentials. After all, I had to explain why I had no bag and why I was temporarily short of cash. She went on and *on* about it. I bought a new purse—this one—and it wasn't till the end of the day when I was in bed again that I realized that I had not made it my business to repay the young man *first thing*. Being with family had just preoccupied me. And then the real tragedy struck me."

Mrs. Lindemann stopped and tried to keep her face from crumpling but failed. She began to weep quietly and to reach desperately into her bag for a handkerchief.

Henry said softly, "Would you care to rest awhile, Mrs. Lindemann?"

Rubin said, just as softly, "Would you like a cup of tea, Mrs. Lindemann, or some brandy?" Then he glared about as though daring anyone to say a word.

Mrs. Lindemann said, "No, I'm all right. I apologize for behaving so, but I found I had forgotten. I don't remember the young man's address, *not at all*, though I must have known it that night because I talked about it. I don't remember his first name! I stayed awake all night trying to remember, and that just made it worse. I went out the next day to try to retrace my steps, but everything looked so different by day—and by night, I was afraid to try.

"What must the young man think of me? He's never heard from me. I took his money and just vanished with it. I am worse than those terrible young hoodlums who snatched my purse. I had never been kind to *them*. They owed *me* no gratitude."

Gonzalo said, "It's not your fault that you can't remember. You had a rough time."

"Yes, but *he* doesn't know I can't remember. He thinks I'm an ungrateful thief. Finally, I told my nephew about my trouble and he was just thinking of employing Mr. Gonzalo for something and he felt that Mr. Gonzalo might have the kind of worldly wisdom that might help. Mr. Gonzalo said he would try, and in the end—here I am. But now that I've heard myself tell the story I realize how hopeless it all sounds."

Trumbull sighed. "Mrs. Lindemann, please don't be offended at what I am about to ask, but we must eliminate some factors. Are you sure it all really happened?"

Mrs. Lindemann looked surprised. "Well, of *course* it really happened. My purse was *gone!*"

"No," said Henry, "what Mr. Trumbull means I think is that after the mugging, you somehow got back to the hotel and then had a sleep that may have been filled with nightmares so that what you remember now is partly fact and partly dream—which would account for the imperfect memory."

"No," said Mrs. Lindemann firmly, "I remember what I do remember perfectly. It was not a dream."

"In that case," said Trumbull, shrugging, "we have very little to go on."

Rubin said, "Never mind, Tom. We're not giving up. If we choose the right name for your rescuer, Mrs. Lindemann, would you recognize it, even though you can't remember it now?"

"I hope so," said Mrs. Lindemann, "but I don't know. I've tried looking in a phone directory to see different first names, but none seemed familiar. I don't think it could have been a very common name."

Rubin said, "Then it couldn't have been Sam?"

"Oh, I'm certain that's not it."

"Why Sam, Manny?" asked Gonzalo.

"Well, the fellow was a Good Samaritan. Mrs. Lindemann called him that herself. Sam for Samaritan. His number and street may have represented the chapter and verse in the Bible where the tale of the Good Samaritan begins. You said his name and address fitted each other and that's the only clue we have."

"Wait," put in Avalon eagerly, "the first name might have been the much less common one of Luke. That's the gospel in which the parable is to be found."

"I'm afraid," said Mrs. Lindemann, "that doesn't sound right, either. Besides, I'm not *that* well acquainted with the Bible. I couldn't identify the chapter and verse of the parable."

Halsted said, "Let's not get off on impossible tangents. Mrs. Lindemann taught American history in school so it's very likely that what struck her applied to American history. For instance, suppose the address were 1812 Madison Avenue and the young man's name was James. James Madison was President during the War of 1812."

"Or 1492 Columbus Avenue," said Gonzalo, "and the young man was named Christopher."

"Or 1775 Lexington Avenue and the name Paul for Paul Revere," said Trumbull.

"Or 1623 Amsterdam Avenue and the name Peter," said Avalon, "for Peter Minuit, or 1609 Hudson Avenue and the name Henry. In fact, there are many named streets in lower Manhattan. We can never pick an appropriate one unless Mrs. Lindemann remembers."

Mrs. Lindemann clasped her hands tightly together. "Oh, dear, oh, *dear*, nothing sounds familiar."

Rubin said, "Of course not, if we're going to guess at random. Mrs. Lindemann, I assume you are at a midtown hotel."

"I'm at the New York Hilton. Is that midtown?"

"Yes. Sixth Avenue and Fifty-third Street. The chances are you could not have walked more than a mile, probably less, before you grew tired. Therefore, let's stick to midtown. Hudson Avenue is much too far south and places like 1492 Columbus or 1812 Madison are much too far north. It would have to be midtown, probably West Side—and I can't think of anything."

Drake said, through a haze of cigarette smoke, "You're forgetting one item. Mrs. Lindemann said it wasn't just the name and address that fit but what the young man said back there; that is, at the site of the rescue. What did he say back there?"

"It's all so hazy," said Mrs. Lindemann.

"You said he called out roughly at the muggers. Can you repeat what he said?"

Mrs. Lindemann colored. "I could repeat *some* of what he said, but I don't think I want to. The young man apologized for it afterward. He said that unless he used bad language the hoodlums would not have been impressed and would not have scattered. Besides, I know I couldn't have referred to *that* at all."

Drake said thoughtfully, "That bites the dust then. Have you thought of advertising? You know, 'Will the young man who aided a woman in distress—' and so on."

"I've thought of it," said Mrs. Lindemann, "but that would be *so* dreadful. He might not see it and so many imposters might arrive too make a claim.—Really, this is so dreadful."

Avalon, looking distressed, turned to Henry and said, "Well, Henry, does anything occur to you?"

Henry said, "I'm not certain.—Mrs. Lindemann, you said that by the time you took the taxi it was late by the clock but not by your insides. Does that mean you arrived from the West Coast by plane so that your perception of time was three hours earlier than the clock?"

"Yes, I did," said Mrs. Lindemann.

"Perhaps from Portland, or not too far from there?" asked Henry.

"Why, yes, from just outside Portland. Had I mentioned that?"

"No, you hadn't," interposed Trumbull. "How did you know, Henry?"

"Because it occurred to me, sir," said Henry, "that the young man's name was Eugene, which is the name of a town only about a hundred miles south of Portland."

Mrs. Lindemann rose, eyes staring. "My goodness! The name *was* Eugene! But that's marvellous. How could you possibly tell?"

Henry said, "Mr. Rubin pointed out the address had to be in midtown Manhattan on the West Side. Dr. Drake pointed out your reference to what the young man had said at the scene of the rescue and I recalled that one thing you reported him to have said besides the bad language you did *not* describe specifically was that you had better get to his place or there'd be a battle.

"Mr. Halsted pointed out that the address ought to have some significance in American history and so I thought it might be 54 West Fortieth Street, since there is the well-known election slogan of '54-40 or fight,' the election of 1844, I believe. It would be particularly meaningful to Mrs. Lindemann if she were from the Northwest since it pertained to our dispute with Great Britain over the Oregon Territory. When she said she was indeed from near Portland, Oregon, I guessed that the rescuer's name might be Eugene."

Mrs. Lindemann sat down. "To my dying day, I will never forget this. That *is* the address. How could I have forgotten it when you worked it out so neatly from what little I did remember."

And then she grew excited. She said, "But it's not too

late. I must go there *at once*. I must pay him or shove an envelope under his door or something."

Rubin said, "Will you recognize the house if you see it?"

"Oh, yes," said Mrs. Lindemann. "I'm sure of that. And it's apartment 4-F. I remembered that. If I knew his last name, I would call, but, no, I want to *see* him and explain."

Rubin said mildly, "You certainly can't go yourself, Mrs. Lindemann. Not into that neighborhood at this time of night after what you've been through. Some of us will have to go with you. At the very least, I will."

Mrs. Lindemann said, "I very much dislike inconveniencing you, Mr. Rubin."

"Under the circumstances, Mrs. Lindemann," said Rubin, "I consider it my duty."

Henry said, "I believe we will all accompany you, Mrs. Lindemann. I know the Black Widowers."

Afterword

I am rather stubborn about keeping my Black Widowers rigidly to the format. I have sometimes thought about getting them out on a picnic in Central Park or having them attend a large convention en masse, or separating them and having each do a bit of detective work with Henry pulling the strings together at last. (I may try that last bit if I ever do a Black Widowers novel, which somehow is not a thought that greatly attracts me.) None of these variations strikes me as safe, however. Once I begin playing games with the formula, the whole thing might fall apart.

And yet even within the rigidity of the game, there are some rules that can be bent. Might we not have a woman guest despite the die-hard male chauvinism of the Black Widowers? Might a woman not be in trouble? And if the Black Widowers themselves are stupid about it, surely *Henry* wouldn't be.

So I deliberately set about writing "The Good Samaritan." I didn't have to. It might just as easily have been a kindly and unsophisticated elderly gentleman who had gotten into trouble with a mob of kids.—But I wanted a woman, if only to watch Manny Rubin throw a fit.

The story appeared in the September 10, 1980, issue of *EQMM*.

The Year of the Action

"Sir Rupert Murgatroyd," caroled Geoffrey Avalon, "his leisure and his RICHes; he ruthlessly employed in persecuting WITCHes—"

He was returning from the men's room and was clearly in a happy mood. His dark eyes twinkled and his formidable eyebrows twitched in friendly fashion.

Except that "caroled" is perhaps not the right word to use in connection with any attempt Avalon ever made in the direction of song. It was not that he was either flat or sharp, for on no occasion in the memory of any member of the Black Widowers had he ever struck a note close enough to the desired one to be either flat or sharp.

Thomas Trumbull turned on his heel as though he had been jabbed in some tender portion of his anatomy with a thumbtack. He said, "Jeff, shut *up*. Five years ago, when you last did this, I told you that any repetition of this vile noise you make, will induce homicidal mania in everyone and that I fully intended to beat them all to the punch."

"Come on, Tom," said Mario Gonzalo complacently, "the man is just in a Gilbert and Sullivan mood. Let's put him to some interesting use. If he doesn't do the words but just hums, we can all try to guess the tune."

"Except," said James Drake, thoughtfully, "that it would be a lost cause. If Jeff hummed 'Yankee Doodle' and then 'Old Man River,' we couldn't tell them apart."

Roger Halsted said, "I don't think the experiment should be tried without earplugs."

Avalon would have drawn himself up, had not his natural stance placed him in a perpetual seventy-four-inch up-drawn position. His voice, in its natural rich baritone—when he was speaking—was distinctly aggrieved in tone as he said, "I had not intended to continue singing after I had emerged from the men's room, and I will cheerfully stop. But might I remind you that as tonight's banquet host I am within my rights in declaring myself permitted to sing?"

"To do something," said Trumbull, gratingly, "that someone, somewhere, at some time, in a state not too close to drunken insensibility can call singing, yes. That does not, however, include what *you* do."

Henry, that best of waiters, who had listened blandly as he completed the table setting, raised his voice without, somehow, seeming to, and said, "Gentlemen, please seat yourselves."

They did, and Emmanuel Rubin, who had been talking to Avalon's guest of the evening during the altercation, now drew the guest into the seat next to his.

Henry held the seat for the guest and said, "Welcome to the Black Widowers, Mr. Graff."

The guest looked up in surprise. "Do you know me?"

He was rather short, not much taller than Rubin, round-faced, with a generous mustache like that of a baby walrus, and thick graying hair that covered most of his ears.

Henry said, "I attended a lecture of yours at New York University about a year ago and enjoyed it very much."

Graff beamed. He said to Rubin, "See, who needs intellectuals? With waiters, I'm big."

Rubin said, "Don't dismiss Henry that easily, Graff. We intellectuals bask in his reflected glory."

Graff said, "Listen, do you guys talk like this all the time? I never heard such fighting. Over every little thing, too. With words. With whole sentences.—And call me Herb."

Rubin said, "You have to understand, Herb, that each of us spends most of his time with ordinary people. We can't pick on them; it wouldn't be fair. Once a month, we're here, and we can let loose."

"But you sound as though you're getting mad. Look at Jeff Avalon. In one minute, he'll take his knife and carve up everyone here."

"Not at all," said Rubin. "I give him five mintues and he'll be pontificating. Listen—"

Rubin waited five minutes and then, as the roast goose was placed before him, he said, "Of course, Jeff, it is really unjust to say Gilbert and Sullivan. It should be Sullivan and Gilbert. In any of the numerous parodies of the operettas, Gilbert's words are invariably changed but no one would dream of changing a note of Sullivan's music."

Jeff said, "You are quite wrong, Manny. There were other light-opera composers in Sullivan's time and after— Offenbach, Strauss, Lehar, Romberg, and so on. Many tunes of each one of these lives. But only in the case of Sullivan are any of the tunes ever sung by ordinary people. No one knows the words—except in the case of Sullivan, because only Sullivan had the greatest lyricist in the English language working with him."

His ill temper seemed to have evaporated. "Gilbert is the one lyricist who used the full strength of the English language and the full vocabulary. He rhymes 'executioner' with 'ablutioner,' 'diminutioner,' and '*you*-shun-her.' He—"

Rubin turned to Graff and said in a low voice, "See?"

Henry was making the rounds with the brandy bottle, and Avalon bestirred himself. Rattling his spoon on the water glass, he said, "Gentlemen, we come now to the important portion of the evening. Manny, since you were the one person who, earlier in the evening, refrained from needless pseudo-wit at my expense, and showed an odd and unaccustomed gentlemanliness of behavior—"

"Odd and unaccustomed?" said Rubin indignantly, his sparse beard quivering. "If you're intending that as a compliment, it's a hell of an ungracious way of doing it."

"Odd and unaccustomed is what I said," said Avalon, loftily. "And I am asking you to be in charge of the grilling."

"What grilling?" said Graff, looking startled.

"The question-and-answer period, Herb," said Avalon, in what was for him a low voice. "I told you."

Graff, recollecting, nodded his head.

Rubin intoned, "May I ask you, Herb, just how you justify your existence?"

Graff sat back in his seat and stared in astonishment at Rubin for a moment, before answering. "Justify my existence?" he said, with a strong upward inflection. "Listen, you step out into the street and take a look at the cockamamie people passing by. You ever get into an elevator and listen to them talking? Three things you hear. Three. 'What did you watch on television last night?,' 'Where are you going to go on vacation?,' 'You think the Mets will win today?'—That is, if they can talk at all. I should justify *my* existence? Let them all justify *their* existence, and I'll justify mine. Not before."

Rubin nodded his head. "There's something in what you say."

Trumbull interrupted. "You know, Jeff's right about you, Manny. Are you sure you're Emmanuel Rubin, or are you a lookalike sent here to drive us mad with unaccustomed sweetness?"

Rubin said, "I received word of a very nice paperback sale yesterday, so I'm in a good mood, but don't presume upon it. For instance, I'll just say politely *once* not to return to that subject.—Now, Herb, putting the question of your existence's justification out of court, what is it you do?"

Graff said, "I'm a movie maven."

"A what?" muttered Gonzalo.

"Maven," said Rubin, "is from the Yiddish, for 'expert.'"

"You mean you make movies?" said Gonzalo.

"Not actually," said Graff. "I talk about them. I have, or

I can get, almost any old movie that's been made and I show them, or I show clips, and I lecture on them. People like it. I give lecture tours, especially on college campuses, and I make a living.—Henry, tell these guys about my lectures."

Henry's unlined, sixtyish face creased briefly into a gentle smile. "It was indeed an entertaining evening. I believe the audience, generally, enjoyed themselves."

Graff said, "There you are, an unpaid testimonial. But just the same, I might actually be making a movie, or helping make one, if I can only figure out how to handle the crazies."

"What kind of movie?" asked Rubin.

"Gilbert and Sullivan, actually," said Graff, with what seemed a trace of embarrassment. "I've been talking to Jeff Avalon about it on the way here and that's what put him into—you should excuse the expression—a singing mood."

"Is there money in Gilbert and Sullivan in the movies?" asked Drake skeptically. "I should think it just has a small cult following."

Graff said, "Bigger than you think, but you're right. You can't make a colossal extravaganza out of it. But then you don't have to spend ten million dollars on it. You can do it small-scale. It's been done. Kenny Baker sang Nanki-Poo in a movie version of *The Mikado* and was cut to ribbons by all the D'Oyly Carte types that supported him. The trouble is, you can't do much with Gilbert and Sullivan except photograph the stage play. You can't change the music or the words or the plot because as soon as you change anything it's not Gilbert and Sullivan and you're nowhere. So if you're just going to photograph the play, you're not taking advantage of the power of the camera and where are you?"

"Where indeed?" said Drake.

Graff said, "But these guys—I didn't tell you about these guys yet, did I? Two kids in their early twenties, but young as they are, they've really got it. You know, in any field of art, it's the young people who look at things with new eyes.

These guys are a pair of crazies, of course, but you've got to expect that. Their names are Sam Appelbaum and Tim Mentz and they're pupils of mine. I give a course on moving making at the New School and that's how I met them. They want to do *The Pirates of Penzance*, one of the Gilbert and Sullivan operettas, because they'd seen a performance by the Village Light Opera Group and were enthusiastic.

"They joined the Gilbert Sullivan Society, which seems to be a very active group here in New York, and they met Jeff Avalon, who's a Gilbert and Sullivan aficionado.—Is that the way you pronounce the word?"

"Quite," said Avalon. "Though my singing voice may not be approved by all, I presume that not even the most captious will try to prevent me from listening to music and I know virtually all of Gilbert and Sullivan by heart."

Trumbull growled, "You may know Gilbert's words by heart, but if you know a single note of Sullivan's music—or anyone's—may I be struck by lightning right now."

"In any case," said Graff, "I met Jeff through Appelbaum and Mentz, and a couple of months ago we were talking about what strategy to use in making a movie of *Pirates*, and how limited we were in handling it, and Avalon suggested an animated cartoon. Appelbaum and Mentz fell over themselves to grab the idea. You have the voices, the words, the notes, and you have a free hand to be as fantastic as you want. Gilbert and Sullivan operettas are always overacted, anyway, on principle. I'm certain that if Gilbert and Sullivan had worked in the 1970s instead of the 1870s, they would have written the operettas for animation in the first place."

James Drake stubbed out his cigarette with a violent motion and said, "I think that's disgusting. You'll have a whole bunch of cutesie choruses dancing around Prince Charming Frederic and Snow White Mabel."

"No!" said Graff, earnestly. "What do you think? Disney is all there is? Besides, who can spend the money on the kind of animation that Disney used in the days of slave labor where you make a thousand different drawings to show Dopey picking his nose realistically. We're counting on surrealism. In fact, these guys are going to use the techniques of modern art to evoke humor and fantasy in a whole new way. I can't explain how it will work. After all, am I an artist? But when they're through, it will work and you'll see how it works. It will start a whole new fashion and, on top of that, it will make them trillionaires and it would make me a few shiny pennies, too. *If* they do it, that is."

"Why *if?*" said Halsted.

"Because they had a fight, that's why. And they're still fighting," said Graff. "And go try and settle it. They've got all the money in the world waiting to be scooped in and neither one will move unless the other gives in."

"What are they fighting about?" asked Rubin. "Are they both in love with the same soprano?"

Graff shook his head. "You don't know the crazies of this world, do you? Crazies don't fight over a woman or over anything sensible. That's for plain people like you and me. Crazies fight over things you can't imagine—like when did the action of the play take place. Appelbaum says the action begins on March 1, 1877, and Mentz says March 1, 1873, and neither one will give in.

"You see, you guys in the Black Widowers argue, but you forget, because you've got a million things to argue about, so you drop each particular argument in favor of another. I've been listening to you do it all through dinner. My two guys are big talents but they're limited. They've only got one thing to fight over so there's no chance of their forgetting. With them it's 1873, 1877, 1873, 1877, till you can get sick and die."

"I take it," said Halsted, "that Gilbert gives no indication which it is."

"No," said Graff.

Trumbull said, with clear contempt, "Does it make a difference?"

Graff said, "Actually, it does. The guys want to keep up a running set of montages dating back to Victorian times to keep pace with the words and music. These would be accompaniments and references to whatever was happening, sometimes so fast you couldn't really make out the details, but you would get it, uh, subliminally.—Is that how you say it?—It would be a kind of running visual gag, and it could start a cult. You know, people would say, did you see that picture of Disraeli, and who was the other guy with him and what was he doing, and they'd go several times just to try to pick up all the clues they could. Well, there are places where what you show would depend on whether it was 1873 or 1877."

Trumbull said, "Then let them pick one of the two years and get going. Who would care?"

Graff said, "*They* would care. Neither one will give in. It's life and death with them. Look, do you know the play?"

"I don't," said Trumbull, flatly.

Drake said, "I suppose Jeff knows it by heart, but I just know the Major-General's patter song, which is an example of what Jeff was talking about with its fancy vocabulary and ingenious rhymes." Rather surprisingly, he lifted his soft, hoarse voice in song, and with a fair approximation of the notes, went, " 'Then I can hum a fugue of which I've heard the music's din afore, and whistle all the airs from that infernal nonsense, *Pinafore*.'—Which shows," he added, "that Gilbert could make a little fun of himself, too, since *Pinafore* was his big early success."

Graff said, hastily, "Well, let me just outline the plot quickly, so you can see where the trouble is. Is that all right?"

"Go ahead, Herb," said Avalon, indulgently. "I'm host and what I say goes—or should go," and he bent his formidable frown at Trumbull, who shrugged and muttered something under his breath.

Graff said, "Frederic is a pirate-apprentice. It was all a mistake because his nursery-maid, Ruth, had been told to apprentice him to a pilot, but had misheard the word. Unable to return home and explain the mistake, she, too, joined the pirate band.

"As the play opens, Frederic has just turned twenty-one and entered his twenty-second year so his apprenticeship is over. As the slave of duty he has remained with the pirates, but now that he has served his term, he will abandon them and, because he is also the soul of honor, he will devote himself to their examination.

"Ruth, a maiden of forty-seven, wants to go with him for she loves Frederic. But then they encounter the daughters of Major-General Stanley, and Frederic, realizing that Ruth is old and plain, falls in love instead with Mabel, the prettiest of the daughters.

"The pirates surprise them and make ready to marry all the daughters—anything but marriage being inconceivable to good old Gilbert—when their father arrives and sings the Major-General's song that Jim Drake mentioned. The Major-General persuades the pirates to give up their scheme for marrying his daughters by claiming, falsely, to be an orphan boy. The tenderhearted pirates burst into tears and the first act ends happily.

"In the second act, Frederic prepares to lead the police against the pirates. Before he can leave with his band, however, the Pirate King, together with Ruth, come upon him alone and tell him they have just remembered that he was born on leap day, February 29. The apprenticeship papers say he must serve till his twenty-first *birthday* and, strictly speaking, he has had only five.

"Frederic, the slave of duty, at once rejoins the band and, as a loyal pirate, now tells them of the Major-General's lie. The furious pirates attack the Major-General's estate and, in a battle with the police, emerge the winners.

"However, the police produce a Union Jack and demand the pirates yield in Queen Victoria's name. The pirates promptly do so, saying, 'With all our faults, we love our Queen.' As the pirates are about to be led away to jail, Ruth quickly explains that all the pirates are just noblemen gone wrong. The Major-General at once frees them saying, 'With all our faults, we love our House of Peers,' and everything ends happily."

Graff beamed around the table and said, "It's actually a very funny and happy play. There's just one line that creates the problem. When Frederic finds out his apprenticeship goes by birthdays and not by years, he explains to Mabel, 'In 1940 I of age shall be.' That means that on February 29, 1940, he'll celebrate his twenty-first birthday."

Drake nodded. He had lit a new cigarette and he blinked his eyes slowly. "On February 29, 1940, the New York *Times* ran an editorial on Frederic's being out of his indentures. I remember reading it."

Graff said, "All right, but if there's a leap day every four years—"

Roger Halsted interrupted. "But there isn't—"

Graff shook his head violently. "Just wait a minute. If there's a leap day every four years, then Frederic was eighty-four years old on his twenty-first birthday, and he was born in 1856. He was twenty-one years old in 1877, a year after his fifth birthday. He would have had to celebrate his coming of age on March 1, 1877, since there is no February 29 in that year and, Appelbaum says, that is therefore the day on which the action of the play opens."

"But—" said Halsted.

"But," said Graff, raising his voice, "apparently the year 1900 should have been a leap year but wasn't. There was no February 29, 1900. That's what you're trying to say, isn't it, Roger? I don't know why that should be. Some Pope arranged it."

Halsted said, "Pope Gregory XIII in—"

"That part doesn't matter," said Graff, impatiently. "The point is that one leap day is missing, so to get twenty-one of them, you have to move four years further back. Frederic would have to have been born in 1852 and become twenty-one in 1873, so that the action of the play opens on March 1, 1873. That's what Mentz says.

"*The Pirates of Penzance* opened in early 1880 so 1877 is the logical year, says Appelbaum, and Gilbert either forgot or didn't know that 1900 was not a leap year. Mentz says it is inconceivable that Gilbert would make a mistake about 1900 and that no true aficionado—yes, you told me I said it right—would think so for a minute, so the year was 1873. There they stand. Neither one will give in."

There was a silence around the table. Finally, Gonzalo said, "You really think there's a lot of money in the picture if they make it?"

Graff said, "Who can tell about public taste—but there's a good chance."

"Then can't you make up some argument that would convince them one year or the other was right? You know, something that sounds good?"

"Like what?" said Graff.

"The trouble is," said Avalon, sententiously, "that the world of Gilbert and Sullivan is not a real one and it doesn't lend itself to logical arguments. For instance, though it is clearly stated that Frederic has just turned twenty-one and that his birthday is on February 29, nevertheless the Major-General's daughters, when they first arrive on the scene, decide to take off their shoes and socks and paddle their feet in the sea. The scene is set in Cornwall, where the town of Penzance is located, and you can imagine what it would be like paddling in the English Channel in winter."

"Well," said Graff, "the daughters call themselves 'hardy little lasses' in their first chorus."

Gonzalo said, "Did the Major-General have any sons?"

"No," said Graff, "just daughters. In a full performance, there could be as many as twenty-four daughters, all pretty much the same age and no sign of any mother, either. It *is* unreal, so how are we going to find some way of deciding between 1873 and 1877 that will hold water?"

Trumbull said, "You have to think of something that *sounds* good. It doesn't have to *be* good, or sensible. Look, wasn't Queen Victoria Empress of India, too?—Henry, would you be so kind as to go over to the reference shelf and look up Queen Victoria in the encyclopedia. Maybe it will say when she became Empress."

After some moments, Henry said, "The title was secured for her by Benjamin Disraeli in 1876, sir, and she was proclaimed Empress of India on January 1, 1877."

"Ah, perfect. The whole thing is solved and we can forget about this nonsense."

Graff looked doubtful. "How is it solved?"

"Easy. Victoria loved the new title. Anyone wanting to please her would go around calling her 'Queen-Empress.' You quoted the pirates as saying that, with all their faults, they love their Queen. Well, if the action opens on March 1, 1877, only two months after Victoria gained the imperial title, surely they would refer to her, with pride, as Queen-Empress. The fact that they didn't proves it was 1873."

Graff looked still more doubtful. "'Queen-Empress' wouldn't rhyme or scan."

"Don't be an idiot," said Trumbull. "I told you the argument doesn't have to make *sense*. It just has to *sound* good. It's just a piece of gobbledygook designed to settle the matter."

"I don't think that would win over Appelbaum," said Graff.

"Well, then," said Avalon, "let's think up more arguments like that, but let's keep them all on one particular year, because if we think up ways of arguing for both years, that won't settle matters. What else is there we can use for 1873? It doesn't have to be sensible."

"Anything else about kings and queens?" asked Gonzalo. "Does the Pirate King represent anyone?"

"I don't know that he does," said Avalon, shaking his head slowly, "but there is some mention of kings in the Pirate King's opening solo. He admits he sinks more ships than a well-bred monarch ought to do, but then he says, 'Many a king on a first-class throne, if he wants to call his crown his own, must manage somehow to get through more dirty work than ever I do.' Now can he be referring to some particular king?"

Rubin stared up through narrowed eyes. "Let's see—Who were the first-class thrones in the 1870s? There was William I of Germany. The German Empire had just been established and there was a lot of chicanery there."

Drake said, "That was the chicanery of Otto von Bismarck, Manny. William I was just an old man who did what he was told."

Rubin said, "You're right there, Jim.—Francis Joseph of Austria was a dim sort of monarch and Alexander II of Russia was not bad for a tsar. Those were the only ones whom Gilbert would have considered as sitting on a first-class throne."

Halsted said, "How about Napoleon III of France? Wasn't he ruling about that time?"

"No," said Rubin. "He got kicked out in the Franco-Prussian War in 1870, and France was a Republic in the 1870s and, in fact, ever since. Too bad, too, because Napoleon III was as crooked as a bolt of lightning. He was a conniver and an intriguer who made it to the imperial throne by lying and cheating and he could at no time be trusted to keep his word unless you kept a gun trained at him."

Gonzalo said, "When did he die?"

Rubin said, "I'm not sure. Not long afterward, I think. Henry, would you check that little matter."

Henry did so. "He died on January 9, 1873."

Gonzalo was enthusiastic. "That's perfect. Gilbert wouldn't make snide remarks against a sitting monarch, because that would create an international incident, but—"

Rubin said, "Listen, Gilbert would not hesitate to—"

"No, no, we're just building an argument," said Gonzalo, "so let's say he wouldn't. But a king who was dead would be fair game. If it were 1877, the Pirate King might not think of Napoleon III, but if it were 1873, Napoleon III would have died only two months before, there would have been obituaries and biographies, and he would be fresh in the minds of pirates. Naturally, they would refer to the 'dirty work' he did. So that's two arguments for 1873."

Avalon said, "That won't work, Mario. Napoleon III wasn't a king. He was an emperor. France, Germany, Austria-Hungary, and Russia were all empires in Victoria's time. So was Japan, for that matter. That was one reason why Victoria was so pleased with the imperial title. Without it, every other important monarch outranked her."

"So?" said Gonzalo.

"So," said Avalon, "Tom's argument is that it had to be 1873 because Victoria was called a Queen and not a Queen-Empress. But if you're going to be so picky about titles you can't have the Pirate King talk about kings when he is referring to Napoleon III, who was an emperor."

"On this point, Jeff," said Rubin, "I side with Mario. Gilbert, as a loyal Britisher, would certainly not abate one jot of the title of Victoria. However, he isn't going to worry about some French monarch. In Gilbert's time, France was still the traditional enemy of Great Britain through a series of wars stretching back to Henry II seven centuries before."

Graff nodded. "There's something to that. In *Ruddigore*, there's a song by the sailor, Richard Dauntless, which makes mild fun of the French and calls them 'froggies,' 'parley-voos,' and 'darned Mounseers.'"

"Exactly," said Rubin. "Gilbert wouldn't worry about the precise title of a darned Mounseer, so that's two arguments in favor of 1873."

Graff said, "Yes, but they're—" He wiggled his hand in a rapid roll.

"All right, then," said Avalon. "Anything else?"

Silence.

Finally, Halsted muttered, "I wish I knew the play better. Listen, Herb, did you say the pirates were members of the House of Peers?"

"They have to be," said Graff. "When the Major-General hears that the pirates are noblemen gone wrong, he says, 'No Englishman unmoved that statement hears, because, with all our faults, we love our House of Peers.' Then he goes on to say to the pirates, 'Peers will be peers, and youth will have its fling. Resume your ranks and legislative duties—' So I suppose they're part of Parliament.''

"Ah," said Halsted, "then that settles it. In the 1870s, Great Britain was the dominant economic power on earth. In particular, there were heavy British investments in the United States. *If* a bunch of notorious pirates were suddenly to flood into Parliament, that would make Americans feel pretty shaky about the status of the British investments. You can't trust pirates. They might withdraw those investments. That would unsettle the American economy and—"

"You would have the Panic of 1873," said Rubin, triumphantly.

"Exactly," said Halsted.

Rubin said, "That really does it. There *was* a Panic of 1873. It was the worst economic downturn the United States had up to the Great Depression of the 1930s."

Avalon said, "There you are, Herb. Three arguments in favor of 1873. Each one by itself is weak, perhaps, but surely all three combined have force. One: Victoria would have been referred to as Queen in 1873, but not in 1877 when she was Empress as well. Two: Napoleon III would have been referred to as an example of a royal conniver in 1873, soon after he died, but not in 1877 by which time he might have been out of mind. Three: the return of the pirates to Parliament could and did set off an American depression in 1873, while there was none in 1877."

Graff nodded gloomily. "Yes, that's very nice and I hope it works. Maybe it will work. Anyway, I want to thank you all very much. If I can get Appelbaum to see the force of these arguments—" He paused, then said wistfully, "There wouldn't be anything else you could feed me, would there? Something, I mean, that doesn't have all that subtle logic. Something simple."

His eyes went from one to the other and met only blankness.

Afterword

I have a number of wild enthusiasms, and one of them is Gilbert and Sullivan. I am a member of The Gilbert and Sullivan Society and occasionally I like to drag some G & S reference into a story. Finally, I managed to think of a plot in which a G & S angle is central and then you can bet that nothing could stop me from writing the story at once. Fred Dannay changed the title to "The Gilbert and Sullivan Mystery" but that struck me as too prosaic, so I kept my own title for this collection.

Incidentally, the character Herb Graff in the story is, in a way, a real person. He is a dear friend of mine in the Dutch Treat Club, another organization I belong to. He asked me to put him into a story, using his real name, description, and hobby. I was doubtful and asked him to give me a piece of paper with his signature on it, giving me permission to do so. He gladly did so.

I thereupon wrote him into "The Year of the Action" and gave him a copy of the January 1, 1981, issue of *EQMM*, in which the story appeared. That was at a Dutch Treat luncheon, something we have every Tuesday.

The following Tuesday I said, "How did you like the story?," for I thought he would be pleased at how well I had captured his essence (and he's really one of the nicest guys in the world—funny, intelligent, and with a heart of gold).

However, I had used a word he had disapproved of and that spoiled everything. He drew himself up, fixed me with a piercing eye, and said, "Plump???"

No word is worth hurting the feelings of a friend, so you won't find it in the version of the book. I have removed it.

Can You Prove It?

Henry, the smoothly functioning waiter at the monthly Black Widowers banquet, filled the water glass of the evening's guest as though knowing in advance that that guest was reaching into his shirt pocket for a small vial of pills.

The guest looked up. "Thank you, waiter—though the pills are small enough to go down au jus, so to speak."

He looked about the table and sighed. "Advancing age! In our modern times we are not allowed to grow old ad lib. Doctors follow the faltering mechanism in detail and insist on applying the grease. My blood pressure is a touch high and I have an occasional extrasystole, so I take a pretty little orange pill four times a day."

Geoffrey Avalon, who sat immediately across the table, smiled with the self-conscious superiority of a man moderately stricken in years who kept himself in good shape with a vigorous system of calisthenics, and said, "How old are you, Mr. Smith?"

"Fifty-seven. With proper care, my doctor assures me I will live out a normal lifetime."

Emmanuel Rubin's eyes flashed in magnified form behind his thick spectacles as he said, "I doubt there's an American who reaches middle age these days who doesn't become accustomed to a regimen of pills of one kind or another. I take zinc and vitamin E and a few other things."

James Drake nodded and said in his soft voice as he peered through his cigarette smoke, "I have a special weekly pillbox arrangement to keep the day's dosages correct. That way you can check on whether you've taken the second pill of a particular kind. If it's in the Friday compartment still—assuming the day is Friday—you haven't taken it."

Smith said, "I take only this one kind of pill, which simplifies things. I bought a week's supply three years ago—twenty-eight of them—on my doctor's prescription. I was frankly skeptical, but they helped me tremendously and I persuaded my doctor to prescribe them for me in bottles of a thousand. Every Sunday morning, I put twenty-eight into my original vial, which I carry with me everywhere and at all times and which I still use. I know at all times how much I should have—right now, I should have four left, having just taken the twenty-fourth of the week, and I do. In three years, I've missed a pill only twice."

"I," said Rubin, loftily, "have not yet reached that pitch of senility that requires any mnemonic devices at all."

"No?" asked Mario Gonzalo, spearing his last bit of baba au rhum. "What pitch of senility *have* you reached?"

Roger Halsted, who was hosting the banquet that night, forestalled Rubin's rejoinder by saying, hastily, "There's an interesting point to be made here. As increasing numbers of people pump themselves full of chemicals, there must be fewer and fewer people with untampered tissue chemistry."

"None at all," growled Thomas Trumbull. "The food we eat is loaded with additives. The water we drink has purifying chemicals. The air we breathe is half pollution of one sort or another. If you could analyze an individual's blood carefully enough, you could probably tell where he lived, what he eats, what medicines he takes."

Smith nodded. His short hair exposed prominent ears, something Gonzalo had taken full advantage of in preparing his caricature of the evening's guest. Now Smith rubbed one of them thoughtfully, and said, "Maybe you could file everyone's detailed blood pattern in some computer bank. Then if all else fails, your blood would be your identification. The pattern would be entered into the computer which would compare it with all those in its memory files and, within a minute, words would flash across a screen saying, 'The man you have here is John Smith of Fairfield, Connecticut,' and I would stand up and bow."

Trumbull said, "If you could stand up and bow, you could stand up and identify yourself. Why bother with a blood pattern?"

"Oh, yes?" said Smith, grimly.

Halsted said, "Listen, let's not get involved in this. Henry is distributing the brandy and it's past time for the grilling. Jeff, will you assume the task?"

"I will be glad to," said Avalon in his most solemn tone.

Bending his fierce and graying eyebrows over his eyes, Avalon said, with incongruous mildness, "And just how do you justify your existence, Mr. Smith?"

"Well," said Smith, cheerfully, "I inherited a going business. I did well with it, sold it profitably, invested wisely, and now live in early retirement in a posh place in Fairfield—a widower with two grown children, each on his own. I toil not, neither do I spin and, like the lilies of the field, my justification is my beauty and the way it illuminates the landscape." A grin of self-mockery crossed his pleasantly ugly face.

Avalon said, indulgently, "I suppose we can pass that. Beauty is in the eye of the beholder. Your name is John Smith?"

"And I can prove it," said Smith quickly. "Name your poison. I have my card, a driver's license, a variety of credit cards, some personal letters addressed to me, a library card, and so on."

"I am perfectly willing to accept your word, sir, but it occurs to me that with a name like John Smith you must frequently encounter some signs of cynical disbelief—from hotel clerks, for instance. Do you have a middle initial?"

"No, sir, I am the real thing. My parents felt that any modification of the grand cliché would spoil the grandeur. I won't deny that there haven't been times when I've longed to say my name was Eustace Bartholomew Wasservogel, but the feeling passes. Of the Smiths I am, and of that tribe—variety, John—I remain."

Avalon cleared his throat portentously and said, "And yet, Mr. Smith, I feel you have reason to feel annoyance at your name. You reacted to Tom's suggestion that you could merely announce your name and make the blood identification unnecessary with a clear tone of annoyance. Have you had some special occasion of late when you failed to identify yourself?"

Trumbull said, "Let me guess that you did. Your eagerness to demonstrate your ability to prove your identity would show that some past failure to do so rankles."

Smith stared around the table in astonishment, "Good God, does it show that much?"

Halsted said, "No, John, it doesn't, but this group has developed a sixth sense about mysteries. I told you when you accepted my invitation that if you were hiding a skeleton in your closet, they'd have it out of you."

"And I told you, Roger," said Smith, "that I had no mystery about me."

"And the matter of inability to prove identity?" said Rubin.

"Was a nightmare rather than a mystery," said Smith, "and it is something I've been asked not to talk about."

Avalon said, "Anything mentioned within the four walls of a Black Widowers banquet represents privileged communication. Feel free."

"I can't." Smith paused, then said, "Look, I don't know what it's all about. I think I was mistaken for someone once when I was visiting Europe and after I got out of the nightmare, I was visited by someone from the—by someone, and asked not to talk about it. Though come to think of it, there is a mystery of a sort."

"Ah," said Avalon, "and what might that be?"

"I don't really know how I got out of the nightmare," said Smith.

Gonzalo, looking pleased and animated, said, "Tell us what happened and I'll bet we tell you how you got out of it."

"I can't very well—" began Smith.

Trumbull's frowning face, having attempted to wither Gonzalo, turned to Smith. "I understand such things, Mr. Smith," he said. "Suppose you omit the name of the country involved and the exact dates and any other such indentifiable paraphernalia. Just tell it as a story out of the Arabian Nights—if the nightmare will stand up without the dangerous detail."

Smith said, "I think it will, but seriously, gentlemen, if the matter does involve national security—and I can imagine ways in which it might—how can I be sure you are all to be trusted?"

Halsted said, "If you trust me, John, I'll vouch for the rest of the Black Widowers—including, of course, Henry, our esteemed waiter."

Henry, standing at the sideboard, smiled gently.

Smith was visibly tempted. "I don't say I wouldn't like to get this off my chest—"

"If you choose not to," said Halsted, "I'm afraid the banquet ends. The terms of the invitation were that you were to answer all questions truthfully."

Smith laughed. "You also said I would not be asked anything designed to humiliate me or to put me in a disgraceful light—but have it your way."

"I was visiting Europe last year," said Smith, "and I'll put the location and date no closer than that. I was a recent widower, a little lost without my wife, and rather determined to pick up the threads of life once again. I had not been much of a traveller before my retirement and I was anxious to make up for that.

"I travelled alone and I was a tourist. Nothing more than that. I want to stress that in all truthfulness. I was not serving any organ of the government—and that's true of *any*

government, not just my own—either officially or unoffi-
cially. Nor was I there to gather information for any private
organization. I was a tourist and nothing more and so
steeped in innocence that I suppose it was too much to
expect that I not get into trouble.

"I could not speak the language of the country but that
didn't bother me. I can't speak any language but English
and I have the usual provincial American attitude that that's
enough. There would always be *someone*, anywhere I might
be, who would speak and understand English.—And as a
matter of fact, that always proved to be correct.

"The hotel I stayed at was reasonably comfortable in
appearance, though there was so foreign an aura about it
that I knew I would not feel at home—but then I didn't
expect to feel at home. I couldn't even pronounce its name,
though that didn't bother me.

"I only stayed long enough to deposit my luggage and
then it was ho, for the great foreign spaces where I could get
to know the people.

"The man at the desk—the concierge, or whatever he
might be called—spoke an odd version of English that, with
a little thought, could be understood. I got a list of tourist
attractions from him, some recommended restaurants, a
stylized map of the city (not in English, so I doubted it
would do me much good), and some general assertions as to
how safe the city was and how friendly the inhabitants.

"I imagine Europeans are always eager to impress that on
Americans, who are known to live dangerously. In the
nineteenth century they thought every American city lay
under imminent threat of Indian massacre; in the first half of
the twentieth century, every one was full of Chicago
gangsters; and now they are all full of indiscriminate
muggers. So I wandered off into the city cheerfully."

"Alone? Without knowing the language?" said Avalon,
with manifest disapproval. "What time was it?"

"The shades of evening were being drawn downward by
a cosmic hand and you're right in the implication, Mr.

Avalon. Cities are never as safe as their boosters claim, and I found that out. But I started off cheerfully enough. The world was full of poetry and I was enjoying myself.

"There were signs of all kinds on buildings and in store windows that were beginning to be lit up in defense against the night. Since I could read none of them, I was spared their deadly prosiness.

"The people *were* friendly. I would smile and they would smile in return. Many said something—I presume in greeting—and I would smile again and nod and wave. It was a beautiful, mild evening and I was absolutely euphoric.

"I don't know how long I was walking or how far I had gone before I was quite convinced that I was lost, but even that didn't bother me. I stepped into a tavern to ask my way to the restaurant where I had determined to go and whose name I had painstakingly memorized. I called out the name of the restaurant, and pointed vaguely in various directions and shrugged my shoulders and tried to indicate that I had lost my way. Several gathered around and one of them asked in adequate English if I was an American. I said I was and he translated that jubilantly to the others, who seemed delighted.

"He said, 'We don't see many Americans here.' They then fell to studying my clothes and the cut of my hair and asking where I was from and trying to pronounce 'Fairfield' and offering to stand me drinks. I sang 'The Star-Spangled Banner' because they seemed to expect it and it was a real love feast. I did have a drink on an empty stomach and after that things got even love-feastier.

"They told me the restaurant I asked for was very expensive, and not very good, and that I should eat right there and they would order for me and it would be on the house. It was hands across the sea and building bridges, you know, and I doubt if I had ever been happier since before Regina had died. I had another drink or two.

"And then after that my memory stops until I found

myself out in the street again. It was quite dark, much cooler. There were almost no people about, I had no idea where I was, and every idea that I had a splitting headache.

"I sat down in a doorway and knew, even before I felt for it, that my wallet was gone. So was my wristwatch, my pens—In fact, my trousers pockets were empty and so were my jacket pockets. I had been Mickey Finned and rolled by my dear friends across the sea and they had probably taken me by car to a distant part of the city and dumped me.

"The money taken was not terribly vital. My main supply was safely back in the hotel. Still I had no money at the moment, I didn't know where I was, I didn't remember the name of the hotel, I felt woozy, sick, and in pain—and I needed help.

"I looked for a policeman or for anyone in anything that looked like a uniform. If I had found a street cleaner, or a bus conductor, he could direct me or, better, take me to a police station.

"I found a policeman. Actually, it wasn't difficult. They are, I imagine, numerous and deliberately visible in that particular city. And I was then taken to a police station—in the equivalent of a paddy wagon, I think. My memory has its hazy spots.

"When I begin to remember a bit more clearly, I was sitting on a bench in what I guessed to be the police station. No one was paying much attention to me and my headache was a little better.

"A rather short man with a large mustache entered, engaged in conversation with a man behind a massive desk, then approached me. He seemed rather indifferent, but to my relief he spoke English and quite well, too, though he had a disconcertingly British accent.

"I followed him into a rather dingy room, gray and depressing, and there the questioning began. It was the questioning that was the nightmare, though the questioner remained unfailingly, if distantly, polite. He told me his name but I don't remember it. I honestly don't. It began with a *V,* so I'll just call him 'Vee' if I have to.

"He said, 'You say your name is John Smith.'

"'Yes.'

"He didn't exactly smile. He said, 'It is a very common name in the United States and, I understand, is frequently assumed by those who wish to avoid investigation.'

"'It is frequently assumed *because* it is common,' I said, 'and since it is common, why shouldn't I be one of the hundreds of thousands who bear it?'

"'You have identification?'

"'I've been robbed. I've come in to complain—'

"Vee raised his hand and made hushing noises through his mustache. 'Your complaint has been recorded, but I have nothing to do with the people here. They merely made sure you were not wounded and then sent for me. They have not searched you or questioned you. It is not their job. Now—do you have identification?'

"Wearily, and quietly, I told him what had happened.

"'Then,' he said, 'you have nothing with which to support your statement that you are John Smith of Fairfield, Connecticut?'

"'Who else should I be?'

"'That we would like to find out. You say you were mistreated in a tavern. Its location, please.'

"'I don't know.'

"'Its name?'

"'I don't know.'

"'What were you doing there?'

"'I told you. I was merely walking through the city—'

"'Alone?'

"'Yes, alone. I told you.'

"'Your starting point?'

"'My hotel.'

"'And you have identification there?'

"'Certainly. My passport is there and all my belongings.'

"'The name of the hotel?'

"I winced at that. Even to myself my answer would seem too much to accept. 'I can't recall,' I said in a low voice.

" 'Its location?'

" 'I don't know.'

"Vee sighed. He looked at me in a nearsighted way and I thought his eyes seemed sad, but perhaps it was only myopia.

"He said, 'The basic question is: What is your name? We must have some identification or this becomes a serious matter. Let me explain your position to you, Mr. Blank. Nothing compels me to do so, but I am not in love with every aspect of my work and I shall sleep better if I make sure you understand that you are in great danger.'

"My heart began to race. I am not young. I am not a hero. I am not brave. I said, 'But why? I am a wronged person. I have been drugged and robbed. I came voluntarily to the police, sick and lost, looking for help—'

"Again, Vee held up his hand. 'Quietly! Quietly! Some speak a little English here and it is better we keep this between ourselves for now. Things may be as you have described, or they may not. You are an American national. My government has cause to fear Americans. That, at least, is our official position. We are expecting an American agent of great ability to penetrate our borders on a most dangerous mission.

" 'That means that any strange American—any American encountered under suspicious circumstances—has, for a week now, been referred instantly to my department. Your circumstances were suspicious to begin with and have grown far more suspicious now that I have questioned you.'

"I stared at him in horror. 'Do you think *I*'m a spy? If I were, would I come to the police like this?'

" 'You may not be *the* spy, but you may still be *a* spy. There are people who will think so at once. Even I view it as a possibility.'

" 'But *no* kind of *spy* would come to the police—'

" 'Please! It will do you good to listen. You may be a distraction. If you play chess, you will know what I mean when I say you may be a sacrifice. You are sent in to confuse and distract us, occupying our time and efforts, while the real work is done elsewhere.'

"I said, 'But it hasn't worked, if that's what I'm supposed to be. You're not confused and distracted. No one could be fooled by anything as silly as this. It's not a reasonable sacrifice and so it's no sacrifice at all. It's nothing but the truth I've been telling you.'

"Vee sighed. 'Then what's your name?'

"'John Smith. Ask me a million times and it will stay my name.'

"'But you can't prove it.—See here,' he said, 'you have two alternatives. One is to convince me in some reasonable way that you are telling the truth. Mere statements, however eloquent, are insufficient. There must be evidence. Have you nothing with your name on it? Nothing material you can show me?'

"'I told you,' I said, despairingly. 'I've been robbed.'

"'Failing that,' he said, as though he hadn't heard my remark, 'it will be assumed that you are here to fulfill some function for your country that will not be to the interest of my country, and you will be interrogated with that in mind. It will not be my job, I am glad to say, but those who interrogate will be most thorough and most patient. I wish it were not so, but where national security is at stake—'

"I was in utter panic. I said, stuttering, 'But I can't tell what I don't know, no matter how you interrogate.'

"'If so, they will finally be convinced, but you will not be well off by then. And you will be imprisoned, for it will not then be politic to let you go free in your condition. If your country succeeds in what it may be attempting, there will be anger in this country and you will surely be the victim of that and will receive a long sentence. Your country will not be able to intercede for you. It will not even try.''

"I screamed. 'That is unjust! That is unjust!'

"'Life *is* unjust,' said Vee, sadly. 'Your own President Kennedy said that.'

"'But what am I to do?' I babbled.

"He said, 'Convince me your story is true. Show me something! Remember something! Prove your name is John Smith. Take me to the tavern; better yet to the hotel. Present me with your passport. Give me anything, however small, as a beginning, and I will have sufficient faith in you to try for the rest—at some risk to myself, I might add.'

"'I appreciate that, but I cannot. I am helpless. I cannot.' I was babbling. All I could think of was that I was facing torture and an extended prison term for the crime of having been drugged and robbed. It was more than I could bear and I fainted. I'm sorry. It is not a heroic action, but I told you I wasn't a hero.''

Halsted said, "You don't know what they had put in your drink in the tavern. You were half-poisoned. You weren't yourself.''

"It's kind of you to say so, but the prospect of torture and imprisonment for nothing was not something I could have faced with stoicism on my best day.

"The next memory I have is that of lying on a bed with a vague feeling of having been manhandled. I think some of my clothing may have been removed.

"Vee was watching me with the same expression of sadness on his face. He said, 'I'm sorry. Would you care for some brandy?'

"I remembered. The nightmare was back. I shook my head. All I wanted was to convince him of my utter innocence somehow. I said, 'Listen! You *must* believe me. Every word I have told you is true! I—'

"He placed his hand on my shoulder and shook it. 'Stop! I believe you!'

"I stared at him stupidly. 'What!'

"He said, 'I believe you. For one thing, no one who was sent on a task such as yours might have been, could have portrayed utter terror so convincingly, in my opinion. But that is only my opinion. It would not have convinced my superiors and I could not have acted on it. However, no one could be as stupid as you have now proved to be without having been sufficiently stupid to step into a strange tavern so confidingly and to have forgotten the name of your hotel.'

" 'But I don't understand.'

" 'Enough! I have wasted enough time. I should, properly, now leave you to the police, but I do not wish to abandon you just yet. For the tavern and the thieves within, I can do nothing now. Perhaps another time after another complaint. Let us, however, find your hotel.—Tell me everything you remember—the décor—the position of the registration desk—the hair color of the man behind it—were there flowers? Come, come, Mr. Smith, what kind of street was it on? Were there shops? Was there a doorman? Anything?'

"I wondered if it were a scheme to trap me into something, but I saw no alternative but to try to answer the questions. I tried to picture everything as it had been when I had walked into the hotel for the first time less than twelve hours before. I did my best to describe and he hurried me on impatiently, asking questions faster than I could answer.

"He then looked at the hurried notes he had taken and whispered them to another official of some sort, who was on the spot without my having seen him enter—a hotel expert, perhaps. The newcomer nodded his head wisely and whispered back.

"Vee said, 'Very well, then. We think we know what hotel it was, so let us go. The faster I locate your passport, the better all around.'

"Off we went in an official car. I sat there, fearful and apprehensive, fearing that it was a device to break my spirit by offering me hope only to smash it by taking me to prison instead. God knows my spirit needed no breaking.—Or what if they took me to a hotel, and it was the wrong one, would they then listen to anything at all that I had to say?

"We did speed to a hotel, however. I shrugged helplessly when Vee asked if it was *the* hotel. How could I tell in pitch-darkness? And I feared committing myself to what would turn out to be a mistake.

"But it *was* the correct hotel. The night man behind the desk didn't know me, of course, but there was the record of a room for a John Smith of Fairfield. We went up there and behold—my luggage, my passport, my papers. Quite enough.

"Vee shook hands with me and said, in a low voice, 'A word of advice, Mr. Smith. Get out of the country quickly. I shall make my report and exonerate you, but if things go wrong in some ways, someone may decide you should be picked up again. You will be better off beyond the borders.'

"I thanked him and never took anyone's advice so eagerly in all my life. I checked out of the hotel, grabbed a taxi to the nearest station, and I don't think I breathed till I crossed the border.

"To this day, I don't know what it was all about—whether the United States really had an espionage project under way in that country at that time or whether, if we did, we succeeded or failed. As I said, some official asked me to keep quiet about the whole thing, so I suppose the suspicions of Vee's government were more or less justified.

"In any case, I never plan to go back to that particular country."

Avalon said, "You were fortunate, Mr. Smith. I see what you mean when you said you were puzzled by the ending. Vee, as you call him, did make a sudden about-face, didn't he?"

"I don't think so," interposed Gonzalo. "I think he was sympathetic to you all along, Mr. Smith. When you passed out, he called some superior, convinced him you were just a poor jerk in trouble, and then let you go."

"It might be," said Drake, "that it was your fainting that convinced him. If you were actually an agent, you would know the dangers you ran, and you would be more or less steeled for them. In fact, he said so, didn't he? He said you couldn't fake fear so convincingly and you therefore had to be what you said you were—or something like that."

Rubin said, "If you've told the story accurately, Mr.

Smith, I would think that Vee is out of sympathy with the regime or he wouldn't have urged you to get out of the country as he did. I should think he stands a good chance of being purged, or has been since that time."

Trumbull said, "I hate to agree with you, Manny, but I do. My guess is that Vee's failure to hang on to Smith may have been the last straw."

"That doesn't make me feel very good," muttered Smith.

Roger Halsted pushed his coffee cup out of the way and placed his elbows on the table. He said earnestly, "I've heard the bare bones of the story before and I've thought about it and think there's more to it than that. Besides, if all five of you agree on something, that must be wrong."

He turned to Smith. "You told me, John, that this Vee was a young man."

"Well, he struck me as being in his early thirties."

"All right, then," said Halsted, "if a youngish man is in the secret police, it must be out of conviction and he must plan to rise in the ranks. He isn't going to run ridiculous risks for some nonentity. If he were an old man, he might remember an earlier regime and might be out of sympathy with the new government, but—"

Gonzalo said, "How do you know this Vee wasn't a double agent? Maybe that's why our government doesn't want Smith to be talking about the matter."

"If Vee were a double agent," said Halsted, "then, considering his position in the government intelligence there, he would be enormously valuable to us. All the more reason that he wouldn't risk anything for the sake of a nonentity. I suspect that there's more than sympathy involved. He must have thought of something that authenticated John's story."

"Sometimes I think that's it," said Smith, morosely. "I keep thinking of his remark after I came out of my faint to the effect that I was too stupid to be guilty. He never did explain that remark."

"Wait a minute," said Rubin. "After you came out of

your faint, you said you seemed to be in disarray. While you were out, they inspected your clothes closely, realized they were American make—"

"What would that prove?" demanded Gonzalo, scornfully. "An American spy is as likely to wear American clothes as an American jerk is.—No offense, Mr. Smith."

"None taken," said Smith. "Besides, I had bought the clothes I was then wearing in Paris."

Gonzalo said, "I guess you didn't ask him why he thought you were stupid."

Smith snorted. "You mean did I say to him, 'Hey, wise guy, who're you calling stupid?' No, I didn't say that, or anything like it. I just held my breath."

Avalon said, "The comments on your stupidity, Mr. Smith, need not be taken to heart. You have said several times that you were not yourself at any time during that difficult time. After being drugged, you might well have *seemed* stupid. In any case, I don't see that we'll ever know the inwardness of Vee's change of mind. It would be sufficient to accept it and not question the favors of fortune. It is enough that you emerged safely from the lion's mouth."

"Well, wait," said Gonzalo. "We haven't asked Henry for his opinion yet."

Smith said, with astonishment, "The waiter?" Then, in a lower voice, "I didn't realize he was listening. Does he understand this is all confidential?"

Gonzalo said, "He's a member of the club and the best man here.—Henry, can you understand Vee's change of heart?"

Henry hesitated. "I do not wish to offend Mr. Smith. I would not care to call him stupid, but I can see why this foreign official, Vee, thought so."

There was a general stir about the table. Smith said, stiffly, "What do you mean, Henry?"

"You say the events of the nightmare took place some time last year."

"That's right," said Smith.

"And you say your pockets were rifled. Were they completely emptied?"

"Of course," said Smith.

"But that is clearly impossible. You've said you still carry the original vial of pills, and that you have carried it everywhere and at all times, so that I suppose you had it with you when you travelled abroad and that you had it with you when you entered the tavern—and therefore still had it with you when you left the tavern."

Smith said, "Well, yes, you're right. It was in my shirt pocket as always. Either they missed it or decided they didn't want it."

"You didn't say anything about that in the course of the tale you have just told us."

"It never occurred to me."

"Nor did you tell Vee about them, I suppose?" said Henry.

"Look here," said Smith, angrily, "I didn't think of them. But even if I did, I wouldn't voluntarily bring up the matter. They would use it to place a trumped-up charge of carrying dope against me and in that way justify an imprisonment."

"You'd be right, if you thought of the pills only, sir," said Henry.

"What else is there to think of?"

"The container," said Henry, mildly. "The pills were available only by prescription and you told us it was the original vial. May we see it, Mr. Smith?"

Smith withdrew it from his shirt pocket, glanced at it and said, vehemently, "Hell!"

"Exactly," said Henry. "On the label placed on the vial by the pharmacist, there should be printed the pharmacist's name and address, probably in Fairfield, and *your* name should be typed in as well, together with directions for use."

"You're right."

"And after you had denied having any identification on you, even in the face of torture, Vee looked through your pockets while you were unconscious, and found exactly what he had been asking you to give him."

"No wonder he thought I was stupid," said Smith, shaking his head. "I *was* stupid. Now I *really* feel rotten."

"And yet," said Henry, "you have an explanation of something that has puzzled you for a year, and that should make you feel good."

Afterword

Here's another story in which I accepted Fred's title and discarded my own. I had called this story "What's My Name?" and it seems to me that "Can You Prove It?" is much more successful. There's an air of hostility about "Can You Prove It?" that instantly increases the tension even before you begin the story.

Incidentally, this, like "The Driver," is one of those stories that derives its tension from the fact that the world contains two superpowers that have confronted each other for forty years now, each with weapons of destruction so unparalleled that a war between them would mean loss (perhaps irreversible loss) for all mankind.

It is for that reason that I hate to write stories involving the confrontation, or even to read them. It strikes me that anything that serves to increase hatred and suspicion just increases the chances that in a moment of anger or miscalculation the nuclear button will be pushed.

And yet, sometimes, the exigencies of plotting force me into it, and then as I reread the story I can't help but think sardonically that with the change of a very few words, with just a substitution here and there of minor extent, the story could very well have been written by someone on the other side.—And that's rather sad, too.

The story appeared in the June 17, 1981, issue of *EQMM*.

The
Phoenician Bauble

Geoffrey Avalon, a patent lawyer by profession, did not often admit to reading light fiction. On the occasion of this particular Black Widowers banquet, however, he stirred the ice in his second drink (which had reached its halfway point and would be sipped no more) and said, "I read an interesting science fiction story yesterday."

James Drake, a retired chemist, who had spent the better part of an otherwise misspent life in reading every kind of popular fiction periodical, said, "Did it hurt?"

"Not at all. I was at a friend's place, saw a magazine, leafed through it, began reading, and, I must admit, rather enjoyed it. The premise was that to a man who had developed total recall there could be no secrets. If I were to recall *everything* you said, Jim, together with intonations and expressions, and combined it with what others said, and what I already knew, I would be able to deduce everything about you. No matter what it was you didn't want me—or anyone—to know, you would give it away a dozen times a day without knowing it. It's only that in real life we pay no attention—or don't hear—or forget—that secrets remain secrets. In the story, of course, the protagonist gets into trouble with his wild talent."

"As they always do," said Drake, unimpressed. "It's a literary convention as old as Midas's golden touch. The story you read was, I suspect, 'Lest We Remember' by Isaac Asimov, in a recent issue of his own magazine."

"That's right," said Avalon.

111

Mario Gonzalo, who had arrived late and had just placed his rubbers and raincoat in the cloakroom (for New York was not really enjoying the rain it badly needed for its reservoirs), ordered his drink from Henry with a small gesture, and said, "Asimov? Isn't he Manny's friend, the one who's even more stuck on himself than Manny is, if you can believe it?"

Emmanuel Rubin turned his entire body to face Gonzalo and pointed his finger. "Asimov is *not* my friend. He merely dogs my footsteps because he needs help on various simple points of science before he can write his so-called stories."

"I looked him up in Books in Print, Manny," said Gonzalo, grinning. "He writes a lot more—"

"Books than I do," Rubin finished. "Yes, I know. That's because I don't sacrifice quality for quantity. Here, meet my guest. Mr. Enrico Pavolini. This is Mario Gonzalo, who represents himself to be an artist and who will disprove the fact by concocting a caricature of you shortly. Mr. Pavolini is curator at the City Museum of Ancient Art."

Pavolini bowed with continental courtesy, and said, "I listen sadly to the science fiction story you are discussing. I fear that even a perfect memory could not penetrate some secrets, except in romances. And always those secrets that badly need penetrating prove the most opaque." His English was perfect but his vowels had a subtle distortion to them that made it clear he was not born to the language.

Trumbull said, "My feeling is that most secrets are safe because no one really *cares*. Most so-called secrets are so damned dull, it is only those who are desperately bored who would take the trouble to ferret them out."

"That may be so in some cases, my dear sir—" began Pavolini, but was interrupted by Henry's quiet announcement that dinner was served. The guests sat down to an array of Greek appetizers that bore a promise of moussaka to come. Roger Halsted made a small sound of pleasure as he draped his napkin over his thighs and Rubin, having speared a stuffed grape leaf, looked at it approvingly, placed it in his mouth, and ground it to nothingness.

Rubin then said (his mind clearly running on his earlier reference to quality versus quantity), "One of the unfortunate consequences of the era of pulp fiction, between 1920 and 1950, is that it raised a generation of Asimovs who learned to write without thought, in the pursuit of quantity only."

"That's not entirely bad," said Drake. "It's far more common for a writer to fall into the opposite trap of postponing execution in a useless search for nonexistent perfection."

"I'm not talking about perfection," said Rubin. "I'm suggesting just a little extra trouble to move away from abysmal junk."

"If you'll *read* some of the better pulp, you'll find it is far away from abysmal junk," said Drake, stiffly. "A lot of it, in fact, is recognized now as an important contribution to literature and its techniques are well worth study. Dashiell Hammett, Raymond Chandler, Cornell Woolrich—Come on, Manny, it's your own field. Don't knock it."

"They weren't pulp. They were real writers who had to make use of the available markets—"

Drake laughed. "It's easy to prove that all pulp is bad, if, when examples of the contrary are cited, you say 'If it's good, it isn't pulp.'"

Gonzalo said, "Once something is old, it gets slavered over by critics who would slap it down hard if they were contemporaries of the object criticized. I've heard Manny say a hundred times that Shakespeare was a hack writer who was despised in his own day."

"For every Shakespeare," said Rubin, violently, his sparse beard bristling, "who was far ahead of the puny minds of his time, there were a hundred, or maybe a thousand, scribblers who were dismissed as zeroes in their own time and who are exactly zero today, if they are remembered at all."

"That's the point," said Pavolini. "Surely survival is the best testimony of worth."

"Not always," said Rubin, characteristically shifting ground at once. "Accident must play a role. Aeschylus and Sophocles wrote over ninety plays each, and in each case only seven survive. Who can possibly say those were the seven best? Sappho was considered by the ancient Greeks to be in a class with Homer himself, and yet virtually nothing of her work survives."

A curious silence fell over the Black Widowers, as though in appreciation of true tragedy—the loss of the irreplaceable work of human genius. The conversation was quieter and more general thereafter.

And finally, Rubin, as host, called for the grilling. "Not you, Mario," he said. "You'll try to prove you're an artist and bore Mr. Pavolini to death and he's too good a friend for me to lose. Jim, do the honors."

Enrico Pavolini looked expectant. His smile, which seemed always radiant, gave every indication of welcoming all questions. He might have been in his fifties, but his neat mustache, his ungraying hair, his unlined face, his unsorrowing eyes, would have made the forties an equally reasonable guess.

Drake cleared his throat and said, "Mr. Pavolini, how do you justify your existence?"

Pavolini showed no surprise at all at the question. He said, "By doing what one man can do to prevent the tragedy of which we spoke earlier in the dinner. I labor to save those products of artistic genius that might otherwise be lost. In so doing, of course, I must deal, often, with thieves and criminals, and compound their felonies—but the nature of my work justifies even that."

Drake said, "Who are these thieves and criminals you speak of?"

"Throughout history," said Pavolini, "works of art have been hidden; sometimes purposely as when they are buried with dead rulers or aristocrats, or when they are concealed from marauding bands of armed men; sometimes accidentally as when a temple is destroyed by an earthquake or a ship sinks at sea. And throughout history, there have been people in search of treasure, persistent robbers with spades who break into pyramids and tombs, who follow the legends of buried treasure, who poke about in sunken ships. Caches of coins, ingots of precious metals, jewels, works of art, are always turning up. Sometimes they are broken up, melted down, sold as bullion or stones. Sometimes, especially in the last two hundred years, they are left intact and placed on the open market. That's where I, and others like myself, come in. We bid for the material. Every museum of art in the world is filled with illegal loot."

Drake said, "What makes these so-called looters criminals? Are they supposed to leave works of art buried—the property of, for instance, a pharaoh who has been dead for thirty-five centuries?"

"In the first place," said Pavolini, "many looters are criminals against humanity. They are ignorant people who may come across a treasure either by accident, or design, but who, from the start, or in the end, are interested only in the negotiable. Everything they do not see as intrinsically valuable, they are liable to destroy, not so much out of malice as out of indifference. They are quite likely to break up priceless artwork in order to salvage a few emeralds or strips of gold.

"Secondly, they are criminals in the eyes of the law. Over the last century, nations have come increasingly to consider various relics of the past as part of their national heritage and therefore the property of the state. Searches should, in theory, be conducted under strict supervision, and finds cannot be sold to foreign museums. Even trained archeologists who flout these rules are, strictly speaking, criminals.

"Still, many governments are too inefficient to conduct proper searches, too corrupt to resist bribery; and human cupidity is such that consideration of national pride can almost never compete with the fact that a better price can be obtained from foreigners."

Drake said, "If all museums combined in a policy of refusing to deal with looters—"

Pavolini shook his head vigorously. "It would do no good. The museums are run by human beings, or by governments, with their own prides, cupidities, and corruptibilities. No museum would want to lose a real find to another museum. And even if the museums were to stand firm as a group, items might be sold to private collections— or be broken up and melted down. Some looters have resorted to blackmail and have used the threat of destruction to force a higher price."

Drake said, "Is it all worth it? Surely not everything is a great work of art?"

"Some is," said Pavolini, smiling with a touch of condescension, "by any standards, as, for instance, the bust of Nefertiti, the Cretan snake goddess, Venus de Milo. That, however, is secondary, in a way. Every artifact of a past era is important as a living evidence of a society that is gone. The commonest pot of terra-cotta was once used, was part of a way of life, was formed to fill a purpose. Each is as important and as indispensable to an archeologist as the fossil tooth of an extinct shark would be to a paleontologist."

Trumbull said, "May I interpose, Jim?—I presume the City Museum of Ancient Art has its share of past artifacts, Mr. Pavolini?"

Pavolini's smile broadened. "It certainly has, Mr. Trumbull. You must come visit us sometime and see for yourself. We are a comparatively young museum and do not have the resources of the Metropolitan, but we are more finely focussed and our collection of pre-Columbian Mexican art is world-famous."

"I will certainly visit you at my first opportunity," said Trumbull, "but I seem to remember that before dinner, you said something about secrets not being easily penetrated."

Pavolini looked suddenly grave. "Did I?"

"Yes. There was some mention of some idiotic science fiction story about a perfect memory being all that was required to penetrate any secret and you said—"

"Ah, yes, I remember."

"Well, then, were you referring to anything specific, anything that had to do with your work?"

"As a matter of fact, yes." Pavolini shrugged his shoulders. "A small thing that has been haunting me for some time, but of no importance outside my own feelings, I suppose."

"Tell us about it," said Trumbull, conjugating himself abruptly into the imperative.

Pavolini blinked. "As I said, utterly unimportant."

Rubin put in gently, "Tell us anyway, Enrico. It's the price of the dinner. You remember I explained about the grilling."

"Yes, Emmanuel," said Pavolini, "but it is not a thing I can discuss indiscriminately. From a strictly legal standpoint—"

Rubin said, "We are all as silent as one of your pre-Columbian artifacts. That includes, particularly, our esteemed waiter and fellow member, Henry. Please continue, Enrico."

Pavolini smiled, ruefully. "Our artifacts are not by any means silent, since they speak to us eloquently of past cultures, so it was an unfortunate simile. However—There was a Phoenician bauble on the market of the museum world—the *black* market, I suppose.

"It had been dug up in Cyprus, where the confusion of the past decade has made it possible for looters to obtain and smuggle out valuable material. This was a small cup of gold and enamel, dating back to some time about 1200 B.C. There was some question as to whether it showed Mycenean influence and it bore promise of modifying some of our notions of events in the time of the Trojan war.

"Naturally, we wanted it, and so, I imagine, did a dozen

other major museums in the world. It wasn't, of course, a matter of mere bidding. The person offering it for sale had to cover his tracks for he wanted to get back to Cyprus, to obtain other pieces perhaps, without being stripped of his gains and being thrown into prison besides by the Cypriot authorities. For that reason, he needed to have certain precautions accepted, certain guaranties made. And, of course, it helped to have a good man on the spot, a persuasive man."

Rubin said, "You once told me about one of your people who you said was exactly like that—Jelinsky."

Pavolini nodded. "The name is not merely Jelinsky. You forget how it came about I mentioned him to you in the first place. His full name was Emmanuel Jelinsky. That is actually how I came to know *you*, Emmanuel. It is an unusual first name and when I was introduced to you, I thought at once of *my* Emmanuel. It drew my attention to you. We talked about him and then I had my chance to get to know you. *My* Emmanuel, however, is now dead."

"I'm sorry," said Rubin.

"A heart attack. He was sixty-five and it was not entirely unexpected, but, if I may be permitted to view it selfishly, it was tragic, for with his death went all chance of obtaining the Phoenician bauble." Pavolini sighed heavily. "To be honest, it was with the greatest difficulty that I persuaded myself to attend the banquet tonight—but I had accepted your invitation nearly a month ago and my wife rather insisted I go. She said she did not want me brooding and tearing my hair. She said, 'Have one evening out. Forget.' So here I am, and I'm not forgetting after all."

There was an uneasy silence at that, and then Gonzalo, the ever-hopeful, said, "Sometimes it turns out that we can help people with problems."

Trumbull said with instant fury, "*Will* you stop making ridiculous statements like that?"

"I said *sometimes*," said Gonzalo, defensively, "and I intend to continue the grilling. How about it, Manny? You're the host."

Rubin looked uncomfortable. "Do you mind if we continue, Enrico?"

Pavolini managed a smile. "Not talking will not bring him back, nor the bauble, either."

"All right then," said Gonzalo. "You said that Jelinsky's death lost you that Phoenician whatever-it-was. Which museum got it?"

"I wish one of them did. That would be better for the world generally. The trouble is that the object has simply disappeared."

"How? Why?" burst out Trumbull.

Pavolini sighed. "Well, then, from the beginning. Let me explain about Jelinsky. He was with the museum longer than I was and he was simply invaluable. I don't wish to overdramatize but in some respects museums must engage in activities that have about them some of the atmosphere of espionage work. There are delicate negotiations to be carried through; clandestine contacts to be made; objects to be purchased illegally and, therefore, secretly; other museums to spy on and measures to be taken to foil the spies of others.

"Of course, it is all small potatoes since the apparatuses involved and the stakes, too, are far smaller than those which governments or even industries can dispose of. On the other hand, we don't have great power to fall back on for protection, and to us, at least, if to no one else, the stakes are high.

"Jelinsky was what we would consider a master spy, if he were an employee of the CIA. He could trace valuable items and make his contacts before anyone else was fairly in the field. He was persuasive, could talk a bird out of a tree and into his hand, could close a deal to the greatest advantage of ourselves even while others were after the same item with offers that were double what we could offer. We never knew how he did it.

"I asked him once about that but he just let one eyelid close and said, 'You'll never know, Enrico. After all, if you ever fire me, I would have to find work elsewhere and it would be inconvenient if you knew my methods then.'

"He had one peculiarity, however, that we all knew about. It was impossible to miss. He doodled! He was never without a scratch pad and at any time that scratch pad had the top sheet covered with fascinating abstractions. They were never quite the same but they were always neatly geometric—triangles, squares, trapezoids, octagons, either alone or in bizarre combinations. Sometimes there would be words built up of letters neatly printed in geometric form. Sometimes I could tell it was a word that occupied his mind at the time of the doodling. I remember once, when we were in conference, he wrote the first few letters of my name, each letter constructed in a series of egg-shaped segments. I asked him if he would let me have it as a curio and he looked at it with astonishment as if not aware he had done it. He gave it to me with an air of wondering why I could possibly want it. I still have it.

"I asked him once why he doodled and he said he wasn't sure. He said, 'Maybe it is what I do instead of jiggling my feet or tapping my fingernails. I have a restless mind and this focuses it and keeps it from darting off in unwanted directions. Maybe. And maybe it just serves as an outlet for some artistic impulse that lies dormant in me. I don't know. In any case, I never notice that I'm doodling when I'm doodling. But at least I stick to geometry so I never give away my thoughts.'

"'Except when you write letters,' I said, and he flushed and insisted they never meant anything."

Gonzalo said, with satisfaction, as he sipped at his brandy and then held up the glass for Henry to renew the infusion, "I'll bet one of Jelinsky's doodles has a part in all this."

"Yes," said Pavolini, sadly, "or I should not have gone on at such length about it. Obviously. Two weeks ago, I received a call from Jelinsky. He was in Halifax. He did not speak of the Phoenician artifact directly for—and again I do not wish to overdramatize—he well knew this room might be bugged or his wire tapped. Some of our competitors are at least as unscrupulous as we ourselves are.

"I understood well the significance of what he was saying, however. He had closed the deal and he had the object. Why the deal was closed in Halifax, I don't know and didn't ask. The looter may have been Canadian or Jelinsky may have persuaded him to come to that unlikely city to throw off the scent as far as the others in the field were concerned. It didn't matter.

"Though Jelinsky had physical possession of the object, he did not intend to carry it with him to New York. He had checked it in an unobtrusive place in the form of a package that gave no outward clue to its contents or its value, and under conditions where it was clear to the people keeping it that it might be some time before it was called for. He was coming to New York with the information and someone else would fly to Halifax to get the object. All this was told me most indirectly; virtually in code."

"Isn't all this indirection overdrawn?" said Halsted.

"I know it sounds paranoid," said Pavolini, "but Jelinsky was a known man. He might be followed, his baggage might be tampered with. After all, why hesitate to steal an object that was already stolen? In any case, Jelinsky did not feel it safe to carry the object to New York. We could send some unknown to carry the object, someone who would be safe *because* he was unknown."

"Except that he died," said Gonzalo, excitedly, "before he could pass on the necessary information."

"Of a heart attack, as I told you," said Pavolini, "at Kennedy airport. Naturally, he never had a chance to tell us where he had checked the object."

Avalon looked grave and said, "I scarcely wish to outdo you in overdramatizing the matter, so I will ask you to reassure us and tell us that there is no chance that Jelinsky was murdered and the information taken from his body."

"Not at all possible," said Pavolini. "There were those

who saw him collapse, there was his history of heart disease, and there was a careful autopsy. There was no question but that it was a natural death, and a most unfortunate one for us. For one thing, we had lost an irreplaceable man, but he would have died eventually. It was the precise moment of his death that was the calamity.

"We don't know where the object is. We presume it is somewhere in Halifax—but that is all. Essentially, the Phoenician bauble is once again buried, and it will be recovered only by accident and by—who can tell who.

"Even if it were found by someone and were placed on the market again, the fact that we have already paid a substantial sum for it would mean nothing. We are not likely to be able to prove ownership and, what is worse, we are even less likely to prove legal ownership. If found, and if the find is publicized too openly, the Greek Cypriot Government will claim it and will probably receive it. We can live with the loss of the money, but the loss of the object itself is hard to bear. Very hard." Pavolini shook his head despondently.

Pavolini went on, "What makes it more frustrating is that there is absolutely no reason to think he was robbed. He was under observation by many, as I said, when he collapsed, and airport guards were at his side almost at once. His pockets were filled with the usual—a wallet reasonably supplied with cash, including both American and Canadian bills. There were coins, credit cards, keys, handkerchief, and so on."

"Nothing of interest at all?" asked Halsted, incredulously.

"Well, one of the items was a claim check. We, as his employers, were able to effect a claim to that—though not without considerable legal problems. However, it doesn't help us at all. I suspect—I hope—that the claim check is for the package containing the object, but what good does that do me? The claim check is entirely without distinguishing mark. It is red and rectangular and made of cardboard. On it in black block letters is the number 17. On the other side is nothing. There is no way of identifying where on earth—or, at least, where in Halifax—the ticket belonged."

Trumbull said, "Nothing else. No address book. No folded slip of paper in his wallet."

"Believe me, we went over everything in his pockets and in his baggage; under the eyes of the police, I might add— and there seemed nothing that could indicate the place where he had checked the package. There was an address book, of course, but in it was not one Halifax address; nor was there one non-Halifax address that seemed in any way suspicious. There was his scratch pad, too. If that had not been present, I would have been sure he was robbed. Still, under the closest scrutiny, there was no address on any page of it. We might have tested everything for secret writing—I thought of that—but why on earth should he have gone to such lengths?"

"I suppose," said Halsted, "you might use force majeure. You might go to every place in Halifax that could conceivably use such claim checks and try to recover a package at each one."

"Every hotel? Every restaurant? Every train or bus terminal? Every airport?" said Pavolini. "That would truly be an act of desperation. No!—We tried cutting down the possibilities instead."

"The doodles!" cried out Gonzalo.

"You haven't forgotten," said Pavolini. "Yes, there were doodles on the top page of the scratch pad. They might have been made on the plane, but he doodled chiefly when in conference, and that must have been in Halifax."

"But you said," Avalon pointed out, "that there was no address on any page of the scratch pad."

"That's right, but there were other things. There were his characteristic geometric constructions, as identifiable as fingerprints. If that were all there was, it would be useless, but there was more. It was one of those rare occasions when he constructed letters and I knew there must have been some word, some phrase, which had attracted his attention. Unfortunately, he had written down only part of it. There was a capital *B*, a small *i*, and a small *f*, each in ornate script. Those letters were absolutely identifiable as his handiwork, too. In other words, 'Bif' was the beginning of some word that had caught his attention, when he was negotiating the sale, and if we could work out what the word was and where he had seen it, I have the feeling we would know where he had checked the package.''

Trumbull said, ''For all you know, that doodle may have been made the day before the negotiations, or the week before. It may have no connection with the negotiations at all.''

''Possible,'' said Pavolini, ''but not likely. In my experience, Jelinsky never kept them long but disposed of the used top sheet when beginning another. Therefore, it could not have been very old.''

''But you cannot be sure,'' said Trumbull, persisting.

''No, I cannot be sure but I have nothing else to go by,'' said Pavolini, exasperated.

Gonzalo said, eagerly, ''Do you have the paper with you?''

''No,'' said Pavolini, lifting his arms up and then letting them drop. ''How can you think I would carry it with me? It is in my office safe. Could I have imagined this matter would come up in the evening's discussion?''

''It's just that it seemed to me,'' said Gonzalo, ''that if we could see the doodles, we might get something out of it you didn't. Could you reproduce them for us?''

Pavolini lifted his upper lip in disdain. ''I am not an artist. I could not do it. I could not even reproduce the curlicues in the letters. Believe me, there is nothing there but the letters, and nothing of any significance but the letters. Nothing.''

Halsted said, ''The letters don't seem very significant to me. What word starts with 'bif' anyway?''

'' 'Bifurcate,' '' said Rubin, at once.

"Fine!" said Pavolini. "A useful word, indeed. Where would Jelinsky see 'bifurcate' in the course of the negotiations? My friends, I did not sit about and puzzle out the matter. I used the unabridged dictionary. 'Bifurcate' means 'to divide in two.' There is also 'bifid' meaning 'in two parts.' There are chemical terms, 'biformate,' 'bifluoride,' and so on. These are all useless. It is not in the realm of possibility that he was looking at any of these words while he was sitting—wherever he was sitting—with the man who was selling the artifact. There is only one word, *only one*, that seemed as though it might be useful and that word is 'bifocals.'"

Rubin said, "Was the man Jelinsky dealt with an optometrist?"

"I know nothing about the man, but it seems reasonable that the negotiations might have taken place at an optometrist's, or, more likely, across the street from an optometrist's. With the word 'bifocals' staring him in the face, Jelinsky might well have started writing it absently."

"It's possible," said Avalon, judiciously.

But Pavolini folded his arms across his chest, looked sadly at the men assembled about the table, and said, "It did not work. I had a couple of our men scour the city to find optometrists in whose window, or on whose signs, there might be the word 'bifocals.' We have not yet found one. Optometrists do not stress bifocals. Those are for elderly people. They do their best to impress the public with beauty and with the chic qualities of their spectacles. Everything for youth or pretended youth. Nevertheless, we are not done looking."

Drake said, "You might be looking in the wrong direction. If Jelinsky made his letters with curlicues they might not be easily identifiable at all. For instance, it's easy to draw a small *e* and have it look like a small *i*. Jelinsky may not have intended 'bif' at all. He may have intended 'bef.' His pen might have skipped the little curve because the paper was greasy at that spot."

"What would you have with 'bef'?" asked Rubin.

"I don't know. He might have been starting to write 'beforehand,' let us say, because he had outthought his rivals and had gotten to the seller beforehand."

"That wouldn't help find the package," said Rubin.

"Who says it has to?" demanded Halsted. "What Jelinsky wrote might have nothing to do with the package and might be of no help at all. We're only trying to find out the truth, and if the truth doesn't suit us—" Drake spread his arms in fatalistic resignation.

Pavolini said, "No, no. Let me stop you. I cannot say whether it would help us if we penetrated the meaning of the word. Perhaps not. But at least I am quite certain that the word begins with 'bif' and nothing else. The *i* was an *i* and not an *e* because, for one thing, Jelinsky had placed a dot above it. In fact, Jelinsky even curlicued the dot so that it was a triple dot."

"A triple dot?" said Gonzalo. "What do you mean?"

"Like this," said Pavolini. "I can draw this much, anyway. It looked like this." He withdrew a small pad from an inner jacket pocket, tore out a sheet of paper, and drew three short vertical lines, closely spaced.

"There!" he said. "It was very small."

It was at this point that Henry interrupted. "Mr. Pavolini, may I see that piece of paper?"

Pavolini stared at Henry for a moment; then, with a trace of amusement, he said, "If you wish to look at it, waiter, here it is. Perhaps you will have a theory, too."

Gonzalo said, "I wouldn't take that attitude, Mr. Pavolini. Henry might have a theory at that."

Pavolini said, "Very well. Go ahead, waiter. From those three little lines, can you tell me where the package is hidden?"

"Not exactly, Mr. Pavolini," said Henry, with careful deference. "I can think of two places and there may possibly be one or two others, but I can't pin it down precisely to one place."

"Indeed?" said Pavolini.. "You can give me two, possibly four, places, and the package will be in one of them?"

"I believe so, sir."

"You believe so. Wonderful! In that case just give me the four.—I challenge you." Pavolini's voice had risen to a shout.

"May I first point out that since there is no really hopeful word in English that begins with 'bif,' it may be that Mr. Jelinsky was not writing an English word."

"Take my word for it," said Pavolini, freezingly. "Jelinsky knew no language other than English. He was not an educated man and—except for his specialty—really knew very little."

"I will accept that," said Henry, "but we have to ask ourselves not which word he knew and understood, but which word he encountered in the place in which he was negotiating the sale. If they were seated in a French restaurant, that restaurant—located in a city of British culture—might well sell steak, but would, of course, have it on the menu, or in the window, or on the sign, according to a spelling all their own. 'Beefsteak,' in French, becomes *bifteck.*"

Pavolini said, in a small voice, *"Bifteck?"*

"Yes, sir. I know of two good French restaurants in Halifax and there may be one or two more. I suggest you try the cloakroom in all four, if necessary."

Pavolini said, "You are guessing!"

"Not really, sir. Not after I saw the three little lines you drew. Might those lines have looked a bit more like this, sir?" On the same sheet of paper, Henry drew: ⚜ "Because if they did, that is a fleur-de-lis, which you would find prominently displayed in one place or another in almost any French restaurant. If we take the three letters *and* the fleur-de-lis together, then one can scarcely doubt where Jelinsky was sitting when he prepared this doodle."

Pavolini's mouth was open, and now he closed it with an

audible snap. "By heaven, you are right. I will leave, gentlemen. I will leave *now*. Good-bye to all of you, with my thanks for a wonderful dinner—but I have work to do." He began to hurry out, then stopped and turned. "My thanks to you particularly, Henry, but how did you do it?"

Henry said, gravely, "Restaurants are my specialty, sir."

Afterword

This is the twenty-eighth Black Widowers story that Fred Dannay bought for *EQMM* and, alas, the last, for death (as it must to all) finally came to the man who probably did more for the mystery field than any other single person since Conan Doyle. He will always be missed by all those who read his Ellery Queen stories, by all who dealt with him as editor, and by all who knew him as friend.

In connection with the story you have just read, by the way, I received a letter from a museum curator who pointed out that the story does not describe the actual methods used by museums to obtain their exhibits, and that it perpetuates a false stereotype of museums as promoters of skullduggery.

I'm sure he's right and I apologize to all museums. The fact is that I know nothing about the actual workings of museum acquisitions and I make it all up out of my head in such a way as to have it fit in with the plot. I suspect, though, that that's the way it's got to be, if the hardworking mystery writer is to make a living.

Consider, for instance, the writings of Agatha Christie (that model of everything a mystery writer ought to be, even if she *did* have very peculiar notions about how Americans talk and act). If she were to be taken seriously, there is not an upper-class family in all of England that did not have a member done to death in the library, with a paper knife skewering his heart and a look of indescribable horror on his face, and that did not have another member who did the deed. But we accept that ("suspension of disbelief") and don't expect the world of the mystery to be in one-to-one correspondence with the world of reality.

The story appeared in the May 1982 issue of *EQMM*.

A Monday in April

Charles Soskind was strikingly handsome. That much was obvious from the moment Thomas Trumbull introduced him to the membership of the Black Widowers on the occasion of their monthly banquet.

It was, in fact, obvious even before he was introduced. He was tall, slim, dark-haired. He had a pale complexion with eyes that were all the more startlingly dark for that. He had astonishingly regular features, firm lips with just a trace of sensuousness about them, and an engaging smile. He shook hands with a strong grip and his fingernails were well cared for. He exuded just a trace of after-shave lotion and the paleness of his cheeks was shadowed by the blueness of a buried beard—for there was no visible stubble. He was well-barbered and he seemed like a throwback to a Gibson collar ad.

Trumbull said, "Charles is relatively new at the Department. He took his degree in Slavic studies at the University of Michigan."

Hands were shaken all around and each Black Widower displayed that quite detectable air of distrust with which ordinary males meet an extraordinary specimen of their own kind.

Mario Gonzalo was perhaps most obvious in his reaction. He managed to locate his reflection in the mirror and refurbished the line of his jacket in what he might have thought was an unobtrusive manner.

If so, Emmanuel Rubin promptly disabused him. With a broad grin which showed the pronounced gap between his upper first incisors, Rubin whispered, "Forget it, Mario. You're straight out of the garbage can in comparison."

Gonzalo lifted his eyebrows and stared down at the shorter Rubin in haughty displeasure. "What the hell are you talking about?"

Rubin continued to smile. "You know," he said, "and I know, and surely that's enough."

Just the same, Rubin did manage to run his fingers absently through his straggly beard as though a sudden and impossible desire to have it flow downward in a neat and impressive manner had overtaken him.

Geoffrey Avalon cleared his throat and stood straighter and more stiffly even than was his wont. He was two inches taller than Soskind, and it was clear that he didn't care if the whole world noticed that little fact.

Roger Halsted sucked in his stomach and endured the discomfort of that for nearly two minutes. James Drake, the oldest of the Black Widowers, looked preternaturally indifferent, as though it was only age and nothing more that kept him out of the race—and, what's more, prevented him from winning.

Only Henry, the competent waiter, on whose shoulders the welfare of the banquets rested, seemed truly unaware of anything out of the ordinary as he brought Soskind his straight ginger ale, with a maraschino cherry in it.

Soskind regarded the drink sombrely and then, with the air of someone who had survived questioning on the matter for years, said, even though no one asked, "I order the cherry because that makes it look like an alcoholic drink of some sort and I then don't have to explain why I'm not drinking."

"Why don't you drink?" asked Rubin, with immediate perversity.

"It's not because I'm a member of Alcoholics Anonymous," said Soskind dryly. "I just have a low tolerance for alcohol. One drink gets me distinctly high and since I get no pleasure out of the sensation, I choose not to drink. I don't have to be forced or argued into it."

"If I were you," said Gonzalo, darkly, "I'd get Perrier with a pearl onion in it. That dye they use in maraschino cherries is carcinogenic, I hear."

"So is everything," said Soskind, "if you choose the proper strain of rats to experiment with, and make the doses large enough."

Halsted said, with the usual slight stammer that always seemed to invade his speech as soon as he tried particularly hard to seem a man of the world, "Too bad you're so adversely affected by alcohol. Overdoing it is bestial, but there is nothing quite as civilized as the ritual of the moderate sharing of drinks. It reduces the inhibitions standing in the way of the true grace of social intercourse."

"Believe me," said Soskind, nodding, "I fully appreciate that particular disadvantage under which I labor. I usually avoid cocktail parties simply because I can't participate on equal terms. And that's by no means the worst of it. It's the business lunches that are the real strain. I assure you that if I could drink more easily, I would be glad to do so."

And almost at once, as though on cue, Henry announced the end of the cocktail hour. "Dinner is served, gentlemen."

Drake found himself sitting next to the banquet guest and said, "Are you of Russian extraction, Mr. Soskind?"

"Not as far as I know," said Soskind, his expression lightening a bit at the smoked salmon and onion bits. He reached for a section of the thin-sliced bread and butter and carefully brushed the capers to one side. "My father's father arrived here from Luxemburg, and my mother's parents were both Welsh."

"I asked," said Drake, "because of your degree in Slavic studies. Your doctorate, by the way?"

"Yes, I have the right to be referred to as Dr. Soskind, though I never insist on it. You are Dr. Drake, I presume?"

"Chemistry. But all of us can refer to each other as doctors by virtue of our membership in the club. Even our good Henry, the invaluable waiter of the organization, is Dr. Jackson, if we choose to call him that.—But how did you come to Slavic studies?"

"Oh, that! No personal reasons, if you discount ambition. After all, the United States has been facing the Soviet Union in open competition for forty years now. Many Soviet citizens can speak English and have studied Anglo-American history and culture, while very few Americans have returned the compliment. This puts us under a severe disadvantage and by my making a personal effort to help redress the balance, I am making myself a patriot and, in addition, am opening my way to advancement, since my knowledge is useful."

"You mean in Tom Trumbull's department?"

"I mean," said Soskind, carefully, "in that organ of government in which we both serve."

"I take it then," put in Avalon suddenly from the other side of the table, "that you speak and read Russian quite fluently."

"Yes, sir," said Soskind, "quite fluently, and Polish as well. I can make myself understood in Czech and Serbian. With time, I hope to learn other languages, too. Arabic and Japanese are extremely important in today's world, and I intend to take courses in each as soon as I finish my present damned task."

Trumbull leaned forward from his position at the head of the table, which he occupied by virtue of serving as that evening's host of the banquet.

"Stop it, you idiots! Is this grilling time? Charles, you answer no questions at all until it's time. Right now, you just enjoy your dinner undisturbed.—I don't understand you half-wits. Do the rules of this club have to be explained to you each time?"

"There are no rules," said Rubin, promptly.

"Yes?" said Gonzalo. "I wonder if you'll expound that doctrine the next time I bring in a woman as my guest."

"That's a matter of *tradition!*" howled Rubin. "If you

can't understand the difference between tradition and rules—"

And the discussion degenerated into a verbal free-for-all at once.

The bouillabaisse was done; the hot, scented napkins had been put to their proper use; the baked Alaska was consumed; and the Black Widowers were lingering over their coffee (tea for the guest) when Trumbull rattled the spoon against the water glass and said, "Mario, since you did not display the bad taste to grill my guest before he had been adequately fed, won't you now serve as griller-in-chief?"

Gonzalo jumped slightly. He had produced the needed caricature of the guest, catching him in a spectacularly Byronic profile. He said, "Mr. Soskind, it is customary to begin by asking the guest to justify his existence. Let me answer that question for myself. I judge that you would say in response that you are carrying through the justification by using your Russian to help the American government beat the Soviet Union."

Soskind, who was glaring at the caricature, said, "The word 'beat' has unpleasant connotations. I would prefer to say that I am doing my bit to secure the interests of the United States, which, I take it, means first and foremost the preservation of world peace and the protection of human rights."

Gonzalo said, "But wouldn't you be making a hell of a lot more money if you went into show business?"

Soskind reddened and seemed to be struggling with himself to prevent an explosion. His control burst, however, and he said, "That's an idiotic question to ask, and the proper answer I ought to give you is a punch in the jaw."

For a moment, the gathering froze and then Trumbull said, with totally uncharacteristic mildness, "That's un-called for, Charles. I told you the way in which we play our game when I invited you to dinner. I do not deny that Mario is often idiotic, as are we all—always excluding our good Henry—but he was in this case within his rights. He was asking a question, and he may ask any question. You have been given to understand that you must answer all questions truthfully. Whatever you say will never pass outside this room."

Soskind said, "Of course, Tom. I apologize to you, Mr. Gonzalo, and to all the company." He drew a deep breath and said, not without some signs of continuing anger, "I suppose it might look to some people as though I might be successful in Hollywood, especially if I really looked like that sketch you have drawn, Mr. Gonzalo. I suppose you meant it to represent me but I earnestly hope I don't resemble it altogether.

"Good looks, assuming I have them, might get me into the movies, but I doubt they could make me a success unless I had some minimal acting ability as well—something I do not have. Even then, it could not make me happy unless I had the actor's temperament, which I am poles removed from. I am doing what I want to do—studying the languages of humanity—for the resons I have mentioned and if it returns an adequate compensation, I am quite ready to dismiss the dreams of avarice. Have I made that clear?"

"Very clear," said Gonzalo, "but what makes you think you lack the temperament of an actor? I know a number of actors and they come in all shapes and varieties of temperament. As for acting ability, it seems to me you have the capacity for—histrionics, if Manny will tell me that is indeed the word I want."

"That's the word you want—for once," said Rubin.

Soskind bowed his head for a moment. When he lifted it, it was as though the clouds had thinned and the sun had broken through. His smile was all but irresistible.

"Gentlemen," he said, "I find that I am still making things hard for you. I do not wish to do that. Honestly! It is just that these last ten days or so I have not been myself. I assure you that ordinarily I am not given to histrionics, and I will display none henceforth."

Several of the Black Widowers spoke at once and Trumbull's voice rose piercingly. "Mario has the floor!"

"Thank you, Tom," said Gonzalo, and at once asked what all had been trying to ask. *"Why* are you not yourself? And please don't say that it's private or that it's none of my business. It's my question and I want an answer."

"I understand," said Soskind, calmly. "I'm afraid it's an old, dull story. A young lady with whom I was—am—oh, hell, always may be in love, if you don't mind my sounding like a romantic jackass, betrayed me and—and—Well, what more is there to say?"

"Did she run off with your best friend?" asked Gonzalo.

Soskind looked revolted. "Of course not. Nothing like *that!* She's not that kind of woman."

"Well, then, what happened?" asked Gonzalo.

Avalon's baritone voice boomed out. "Wait! Before you answer, Mr. Soskind—and with your permission, Mario—please tell me if there is any mystery to this."

"Mystery, sir?" Soskind looked nonplussed.

"Yes. Anything you don't understand; anything that puzzles you and that can't be explained."

Soskind said, "Not at all! I wish there were! It's all very plain and, for me, heartbreaking. Claire broke her word, that's all. She took an unfair advantage and didn't even have the decency to be ashamed of it. I couldn't live with that no matter how much I might be in love with her.—But it doesn't make me very happy, not being able to live with it."

"No mystery," said Avalon, smiling. "You might want to let the matter drop then, Mario. Why probe a sore subject just for the sake of probing it?"

"Thank you," said Soskind.

Gonzalo frowned. "Unless Tom makes a host's decision against me, Jeff, I *won't* drop the subject. I'm curious."

Trumbull hesitated. "I'll poll the company. How many want the subject dropped?"

He and Avalon raised their hands, and Trumbull said, "Four to two against dropping the subject. Henry—are you voting?"

Henry, who was just adding a drop of brandy to Drake's glass, said, "Yes, sir. My hand was not raised. I feel that if Mr. Soskind still feels an affection for the young lady, he may have a suspicion that he is misjudging her. It might help if he tells us the details."

Rubin said, "I was pretty much thinking the same thing," and now there was a murmur of agreement about the table.

Soskind looked from face to face and said, "All right, I'll tell you, but you'll find there's simply no doubt about the matter. I have *no* suspicion that I'm misjudging her."

"You know," said Soskind, "it's particularly hard for me to find a young woman I can be interested in. Please don't make mock faces of disbelief. I do attract instant female attention because, I suppose, of my—my appearance, as I would if I were ostentatiously wealthy, or if I were a rock star, but of what value is instant attention for superficial reasons such as those?

"Being human, I sometimes take advantage of such attention, particularly if I am lured into thinking it is something more than a matter of superficial appearance that attracts them, or if I, in turn, am attracted by something or other that is really of no importance. I am, in that case, quickly disillusioned, gentlemen, and so, it may be, are they.

"On the other hand, my appearance is often against me and actually repels young women, and you needn't make exaggerated expressions of disbelief at that, Mr. Gonzalo. There are many women who come to an instant misjudgment concerning me through no fault of my own.

"Unfortunately, the novelists who form our stereotypical beliefs invariably make their heroines incredibly beautiful but only very rarely stress the good looks of the hero. The male protagonist tends to look craggy and charmingly plain. The result is that if I am considered not plain, I arouse instant suspicion.

"I have heard the comments, indirectly. 'Who wants a

boyfriend prettier than I am?' 'I'll have to fight for a chance at the mirror.'

"The feeling is universal that if a man is, quote, good-looking, unquote, as I was accused of being by this assemblage, at least by implication, then he must be vain, self-centered, capricious, and, worst of all, a simpering, brainless fool.

"These days, in fact, women are likely to dismiss me, on sight, as having homosexual tendencies—which I do not, by the way—simply because, quote, that's the way with all these pretty men, unquote.

"As it happens, I am a serious person. I don't mean by that that I lack a sense of humor, or that I do not laugh, or that I do not occasionally enjoy being silly. The point lies in the use of the word 'occasionally.'

"For the most part, I am interested in straightforward application of nose to grindstone, of myself to my career and to my intellectual interests. And I want my women serious, too.

"The women most likely to interest me—the intelligent, serious, ambitious ones—they are the very ones most likely to be put off by me, the very ones who will quickly decide that I am an obnoxious nonentity; that I am, quote, too pretty, unquote.

"Until I met Claire.

"She is in all ways my fellow (if you don't mind the Irish bull). She is a linguist, too, specializing in the modern Romance languages, as I in the Slavic.

"She is quite good-looking—at least I find her so—and quite indifferent to that fact. She is serious, intelligent, hard-driving, and a feminist in fact, rather than in conversation, having driven her way forward, and without much fuss, in a man's world.

"It was not love at first sight. What can one possibly know at first sight but superficialities—and very likely deceiving ones, at that? We met at the library, when we were each engaged in a little research and discovered we had interests in common. I was at the Department, she at Columbia.

"We met again, and then it became periodic. The more we learned about each other, the more satisfied we each became. It turned out we had the same opinions of politics, literature, and art—at least, in general, though there were enough differences in detail to lead to interesting discussions.

"The thing I most approved about her was that where there *was* a disagreement, she expressed her point of view calmly and with cogent arguments, and considered my counterarguments dispassionately and thoughtfully. There were times when she accepted my point of view, and times when I accepted hers, though on most occasions, I must admit, we continued to disagree. I could not argue her into voting Republican, for instance.

"In the end I was in love, by which I do not mean I was overcome by a mooning longing for physical intimacy. That existed, of course, but is not what I consider, quote, love, unquote. I was in love because I desperately wanted a continuing and, if possible, lifelong companionship where we could each pursue our aims and interests; together, if possible, but separately, if necessary—though even in the latter case, each with the interest and support of the other.

"There was talk of marriage and of children and there were also what we might term romantic interludes—neither of us were entirely creatures of the mind—and then, one day, it turned out that neither of us had really studied Latin.

"'We ought to,' said Claire, 'if for no other reason than the mental stimulation. Besides, it would please Professor Trent.'

"I must tell you about Marcus Quintus Trent. He was a Latinist of the old school (and so was his father—hence his name) and he had an emeritus status at Columbia. He had been a friend of Claire's father and had been instrumental in rousing her interest in languages. I had met him and found him genial, interesting, and, above all, urbane. He had the manners of a gentleman, in the non-American meaning of that word, and it made him seem both immensely old-fashioned and immensely civilized.

"His Latinism led him to believe, it sometimes seemed, that he was living in Julius Caesar's time. He was not only Latinate in his way of speaking, but I swear in his way of thinking as well. It seemed an effort for him not to refer to the American President as the Imperator. He would use Latin terms without being aware of it and was as likely to date his letters in the month of Februarius as not.

"I suspect he was a bit woebegone over Claire's having studied all the direct descendants of Latin—even a bit of Catalan and Rumanian—without actually dealing with Latin itself. That may have helped her come to the decision to study it.

"Automatically, I decided to go along with her and thus began what I referred to earlier in the evening as my, quote, present damned task, unquote.

"I do not use the adjective to indicate that the task was difficult. Learning Latin is not the major task a nonlinguist might assume. For me, the case structure of Russian was excellent training for the actually rather simpler case structure of Latin. For Claire, the Latin vocabulary was no problem at all since it was first cousin to Italian, which she spoke like a native. And for both of us, there was a native talent for languages, to say nothing of considerable practice in learning them. No, the task was a damned one for something that had nothing to do with the language itself.

"We discussed, with considerable animation, the matter of which of us would have the final advantage, I with my grammatical head start or she with her vocabularial push forward. Unspoken was the question of which of us might be the better linguist in general.

"Yes, Mr. Rubin, I quite realize that setting up a competition between two ambitious, hard-driving people might well endanger the affection that had grown up between them. Neither of us would have liked being beaten, but we both agreed that our love was strong enough to survive the fact that one of us was bound to be beaten by the other.

"Besides, what was a single defeat? If one of us was a clear loser at this time, he or she might win out on another day in the case of another challenge. The keen edge of intellect, sharpened by the competition, might, in fact, serve to further advance each of us in our profession, and this would more than make up for the trivial score of victories and defeats.

"At least, we persuaded each other that it was so.

"The idea was that we were each, quite independently, to study Latin on our own, using texts and authors of our choice. After six months, Trent would give us a passage of Latin literature to translate and he would judge it on the basis of both accuracy and eloquence of translation. In other words, a word-for-word translation was not enough. Trent intended to look for English that would capture the style as well as the meaning.

"Trent threw himself into the matter with vigor. He chose Cicero as a matter of course since Cicero's Latin is the most elegant in existence and also the most gracefully convoluted. (Trent urged us to read Milton's *Paradise Lost* if we wanted the nearest equivalent in English to Ciceronian style, and to be guided by that.)

"He chose a passage from one of Cicero's lesser essays, one which was likely to be unfamiliar to us, and handed it to each of us in a sealed envelope. The terms were that each of us was to open the envelope at 9 A.M. on the fifteenth of April and hand the translation to him no more than a week later—ample time not only for translation, but for polishing and repolishing in search of that elusive something called style.

"In translating we might use a Latin dictionary but, of course, we were neither of us to search for any already existing translation of the passage. We agreed to this readily, and Trent was gentleman enough to feel quite certain that we would both adhere to all conditions in all honor. As for myself, I knew he would not find me wanting and I assumed he would not find Claire wanting either. It did not even occur to me that Claire could possibly cheat. That was inconceivable.

"The final condition was that Trent would be sole judge of the results and that his decision was to be accepted without argument.

"Claire and I agreed that we would remain completely apart for the testing period, lest the presence of one prove a distraction to the other. In fact, I had to go out of town on Friday, the tenth of April, and was gone for the weekend. I didn't see her from the tenth until after our translations were handed in.

"I remember Trent chuckling over the result. He said we were twin souls indeed, for our translations were so remarkably similar that he could scarcely believe they were independently done. He judged Claire's the superior for reasons he outlined, but by a margin so small that I could scarcely consider it a defeat. I *swear* I held no animosity against Claire for winning. I was proud of her.

"I was human enough to regret one thing. I had opened the sealed passage promptly at 9 A.M. on Wednesday, April 15. Actually, I opened it five minutes after the hour in an exaggerated effort to lean over backward not to break the spirit of the agreement, just in case my watch was a little fast.

"But then, I had not taken the full time. We were allowed seven days, but I took only four. It was a bit of vainglory on my part, I think, but by that time, I had, in any case, grown tired of going over and over the passage and worrying endlessly over whether to say 'of Time's great sway' or 'of Time's mighty hest.' So I just handed it in on the evening of Sunday, the nineteenth.

"Later, of course, I thought that if I had spent three additional days improving my translation, it would have added just that extra bit that would have made me first. After all, Claire told me she had handed in her translation on the afternoon of Monday, the twentieth, so she had nearly a whole extra day. But then, the extra time might simply have resulted in damage through overmuch patching and repatching.

"So I let it go and treated her to a late-evening champagne victory celebration, and we got along marvellously well. After all, we had not seen each other for nearly two weeks and we improved the occasion as lovers will.

"And then, not too long ago, I met an old friend who asked me how Claire was. I said, 'Fine. Why? You sound concerned.'

"He said, 'I met her in the Columbia library last month, sweating over a Latin dictionary and she seemed odd. She snapped at me.'

"'Do you remember when it was?'

"'In April. I know it was a Monday—'

"'Monday, the twentieth,' I said at once. 'She had a paper due then and was making final corrections. I imagine she didn't welcome distractions and she considered you one.' I laughed, rather jovially, at the thought.

"But he said, 'No. It wasn't then. I remember that the day after my wife complained of a sore throat and we had to cancel a dinner engagement. Then I remember thinking of Claire the day before and wondering if something was going around. That dinner was on Tuesday, the fourteenth. I remember that well. So I saw Claire in the library on Monday, the thirteenth.'

"I snapped, 'Impossible!'

"He said, coolly, 'I don't see why it should be impossible. That was when I saw her.'

"That ended that, but I clung to the hope that Claire had been at work in the library on some other aspect of the Latin competition on that day. I sought her out.

"'Claire!' I said. 'Did you start translating the passage on the thirteenth?'

"She looked at me in surprise. 'Of course!'

"I couldn't believe it. 'Not on the fifteenth?'

"'Why on the fifteenth?' she countered. 'I wanted as early a start as possible. I love you, darling, but I intended to win.'

"I turned on my heels and walked away. That was a week ago and I haven't seen her or communicated with her since. She called me once, but I simply hung up.

"Perhaps I could understand her eagerness causing her to break the rules, but what put her over the edge as far as I was concerned was her calm assumption that cheating was permissible—the implication that if I was fool enough to follow the rules, I deserved to lose. She had no conscience in the matter, and no honor, and that meant she was not the woman I thought she was and I could not continue the relationship.

"That's the story and, as I told you, there's no mystery about it."

There was a silence for several moments when Soskind had finished, and then Halsted said, "You didn't put it to her directly, Mr. Soskind. You didn't say 'Why did you cheat, Claire?'"

"I didn't have to. It was clear enough."

There was another silence. Soskind said, defensively, "Come on. Are you saying I should have overlooked the matter? Forgive and forget?"

Rubin said, "You might have misheard. Perhaps the professor said—"

"The rules were in writing," said Soskind. "No mistake was possible."

Avalon said, hesitantly, "Since the young woman was so suitable in all other respects, and since you still seem to be in love with her—"

Soskind shook his head violently. "That lack of honor cancels out everything. If I am still in love, that's a problem that time will cure."

Drake peered through a cloud of cigarette smoke. "If *you* had won instead of her, would you be making all this fuss?"

"I certainly hope so. If I acted otherwise, I would be as bad as she."

Drake shrugged. "You're a stiff-necked moralist, Mr.

Soskind. The club's own stiff-necked moralist is Henry. What do you say, Henry?"

Henry, who was standing thoughtfully at the sideboard, said, "I believe there *is* a mystery to this. The young woman seems to have acted out of character."

Soskind said, "I prefer to think I didn't understand her character until she finally revealed it."

"If I may speak freely, Mr. Soskind—"

"Go ahead," said Soskind, with a bitter snort. "Say what you want. It can neither hurt nor help."

Henry said, "Isn't it possible, sir, that Miss Claire was entirely in the right and that you have behaved hastily and unfairly?"

Soskind reddened. "That's ridiculous!"

"But was the fifteenth of April indeed the starting point?"

"I have already said that that was in writing."

"But, Mr. Soskind, you also told us that Professor Trent tended to be Latinate in expression. Did he actually write 'the fifteenth of April' or 'April 15'?"

"Well, of course, he—Oh, I see what you mean. No, he said 'the ides of April,' but what's the difference?"

"An enormous one," said Henry. "Everyone thinks of the ides of March in connection with the assassination of Julius Caesar, and everyone knows that is March 15 on our calendar. It is only natural to suppose that the ides of every month falls on the fifteenth, but I checked the encyclopedia while you were completing your account and that is true only of March, May, July, and October. In all the other months, including April, the ides fall on the thirteenth of the month. Since the ides of April falls on April thirteenth, Miss Claire began on that day, very correctly, and was surprised that you questioned the matter and seemed to expect her to delay two days for no reason."

Halsted was at the encyclopedia. "Henry's right, by God," he said.

Soskind's eyes opened in a fixed glare. "And I started two days late?"

Henry said, softly, "If Professor Trent had known you did not know when the ides of April was, I suspect you would have lost the competition by a somewhat wider margin."

Soskind seemed to collapse inward in his chair. He said, in a mutter, "What do I do now?"

Henry said, "My experience with matters of the heart, sir, is limited, but I believe you had better waste no more time. Leave *now* and try to see the young lady. She may give you a chance to explain and what I know of such matters leads me to think you had better grovel.—Grovel quite abjectly, sir."

Afterword

Eleanor Sullivan was managing editor of *EQMM* all through the period during which I wrote the Black Widowers stories. Since Fred Dannay always worked from his Westchester home, it was to Eleanor that I brought my stories, and it was with her that I carried on an assiduous and platonic flirtation. (Not that I wanted it to be platonic, you understand, but she insisted.)

After Fred had passed on, she took over as editor, and following the grand tradition that Fred established she kept *EQMM* moving onward rock-steady. That includes (I am thankful to say) the occasional appearance of a Black Widower story, and of an occasional Union Club story, too.

This is the first Black Widower story she accepted in her capacity as editor, and I think that is suitable, for it is a romance.

Very few of my Black Widower stories involve a murder or a violent crime of any kind (that's my personal distaste for violence, although that is not absolute as you will know if you have read my story "The Woman in the Bar," which appeared earlier in this collection). What's more very few, if any, of my stories involve romance (mainly because I started writing when I was very young, and before I had had any personal experience at all with romance). Still, I would rather have romance than violence in a Black Widower story, and when I manage to do this I like the result, and so, in this case, did Eleanor, who is very sweet and softhearted indeed.

The story appeared in the May 1983 issue of *EQMM*.

Neither Brute
Nor Human

The monthly dinner of the Black Widowers was well under way and Emmanuel Rubin, his fork uplifted, and waving threateningly in the air, temporarily ignored his rack of lamb and said, "Edgar Allan Poe was the first important practitioner of the modern detective story and of the modern science fiction story. I'll give him that."

"Nice of you," murmured James Drake, the host of the occasion, in a low aside.

Rubin ignored him. "He lifted the horror story to new heights, too. Still, he had a morbid and unhealthy preoccupation with death."

"Not at all," said Geoffrey Avalon, in his deep voice, his thick eyebrows lowering into a frown. "Poe was writing in the first half of the nineteenth century, and there was still virtually no protection against infectious disease at the time. Life was short and death was ever-present. He wasn't being morbid; he was being realistic."

Roger Halsted said, "Absolutely! Read any fiction of the nineteenth century. Read Dickens and the death of Little Nell, or Harriet Beecher Stowe and the death of Little Eva. Children frequently died in fiction because they frequently died in real life."

Rubin's eyes, magnified by his thick glasses, took on a stubborn gleam, and his sparse beard seemed to bristle. "It's not death in itself. It's how you treat it. You can deal with it as the doorway to heaven, and treat the dying person as a saint—see the death of Beth in *Little Women*. That can be sickeningly sentimental, but it is meant to be uplifting.

Poe, on the other hand, dwells with an unholy glee on the elements of degradation and decay. He makes death worse than it is and—Come on, you all know very well what 'morbid' is.''

He returned to his lamb and attacked it with vigor.

Thomas Trumbull growled and said, "Certainly. 'Morbid' is talking about morbidity over what would otherwise be a pleasant dinner.''

"I don't see that it makes any difference whether Poe was morbid or not,'' said Mario Gonzalo, who was neatly dissecting strips of meat off the ribs. "What counts is whether he was a good writer or not, and I suppose no one argues with the fact that he was good.''

Avalon said, judiciously, "Even good writers aren't good all the time. James Russell Lowell described Poe as 'three fifths of him genius and two fifths sheer fudge,' and I would say that was pretty accurate.''

Halsted said, "My feeling is that a seminal writer has to accept some responsibility for his imitators. There is something about Poe that makes it absolutely necessary for his imitators to be awful. Consider H. P. Lovecraft—''

"No,'' said Rubin, violently, "we are *not* discussing Lovecraft; we are talking about Poe—''

And oddly enough, Drake's guest, who, until now, had sat mute through the dinner, said suddenly in a loud, almost metallic voice, *"Why* are we talking about Poe?''

His name was Jonathan Dandle; short, plump around the middle, a round face that was now quite flushed, a large bald head with a fringe of white hair about the ears, and round gold-rimmed bifocals. He looked in his early sixties.

He had startled the company into silence, and even Henry, the imperturbable waiter who was the pride of the Black Widowers, allowed an expression of surprise to flit momentarily across his face.

Drake cleared his throat and stubbed out his cigarette. "We talk about anything we please, Jonathan. Poe is as good a subject as any, especially since Manny Rubin writes mysteries so that Poe might be considered his patron saint. Right, Manny?"

Dandle looked about the table from one to the other and some of the redness drained out of his face and left it a normal hue. He lifted his hands in a kind of shrug. "My apologies, gentleman. It was not my intention to dictate the subject of the conversation."

He looked a trifle unhappy.

Rubin nodded at Dandle in slightly haughty forgiveness, and said, "Actually, if we're talking about the patron saint of mysteries, I could make a good argument in favor of Conan Doyle. The Mystery Writers of America may hand out Edgars, but the archetypical detective, as all of us know—" and, with that, Poe was abandoned.

Dandle listened intently to the further course of the conversation, but said nothing else until Henry had served the coffee, and Gonzalo had produced a quick caricature which he showed the guest.

Dandle regarded it solemnly, then smiled. "It is fortunate, Mr. Gonzalo, that I have no great opinion of my beauty. You make me look like the old-time actor Guy Kibbee. Perhaps you don't remember him."

Gonzalo said, "Certainly, I remember him, and now that you point it out there *is* a resemblance. A clever artist, with a few strokes of the pen, can bare essentials that are not necessarily obvious."

"What a pity, Mario," said Rubin, "that you don't find a clever artist who can teach you to do so."

"And yet," said Gonzalo easily, "you have met any number of clever writers and none has been able to help you."

At which point, Drake rattled his water glass with his spoon. "Grilling time, gentlemen, so that Manny and Mario are requested to shut up.—Jeff, will you do the honors."

Geoffrey Avalon stirred the melting ice in his half-consumed second Scotch with his middle finger, and said, "Mr. Dandle, how do you justify your existence?"

Dandle said, thoughtfully, "A good question. Since I had nothing to do with the initiation of my existence in this unfortunate world, I might justifiably deny any need to defend myself. However, I have accepted my existence for over six decades now—after all, I might have killed myself easily enough—so I will defend. How would it be if I told you I am making it easier for people to communicate with each other. Would that serve as grounds for justification?"

"It depends on what they communicate," said Gonzalo. "Now Manny's attempts at—"

"Mario!" said Avalon, sharply, and turned a frowning look in Gonzalo's direction. Then, more gently, he said, "I have the floor and I would rather that we not descend into anarchy this time.—In what way, Mr. Dandle, do you make it easier for people to communicate?"

"I work in fiber optics, Mr. Avalon, and communication by laser light through glass, rather than by electricity through copper, will make for cheaper and thinner cables that would nevertheless carry more messages. I admit that not all the high technology in the world will of itself serve to improve the quality of those messages."

"And yet, sir, if I may be allowed to interject a personal note, you do not yourself show much tendency to communicate, considering that communication is your business. You have said hardly anything at all during cocktails or dinner. Is there a reason for that?"

Dandle looked about him, his face reddening again. It was quite apparent that he flushed easily, and, like almost all people who do, that he was quite aware of it and seemed the more embarrassed—and to redden more—because of it. He mumbled something.

"I beg your pardon, sir," said Avalon. "I didn't hear you."

Drake, who sat next to his guest, and who looked rather uncomfortable himself, said, "Jonathan, saying 'I've nothing to say' is no answer."

Dandle said, "It's an answer if that's the answer I choose to give, Jim."

"No," said Drake, peering at his guest out of his wrinkle-nested eyes. "That's not among the permitted choices, Jonathan. I explained the deal on this meeting. You receive a good dinner and good company in exchange for substantive answers. No secrets. No evasions. My own experience is that you've always had plenty to say."

Avalon said, "Let me continue, Jim.—Mr. Dandle, I will accept your answer that you have nothing to say, though I wish you would speak up so that others besides your immediate neighbor might hear you. My next question is this: Why is it that you have nothing to say on this occasion considering that, if we are to believe Jim, such silence is not typical of you?"

Dandle spread out his hands and said loudly enough, "Is a man always accountable for his actions, Mr. Avalon? Does he always know the origins of his moods?"

Avalon said, "Then let me ask you another question. You did, on one occasion, interject a question into the general conversation. You asked why we were talking about Poe, and you did so quite forcibly. I interpreted your remark as indicating that you were offended, perhaps outraged, by the discussion. Is that so? And if it is so, why?"

Dandle shook his head. "No, no. I just asked."

Trumbull stood up and passed one hand over his tightly waved white hair. He said, with exaggerated patience, "Jim, as the host, you must make a decision. We are clearly getting nothing out of our guest, and I think that, under the rules of the club, we might be forced to adjourn the meeting now. In fact, I move you consider adjournment."

Drake waved a hand at him petulantly. "Take it easy, Tom.—Jonathan, you've got to answer honestly. Nothing that is said here will ever be repeated outside these walls. Our waiter, Henry, is a member of the club and he is as closemouthed as we are. More so. I know you well enough to know you haven't committed a crime, or are planning to commit one, but even so, we—"

"You're quite wrong," said Dandle, in a rather more

high-pitched voice than before. "I am trying to commit what *I* consider a crime. I'm certainly trying to be dishonest."

Drake said, "You?"

"With what I think is considerable justification, of course."

"After that," said Trumbull, "if Mr. Dandle does not care to elaborate, Jim, then we can go no further."

There was silence. Trumbull remained standing. Drake looked at Dandle and said, "Well, Jonathan?"

Dandle said, "You told me, Jim, I would be grilled on the details of my profession. I did not expect this sort of thing."

"It can't be helped. If you had been yourself, none of this would have come up. What's wrong?"

Dandle looked helpless. He clenched his fist, made as though he was going to bring it down on the table, stopped the motion, and said, "It's my sister."

"Your crackp—" began Drake, and stopped suddenly.

"My crackpot sister," said Dandle. "She's dying. Cancer."

There was a sudden silence.

"We've known it for months," said Dandle, "and she may live for months more, but it does produce problems."

The silence continued. Finally, Henry said, "Brandy, gentlemen?"

Avalon said, absently, "Just a small portion, Henry.— What kind of problems, Mr. Dandle?"

"Her will."

"You mean, all this is a matter of money?" said Halsted, with rather more than a shade of disapproval in his voice.

"Not money at all," said Dandle, lifting his eyebrows. "Please understand, gentlemen, that my wife and I are well off. We have a son and daughter, but both are grown and both are reasonably well off. My sister has a house and some money that she inherited from our parents, but this is not something we lust for. At least, not the money. That she can dispose of as she wishes. She can leave it to a farm for homeless cats, if she wishes. It's the house."

He fell into momentary thought. "It was quite clear that she would never marry by the time my parents died. It made sense to leave the family house to her, even though it was unnecessarily large for one person. Still, it's belonged to the family since it was built; I was born there; lived there till I married; I have a profound emotional attachment to it. Now my sister, Rachel," Dandle looked briefly at Drake, "being, as you say, a crackpot, is planning to leave it to a crackpot organization, and I don't want her to. I'd be willing to have it sold to someone respectable. I'd even be willing to have it torn down in a decent way for a decent purpose. But I'm damned if I'm willing to let the—the Cosmic Order of Theognostics infest it."

"The *what?*" said Gonzalo.

Avalon said, "The word comes from the Greek and means 'knowing God.'"

Dandle said, "What they really know are methods for extracting money from fools and nuts."

Avalon said, "I assume they are extracting money from your sister."

"To some extent, yes, but not very much. She is a shrewd woman, financially, and is quite compos mentis outside her obsession. Still, they're angling to get it all when she dies. And they may."

"What is her obsession, sir?"

"I believe it started with her reading of Poe when she was young. I think she read everything he had written; memorized it, just about; and absorbed the unhealthy morbidity that Mr. Rubin mentioned. And she read Lovecraft, too, and grew inclined to believe in horrors from outer space, in elder intelligences, and so on. She lectured me often enough on that stuff. Naturally, she became part of the UFO mania."

"Naturally," muttered Rubin, with a look of distaste.

"She became convinced that intelligent beings from outer space are actually on Earth and have taken over Earth's leaders, and much of the general population. She thinks

these aliens are themselves invisible, or can make themselves so, and can live within human beings parasitically.
It's all quite mad."

"I suppose," said Avalon, "that if anyone disagrees with
her, or tries to argue against her views, she considers it a
sign the arguer has been taken over."

"Absolutely. I early recognized the mistake of trying to
oppose her."

Halsted said, "Why haven't the aliens taken over
everybody? How does your sister explain that she herself
hasn't been taken over?"

"I gather," said Dandle, "that the Cosmic Order of
Theognostics fights them with prayer and introspection and
meditation and incantation and whatever the devil they
claim to do, and they have taught her the same. She has
tried to teach me and I've just kept silent and listened.
There's a lot of candle burning involved, and the recitation
of whole pages of material that has no meaning whatever
but I suppose she thinks it keeps me safe—so far."

Drake said, through the smoke of his cigarette, "When I
referred to her as a crackpot, Jonathan, I was thinking of the
UFO stuff. I didn't know about this alien intelligences bit."

"It's not something I like to talk about, obviously," said
Dandle, "and wouldn't be talking about now except under
pressure."

Avalon said, "You said you were thinking of committing
a crime. Surely, you're not thinking of mayhem against the
Theognostics."

"Nothing like that. Just a crime in my own eyes. I've
been trying to cheat and deceive my sister, and I'm not
really proud of that."

"Would you be willing to explain that, sir?" asked
Avalon, stiffly.

"Well, since Rachel was found to have cancer, things are
at a crisis. She won't submit to surgery because she is sure
that under anesthesia she will be taken over. She is
suspicious of radiotherapy, too, since radiation is a weapon

of those beings. She is relying entirely on Theognostic ritual, and you can imagine how effective that is."

Rubin said, "The most ridiculous methods can sometimes help if you believe firmly that they will. The mind is a powerful instrument."

"That may be," said Dandle, "but it isn't helping her. She's going downhill, and, about a month ago, she began to talk of leaving the house and her money to the Theognostics so that they could continue the great fight against the aliens.—So I started a plan of my own." He reddened and stopped.

After a short pause, Avalon said, gently, "Yes, Mr. Dandle?"

"To put it bluntly," said Dandle, "I came to her as an enthusiastic convert. I said she had convinced me and that I was heart and soul with her; that she could leave the money to the Theognostics if she wished, but that she should leave the house to me and I would make it the center of the fight against the aliens. I would allow the Theognostics to use it freely but I merely wanted to keep title to it in honor of our parents. I was hypocritical and obsequious."

"No doubt," said Avalon, "but did it work? People who, like your sister, believe in invisible, untestable dangers would be suspicious of everything."

"I'm afraid so," said Dandle. "She's of two minds about me. She *wants* to believe, but, as you say, she is suspicious. She hesitates to tell me what I'm sure she believes to be the 'higher mysteries,' so to speak. I asked for details about the form and attributes of the mysterious aliens, for instance, and she was closemouthed about it—as though she was not sure I was worthy of initiation."

Trumbull said, "Maybe she doesn't know herself."

Rubin said, "She can easily invent anything she wishes and then come to believe it. Such things are very common."

"Last week she said something in a sort of singsong whisper and I thought I was making progress, but then there was nothing more."

"What did she say?"

"Well, they're hermaphroditic and are neither women nor men. And they weren't Earthly, of course. They aren't human beings or animals. And when they infest us they live on our spiritual nature rather than on our physical bodies, I gather, for she seized my arm, with a surprisingly strong grip, too, and whispered into my ear, 'They are *worse* than cannibals, and that is not surprising considering where they come from.'"

"Where do they come from?" asked Gonzalo.

"That's what I asked," said Dandle, "but she didn't say. She said that once you achieve a certain enlightenment, you *know* where they come from; that that is the test of enlightenment. It comes over you like a wave of revelation and gives you a certain power against them. *She* knows, and the Theognostics know; but they don't tell anyone because that's their test for the people who are strong against the aliens. It doesn't really make sense, but if I were to try to say that to her, it would mean the end of my chance to save the house. So I just said, earnestly, that I would meditate and try to gain the knowledge." He looked about the table with a grim face. "I'm supposed to be fasting.—She called me this morning."

"Things are coming to a crisis?" asked Avalon.

"Yes. That's why I've been preoccupied this evening, and didn't say much. I was of two minds whether to come here at all, but I didn't want to let Jim Drake down."

"But what was it your sister said to you this morning?"

"She says she wants to make a decision about her will. She feels herself weakening and she knows that she must become one with the Great Divine—which is the Theognostic term for God, apparently—and she wants to make sure she continues the fight from beyond the grave. She can't let me have the house unless she is certain I won't bar the Theognostics from it. And, of course, barring them is *exactly* what I intend to do so I am trying to flimflam her.—It's not exactly admirable of me."

Trumbull said, loudly, "We're on your side, Mr. Dandle.

You're fighting a group of pernicious and vicious flimflam operators, and if counter-flimflam is required, so be it."

"Thank you," said Dandle, "but I don't see that I will win out. She wants me to visit her tomorrow at noon and tell her where the aliens come from. If I can't, then she can't rely on me to remain strong against them and the Theognostics will get the house. And, of course, I can't tell her where the aliens come from. They're from outer space, I'm sure. That would fit in with her UFO madness, for they undoubtedly reached Earth by UFO. But where in outer space?"

There was a short silence, then Gonzalo said, "She never gave you any hints?"

Dandle shook his head. "Only the remark about their being worse than cannibals and that that somehow was appropriate, considering where they come from. But what does that mean?"

"Nothing else?"

"Not that I can think of. If she did, it went right past me.—So tomorrow I lose the house."

Avalon said, "You know, sir, that you can contest the will."

"No, not really," said Dandle. "You were introduced to me as a lawyer—"

"A patent lawyer," said Avalon. "I am not knowledgeable on the intricacies of testamentary litigation."

"Well, on the one hand, there is a strong tendency to allow a testator to do as he wishes with his own property. It isn't easy to disallow a religious organization in favor of a relative who is already well off. I doubt that I can prove undue influence, nor would I care to try to make my sister seem to have been of unsound mind, if only out of family considerations. Then, even if I really thought I could win, it would be a long-drawn-out fight in which the legal fees would come to considerably more than I would care to pay.—So I'm going to lose the house."

Avalon said, "We might all of us think about this a bit."

A flicker of hope seemed to enliven Dandle. "Are any of you astronomers?"

"Not professionally," said Halsted, "but we have the usual superficial knowledge of the field that any intelligent and reasonably well-read individuals would have."

"Exactly," said Rubin, "and that means I can make a suggestion. We're looking for something in outer space that has cannibalistic associations. I've read articles recently that in clusters of galaxies, there are occasional collisions and that, in such collisions, the larger member gains stars at the expense of the smaller one. The result is that in clusters, there is one galaxy that is larger than any of the others, having cannibalized them."

Halsted nodded vigorously. "You are right, Manny. I've read about it, too. There's one outsize galaxy that has five small bright regions within itself that resemble galactic centers. The thought is that it swallowed five small galaxies whole."

Gonzalo said, "Just for the record—what are galaxies?"

Avalon said, "Large conglomerations of stars, Mario. Our own Milky Way Galaxy has a couple of hundred billion stars in it."

Gonzalo said, "Well, then, has that cannibal galaxy—the one that swallowed up its five little sisters—got a name?"

The Black Widowers stared at each other. Finally, Halsted said, "It may, but if it does, it's probably not an ordinary name. Just a particular catalog number like NGC-IIII, or something like that."

Gonzalo said, "I don't think Miss Dandle would be impressed by that."

Dandle said, "I don't think so, either. I'm grateful to you for your attempts to help, but if galactic cannibalization is a common phenomenon, which cannibal would be the correct one? And I'm sure my sister knows nothing about modern sophistications in astronomy, anyway. Nor would the Theognostics. Where would they hear of this phenomenon?"

Avalon said, "Does you sister read anything at all in the field of astronomy, Mr. Dandle?"

Dandle said, thoughtfully, "She's certainly read everything there is on UFOs and some astronomy—not necessarily correct—is bound to creep in there. She reads up on astrology, of course, which means additional possibly distorted astronomy. And I have seen astronomy popularizations in the house. I haven't actually seen her reading them but I wouldn't be surprised if she did."

"Is she well-read otherwise, sir?"

"Yes. All of Poe as I said, and Lovecraft, and some science fiction. A great deal of general nineteenth-century fiction, I should say, and, of course, she reads the newspapers and a number of magazines thoroughly, if only to find evidence of how far the aliens have taken over the world. I've got to explain to you that there's nothing wrong with her intelligence, outside her—her crackpottery."

"In that case," said Avalon, with a certain sombre satisfaction, "I am quite sure I have the answer." He paused and cast a glance in the direction of the waiter, who was standing at the sideboard, listening with polite but silent attention.

"Henry," said Avalon, "I think that on this occasion we will not need your help."

"Yes, Mr. Avalon," said Henry, quietly.

Avalon cleared his throat. "You see, by far the best-known portion of the Universe, even to astronomers, and *certainly* to the general public, are the planets of our own solar system. This is especially true for people like Miss Dandle, who are interested in astrology and similar aberrations.

"And of the planets, the one which in recent years has received the most attention and which is, in any case, the most spectacular, is the planet Saturn, with its rings and satellites. The Voyager probes have taken close-up photographs of the Saturnian system and these have made all the newspapers and magazines. Miss Dandle cannot have missed them."

Dandle said, "I'm sure she has not. But what then?"

"Saturn," said Avalon, "is named for an early Roman god of agriculture whom the Romans, with scant justice, equated with the Greek god Kronos. Kronos with his brothers and sisters made up the group of gods called the Titans, and they were the children of Ouranos and Gaea, the god of the sky and the goddess of the Earth, respectively. In a series of most unpleasant myths, the Greeks describe Kronos as castrating his father, Uranus, and taking over the rule of the Universe.

"Since the Fates had decreed that Kronos would, in turn, be replaced as ruler by his own son, the new lord of the Universe took to devouring each child as it was born. His wife, Rhea, managed to save one son by offering Kronos a rock wrapped in the baby's swaddling clothes. The rather stupid Kronos swallowed that without noticing the substitution. The son, still uneaten, was then hidden in Crete, and raised to maturity in secret. Eventually, the son, who was named Zeus (Jupiter, to the Romans), warred upon the Titans, defeated them, released his siblings, who were still alive within Kronos, and took over the Universe. All this Miss Dandle, in her reading, might very well have come across.

"Now, then, Saturn was clearly a cannibal. If there are degrees in such things, devouring one's own children is surely worse than fattening on strangers, so he might well be viewed as worse than an ordinary cannibal. Miss Dandle's statement that the aliens were worse than cannibals and that that was not surprising in view of where they came from would make sense if they came from Saturn."

And Avalon smiled at Dandle with self-conscious triumph.

Dandle said, "You think, then, I had better tell my sister the alien beings come from Saturn?"

"I can't say the matter is certain," said Avalon. "She may, after all, suppose them to have come from some entirely fictitious planet such as Zorkel, the fifth planet of the star Xanadu, in the galaxy of Yaanek. If, however, she has a real astronomical body in mind, then I am virtually certain that it is Saturn. It must be."

"It sounds good to me," said Gonzalo.

"It makes sense," admitted Rubin, looking distressed at having to say so.

Halsted said, "It's worth a try."

Trumbull said, "I can't think of anything better."

Drake said, "It seems unanimous. I'd take the chance, Jonathan."

Dandle began, "Well, since I can't think of anything better, either—"

Gonzalo interrupted. "Wait, Henry hasn't said anything. Henry, what do you think?"

Dandle looked up in astonishment at having the waiter referred to.

When Henry said, "May I ask Mr. Dandle if he shared in his sister's enthusiasm for Poe?" Dandle looked more astonished still.

Drake said, "Please answer, Jonathan. Henry is one of us."

Jonathan said, "No, definitely not. I know 'The Raven'; no one can avoid knowing that; but I know nothing else. I stay away from him."

"In that case," said Henry, "I fear that Mr. Avalon's suggestion, although most ingenious, is not the correct answer."

Avalon looked offended. "Inded, Henry? Have you anything better to offer?"

Henry said, "Consider, sir, that Miss Dandle was a great devotee of Poe, and that in describing the aliens she said that they were neither female nor male, animal nor human."

"Well?"

"Well, Mr. Avalon, I, unlike Mr. Dandle but like his sister, am an admirer of Poe, though more so of his poetry than of his prose. Among my favorite poems by Poe is 'The Bells,' in the fourth part of which he describes the tolling of the funeral bells. There you have his morbid preoccupation with death, you see, something that is bound to follow his earlier descriptions of sleigh bells, wedding bells, and fire-alarm bells.''

"Aha," said Rubin.

"Yes, Mr. Rubin," said Henry. "I suspect you already see what I mean. Part of the description of the funeral bells is—if I may quote:

> *"And the people—ah, the people—*
> *They that dwell up in the steeple,*
> *All alone,*
> *And who, tolling, tolling, tolling,*
> *In that muffled monotone,*
> *Feel a glory in so rolling*
> *On the human heart a stone—*
> *They are neither man nor woman—*
> *They are neither brute nor human—"*

Henry paused, then said, "Miss Dandle was undoubtedly quoting those last two lines, I think. You stated that she said them in singsong fashion, Mr. Dandle, but not being a Poe enthusiast, you did not recognize them."

Avalon said, "But even so—How does that help?"

Henry said, "It is the next line that counts, as Poe identifies the people who toll the funeral bells."

And he and Rubin quoted simultaneously: " *'They are Ghouls.'* "

Henry said, "Ghouls are creatures of the Middle Eastern legend who infest graveyards and feed on dead bodies. That might well strike Miss Dandle, or anyone, as worse than ordinary cannibalism, just as vultures are worse than hawks in the general estimation."

Avalon said, "I grant that, but I still don't see the point."

"Nor I," said Trumbull.

Henry said, "There is a constellation in the sky named Perseus, named for the Greek hero who cut off the head of Medusa, a creature so dreadful in appearance that anyone looking at it turned to stone. The constellation is pictured as the hero holding the head of Medusa and that head is marked by a second-magnitude star, Beta Persei. I looked it up in the Columbia Encyclopedia during the discussion, to be sure of that fact.

"Because of its position in the constellation, Beta Persei is sometimes called the Demon Star, in consequence. The Arabs, who adopted the Greek view of the sky, named it *Al Ghul,* meaning 'The Ghoul,' their version of something as horrible as Medusa, and our English version of that Arabic name is 'Algol.' That is now the common name of the star.

"Since Miss Dandle quoted that poem to define the aliens, she meant that they were ghouls, and therefore worse than cannibals, and she must have meant that it was not surprising that they were since they came from the star known as 'The Ghoul'—a fact she could surely have picked up from some book on popular astronomy, as I did, originally. I would suggest, then, Mr. Dandle, that you say, when you see your sister tomorrow, that the aliens come from Algol."

Dandle smiled brightly for the first time that evening and broke into applause. "Henry, I will. That *should* be the answer, and I am sure it is."

Henry said, gravely, "Nothing may be completely sure in this case, sir, but it is worth the gamble."

Afterword

Eleanor worried about this story a bit because it seemed to her (and to me, too) that it wasn't quite admirable of Jonathan Dandle to want to deceive his sister, or of the Black Widowers to help him do so. Still I felt the cause was good enough to warrant the act, and I managed to convince Eleanor of it, too.

When it comes to that, Dandle himself worried about it, and I had nothing to do with that, either. My characters always manage to have a life of their own and they generally do things without my consciously willing them to do so.

Anyway, I have my own list of dislikes and disapprovals, and high on it are nonrational cults of any kind, whether they cover themselves with a cloak of pseudoreligiosity or not. Mind you, this does not extend to honest and rational religious feeling, as I showed in my story "The One and Only East," which appeared in an earlier Black Widowers collection.

Consequently, if I can do one of them in the eye—even if only fictionally—I don't hesitate.

The story appeared in the April 1984 issue of *EQMM*.

The Redhead

Mario Gonzalo, host of that evening's meeting of the Black Widowers, had evidently decided to introduce his guest with éclat. At least he rattled his glass with a spoon and, when all had broken off their preprandial conversations and looked up from their cocktails, Mario made his introduction. He had even waited for Thomas Trumbull's as-usual late arrival before doing so.

"Gentlemen," he said, "this is my guest, John Anderssen—that's an *s-s-e-n* at the end. You can discover anything you want about him in this evening's grilling. One thing, however, I must tell you now because I know that this bunch of asexual loudmouths will never discover it on their own. John has a wife who is, absolutely, the most gorgeous specimen of femininity the world has ever seen. And I say this as an artist with an artist's eye."

Anderssen reddened and looked uncomfortable. He was a blond young man, perhaps thirty, with a small mustache and a fair complexion. He was about five-ten in height and had rather chiseled features that came together to form a handsome face.

Geoffrey Avalon, looking down from his stiff-backed seventy-four inches, said, "I must congratulate you, Mr. Anderssen, although you need not take seriously Mario's characterization of ourselves as asexual. I'm sure that each of us is quite capable of appreciating a beautiful woman. I, myself, although I might be considered to be past the first flush of hot-blooded youth, can—"

Trumbull said, "Spare us, Jeff, spare us. If you are going

to give an embarrassing account of your prowess, you are better off being interrupted. From my point of view, the next best thing to having the young woman in our midst—if our customs allowed it—would be to see her photograph. I imagine, Mr. Anderssen, you carry a photo of your fair wife in your wallet. Would you consent to let us look at it?''

"No," said Anderssen, emphatically. Then, blushing furiously, he said, "I don't mean you can't look at it. I mean I don't have a photograph of her with me. I'm sorry." But he said it challengingly, and was clearly not sorry.

Gonzalo, unabashed, said, "Well, that's your loss, my friends. You should see her hair. It's gloriously red, a live red that just about glows in the dark. And natural, totally natural—and no freckles."

"Well," said Anderssen in half a mutter, "she stays out of the sun.—Her hair *is* her best feature."

Emmanuel Rubin, who had been standing on the outskirts, looking rather dour, said in a low voice, "And temper to match, I suppose."

Anderssen turned to him, and said, with an edge of bitterness, "She has a temper." He did not elaborate.

Rubin said, "I don't suppose there's a more durable myth than the one that redheads are hot-tempered. The redness of the hair is that of fire, and the principles of sympathetic magic lead people to suppose that the personality should match the hair."

James Drake, who shared, with Avalon, the dubious privilege of being the oldest of the Widowers, sighed reminiscently, and said, "I've known some very hot-blooded redheads."

"Sure you have," said Rubin. "So has everyone. It's a self-fulfilling assumption. Redheaded children, especially girls, are forgiven for being nasty and ill-behaved. Parents sigh fatuously and mutter that it goes with the hair, and the one with red hair in the family explains how Great-Uncle Joe would mop up the floor with anyone in the barroom who said anything that was less than a grovelling compliment. Boys usually grow up and have the stuffing knocked out of them by non-redheaded peers and that teaches them manners, but girls don't. And, if they're beautiful besides, they grow up knowing they can indulge their impoliteness to the hilt. An occasional judicious kick in the fanny would do them worlds of good."

Rubin carefully did not look at Anderssen in the course of his comment and Anderssen said nothing at all.

Henry, the indispensable waiter at all the Black Widower functions, said quietly, "Gentlemen, you may be seated."

The chef at the Milano had clearly decided to be Russian for the evening, and an excellent hot borscht was followed by an even more delightful beef Stroganoff on a bed of rice. Rubin, who usually endured the food with an expression of stoic disapproval, on principle, allowed a smile to play over his sparsely bearded face on this occasion, and helped himself lavishly to the dark pumpernickel.

As for Roger Halsted, whose affection for a good meal was legendary, he quietly negotiated a second helping with Henry.

The guest, John Anderssen, ate heartily, and participated eagerly in the conversation which, through a logical association, perhaps, dealt largely with the shooting down of the Korean jetliner by the Soviets. Anderssen pointed out that the ship had been widely referred to as "Flight 007," which was the number on the fuselage, during the first couple of weeks. Then someone must have remembered that 007 was the code number of James Bond, so when the Soviets insisted the liner had been a spy plane, it became "Flight 7" in the news media, and the "00" disappeared as though it had never been.

He also maintained vigorously that the jetliner, having gone off course almost immediately after leaving Alaska, should not have been left uninformed of the fact. He was shouting, red-faced, that failure to do so, when the Soviet Union was known to be on the hair trigger with respect to American reconnaissance planes and to Reagan's "evil empire" rhetoric, was indefensible.

He paid no attention, in fact, to his dessert, a honey-drenched baklava; left his coffee half-finished; and totally ignored Henry's soft request that he make his wishes known with respect to the brandy.

He was actually pounding the table when Gonzalo rattled his spoon against his water glass. Avalon was forced to raise his baritone voice to a commanding, "Mr. Anderssen, *if* you please—"

Anderssen subsided, looking vaguely confused, as though he were, with difficulty, remembering where he was.

Gonzalo said, "It's time for the grilling, and Jeff, since you seem to have the commanding presence needed in case John, here, gets excited, suppose you do the honors."

Avalon cleared his throat, gazed at Anderssen solemnly for a few moments, then said, "Mr. Anderssen, how do you justify your existence?"

Anderssen said, "What?"

"You exist, sir. Why?"

"Oh," said Anderssen, still collecting himself. Then, in a low harsh voice, he said, "To expiate my sins in an earlier existence, I should think."

Drake, who was at the moment accepting a refresher from Henry, muttered, "So are we all.—Don't you think so, Henry?"

And Henry's sixtyish unlined face remained expressionless as he said, very softly, "A Black Widowers banquet is surely a reward for virtue rather than an expiation for sins."

Drake lifted his glass. "A palpable hit, Henry."

Trumbull growled, "Let's cut out the private conversations."

Avalon raised his hand. "Gentlemen! As you all know, I do not entirely approve of our custom of grilling a guest in the hope of searching out problems that might interest us. Nevertheless, I wish to call your attention to a peculiar phenomenon. We have here a young man—young, certainly, by the standards of old mustaches such as ourselves—well-proportioned, of excellent appearance, seeming to exude good health and an air of success in life, though we have not yet ascertained what the nature of his work is—"

"He's in good health and is doing well at his work," put in Gonzalo.

"I am glad to hear it," said Avalon, gravely. "In addition, he is married to a young and beautiful woman, so that one can't help but wonder why he should feel life to be such a burden as to lead him to believe that he exists only in order to expiate past sins. Consider, too, that during the meal just concluded, Mr. Anderssen was animated and vivacious, not in the least abashed by our older and wiser heads. I believe he shouted down even Manny, who is not one to be shouted down with impunity—"

"Anderssen was making a good point," said Rubin, indignantly.

"I think he was, too," said Avalon, "but what I wish to stress is that he is voluble, articulate, and not backward at expressing his views. Yet during the cocktail period, when the conversation dealt with his wife, he seemed to speak most reluctantly. From this, I infer that the source of Mr. Anderssen's unhappiness may be Mrs. Anderssen.—Is that so, Mr. Anderssen?"

Anderssen seemed stricken and remained silent.

Gonzalo said, "John, I explained the terms. You must answer."

Anderssen said, "I'm not sure how to answer."

Avalon said, "Let me be indirect. After all, sir, there is no intention to humiliate you. And please be aware that nothing said in this room is ever repeated by any of us elsewhere. That includes our esteemed waiter, Henry. Please feel that you can speak freely.—Mr. Anderssen, how long have you been married?"

"Two years. Actually, closer to two and a half."

"Any children, sir?"

"Not yet. We hope to have some one day."

"For that hope to exist, the marriage must not be foundering. I take it you are not contemplating divorce."

"Certainly not."

"I take it then that you love your wife?"

"Yes. And before you ask, I am quite satisfied she loves me."

"There is, of course, a certain problem in being married to a beautiful woman," said Avalon. "Men *will* flock about beauty. Are you plagued by jealousy, sir?"

"No," said Anderssen. "I've no cause for it. Helen—that's my wife—has no great interest in men—"

"Ah," said Halsted, as though a great light had dawned.

"Except for myself," said Anderssen, indignantly. "She's not in the least bit asexual. Besides," he went on, "Mario exaggerates. She does have this luxuriant head of remarkable red hair, but aside from that she is not really spectacular. Her looks, I would say, are average—though I must rely now on your assurance that all said here is confidential. I would not want *that* assessment to be repeated. Her figure is good, and *I* find her beautiful, but there are no men caught helplessly in her toils, and I am not plagued by jealousy."

"What about her temper?" put in Drake, suddenly. "That's been mentioned and you've admitted she had one. I presume there's lots of fighting and dish throwing?"

"Some fights, sure," said Anderssen, "but no more than is par for the course. And no dish throwing. As Mr. Avalon has pointed out, I'm articulate, and so is she, and we're both pretty good at shouting, but after we work off our steam, we can be just as good at kissing and hugging."

"Then am I to take it, sir, that your wife is *not* the source of your troubles?" said Avalon.

Anderssen fell silent again.

"I must ask you to answer, Mr. Anderssen," said Avalon.

Anderssen said, "She *is* the problem. Just now, anyway. But it's too silly to talk about."

Rubin sat up at that and said, "On the contrary. Till now, I felt that Jeff was just wasting our time over the kind of domestic irritations that we attend these dinners, in part, to escape. But if there's something *silly* involved, then we want to hear it."

"If you must know," said Anderssen. "Helen says she's a witch."

"Oh?" said Rubin. "Has she always claimed this, or just recently?"

"Always. We joke about it. She would say she put me under enchantment to get me to marry her, and that she would cast spells and get me a promotion or a raise. Sometimes, when she is furious, she'll say, 'Well, don't blame me if you blotch out in pimples just because you're going to be that stupid and mean.' That sort of thing."

Rubin said, "It sounds harmless to me. She probably *did* put you under enchantment. You fell in love with her and any woman of reasonable intelligence and looks can make a young man fall in love with her if she works hard enough being charming. You can call that enchantment if you wish."

"But I *do* get the promotions and raises."

"Surely that could be because you deserve them. Do you get the pimples, too?"

Anderssen smiled. "Well, I managed to trip and sprain an ankle and, of course, she said she had changed the spell because she didn't want to spoil my pretty face."

Halsted laughed and said, "You don't really act disturbed at this, Mr. Anderssen. After all, this sort of playacting by a young and vivacious woman isn't unusual. Personally, I find it charming. Why don't you?"

Anderssen said, "Because she pulled it on me once too often. She did something that I can't understand." He threw himself back in his chair and stared sombrely at the table in front of him.

Trumbull bent to one side as though to look into Anderssen's eyes and said, "You mean you think she really is a witch?"

"I don't know what to think. I just can't explain what she did."

Avalon said, forcibly, "Mr. Anderssen, I must ask you to

explain just what it was that Mrs. Anderssen did. Would you do that, sir?"

"Well," said Anderssen, "maybe I should. If I talk about it, maybe I can forget it.—But I don't think so."

He brooded a bit and the Widowers waited patiently.

Finally, he said, "It was just about a month ago—the sixteenth. We were going out for dinner, just the two of us. We do that once in a while, and we like to try new places. We were trying a new place this time, the door to which was reached by passing through the lobby of a small midtown hotel. It was an unpretentious restaurant, but we had had good reports of it.—The trouble started in the lobby.

"I don't remember exactly what set it off. In fact, I don't even remember what it was all about, really. What happened afterward pushed it out of my mind. What it amounted to was that we had a—a disagreement. In less than a minute, we would have been inside the restaurant and studying the menu, and instead, we were standing to one side of the lobby, under a plastic potted plant of some sort. I can remember the sharply pointed leaves touching my hand disagreeably when I waved it to make a point. The registration desk was across the way, between the door to the restaurant and the door to the street. The scene is still painted in my mind.

"Helen was saying, 'If that's your attitude, we don't have to have dinner together.'

"I swear to all of you, I don't remember what my attitude was, but we're both of us highly vocal, and we were both of us furious, I admit. The whole thing was highly embarrassing. It was one of those times when you and someone else—usually your wife or girlfriend, I suppose—are shouting at each other in whispers. The words are being squeezed out between clenched teeth, and every once in a while one of you says, 'For Heaven's sake, people are staring,' and the other says, 'Then shut up and listen to reason,' and the first one says, 'You're the one who isn't listening,' and it just keeps on and on."

Anderssen shook his head at the memory. "It was the

most intense argument we had ever had up to that time, or since, and yet I can't remember what it was about. Unbelievable!

"Then she suddenly said, 'Well, then, I'm going home. Good-bye.' I said, 'Don't you dare humiliate me by leaving me in public.' And she said, 'You can't stop me.' And I said, 'Don't tempt me, or I *will* stop you.' And she said, 'Just try,' and dashed into the restaurant.

"That caught me by surprise. I had thought she would try to get past me to the door to the street—and I was ready to seize her wrist and hang on. It would have been better to let her go than to make a scene, I suppose, but I was past reason. In any case, she fooled me, and made a dash for the restaurant.

"I was stunned for a moment—two moments—and then I hurried in after her. I may have been twenty seconds behind her.—Let me describe the restaurant. It was not a large one, and it had the deliberate decor of a living room. In fact, the restaurant is called The Living Room.—Are any of you acquainted with it?"

There was a blank murmur about the table, but Henry, who had cleared the dishes with his usual unobtrusive efficiency and was standing by the sideboard, said, "Yes, sir. It is, as you say, a small but well-run restaurant."

"It had about a dozen tables," Anderssen proceeded, "the largest of which would hold six. There were windows with drapes, but not real windows. They had city views painted on them. There was a fireplace in the wall opposite the entrance door with artificial logs in it, and a couch facing it. The couch was real and, I suppose, could be used by people who were waiting for the rest of their party to arrive. At least, there was one man sitting on the left end of the couch. He had his back to me, and was reading a magazine that he held rather high and close to his head as though he were nearsighted. I judged from its typography that it was *Time*—"

Avalon put in suddenly, "You seem to be a good observer

and you are going into minutiae. Is this important that you've just told us?"

"No," said Anderssen, "I suppose not, but I am trying to impress on you that I was not hysterical and that I was entirely myself and saw everything there was to see quite clearly. When I came in, about half the tables were taken, with two to four people at each. There may have been fifteen to twenty people present. There were no waitresses on the scene at the moment and the cashier was stationed just outside the restaurant, to one side of the door in a rather unobtrusive recess, so it really did look like a living room."

Drake stubbed out his cigarette. "It sounds like an idyllic place. What was present there that disturbed you?"

"Nothing was present that disturbed me. That's the point. It was what was absent there. Helen wasn't there.—Look, she had gone in. I saw her go in. I am *not* mistaken. There was no other door on that side of the lobby. There was no crowd within which she might have been lost to view for a moment. My vision was entirely unobstructed and she went in and did not come out. I followed in her tracks and entered, at the most, twenty seconds after her—maybe less, but not more. And she was not there. I could tell that at a glance."

Trumbull growled. "You can't tell anything at a glance. A glance will fool you."

"Not in this case," said Anderssen. "Mario mentioned Helen's hair. There's just nothing like it. At least I've seen nothing like it. There may have been, at most, ten women there and not one had red hair. Even if one of them had been a redhead, I doubt she would have been a redhead in quite the fluorescent and lavishly spectacular way that Helen was. Take my word for it. I looked right—left, and there was no Helen. She had disappeared."

"Gone out to the street by another entrance, I suppose," said Halsted.

Anderssen shook his head. "There was no entrance to the street. I checked with the cashier afterward, and with the fellow at the registration desk. I've gone back there since to order lunch and managed to look over the place. There isn't any entrance to the outside. What's more, the windows are fakes and they're solid something-or-other. They don't open. There are ventilation ducts, of course, but they're not big enough for a rabbit to crawl through."

Avalon said, "Even though the windows are fake, you mentioned drapes. She might have been standing behind one of them."

"No," said Anderssen, "the drapes hug the wall. There would have been an obvious bump if she were behind one. What's more, they only came down to the bottom of the window and there are two feet of bare wall beneath them. She would have been visible to mid-thigh if she were standing behind one."

"What about the ladies' room?" inquired Rubin. "You know, so strong is the taboo against violating the one-sex nature of these things, we tend to forget the one we don't use is even there."

"Well, I didn't," said Anderssen, with clear exasperation. "I looked around for it, didn't see any indication, and when I asked later, it turned out that both rest rooms were in the lobby. A waitress did show up while I was looking around and I said to her in, I suppose, a rather distracted voice, 'Did a redheaded woman just come in here?'

"The waitress looked at me in a rather alarmed way, and mumbled, 'I didn't see anyone,' and hastened to deliver her tray load to one of the tables.

"I hesitated because I was conscious of my embarrassing position, but I saw no way out. I raised my voice and said, 'Has anyone here seen a redheaded woman come in just a moment ago?' There was dead silence. Everyone looked up at me, staring stupidly. Even the man on the couch turned his head to look at me and he shook his head at me in a clear negative. The others didn't even do that much, but their vacant stares were clear enough indication that they hadn't seen her.

"Then it occurred to me that the waitress must have emerged from the kitchen. For a minute, I was sure that

Helen was hiding there and I felt triumphant. Regardless of the fact that my actions might induce some of the staff to call hotel security, or the police, even, I marched firmly through a pair of swinging doors into the kitchen. There was the chef there, a couple of assistants, and another waitress. No Helen. There was one small further door which might have been a private lavatory for the kitchen staff, and I had gone too far to back down. I walked over and flung the door open. It *was* a lavatory, and it was empty. By then the chef and his assistants were shouting at me, and I said, 'Sorry,' and left quickly. I didn't see any closets there large enough to hold a human being.

"I stepped back into the restaurant. Everyone was still looking at me, and I could do nothing but return to the lobby. It was as though the instant Helen had passed through the doorway into the restaurant, she had vanished."

Anderssen sat back, spread his hands in blank despair. "Just vanished."

Drake said, "What did you do?"

Anderssen said, "I went out and talked to the cashier. She had been away from her station for a few moments and she hadn't even seen me go in, let alone Helen. She told me about the rest rooms and that there was no exit to the street.

"Then I went to talk to the room clerk, which demoralized me further. He was busy and I had to wait. I wanted to yell, 'This is a matter of life and death,' but I was beginning to think I would be carried off to an asylum if I didn't behave in a totally proper way. And when I spoke to him, the room clerk turned out to be a total zero, though what could I really have expected from him?"

"And then what did you do?" asked Drake.

"I waited in the lobby for about half an hour. I thought Helen might show up again; that she had been playing some practical joke and that she would return. Well, no Helen. I could only spend my time fantasizing, as I waited, of calling the police, of hiring a private detective, of personally scouring the city, but you know—What do I tell the police? That my wife has been missing for an hour? That my wife vanished under my eyes? And I don't know any private detectives. For that matter, I don't know how to scour a city. So, after the most miserable half hour of my whole life, I did the only thing there was to do. I hailed a taxi and went home.''

Avalon said, solemnly, "I trust, Mr. Anderssen, that you are not going to tell us your wife has been missing ever since.''

Gonzalo said, "She can't be, Jeff. I saw her two days ago.''

Anderssen said, "She was waiting for me when I got home. For a minute, a wave of intense thankfulness swept over me. It had been a terrible taxi ride. All I could think of was that she would have to be missing twenty-four hours before I could call the police and how would I live through the twenty-four hours? And what would the police be able to do?

"So I just grabbed her and held on to her. I was on the point of weeping, I was so glad to see her. And then, of course, I pushed her away and said, 'Where the hell have you been?'

"She said, coolly, 'I told you I was going home.'

"I said, 'But you ran into the restaurant.'

"She said, 'And then I went home. You don't suppose I needed a broomstick, do you? That's quite old-fashioned. I just—pfft—and I was home.' She made a sweeping motion of her right hand.

"I was furious. I had gotten completely over my relief. I said, 'Do you know what you've put me through? Can you imagine how I felt? I rushed in like a damn fool and tried to find you and then I just stood around.—I almost went to the police.'

"She grew calmer and icier and said, 'Well, it serves you right for what you did. Besides, I *told* you I was going home. There was no need for you to do anything at all but go home, too. Here I am. Just because you refuse to believe I have the power is no reason for you to begin scolding me, when I did exactly what I told you I would do.'

"I said, 'Come on, now. You didn't *pfft* here. Where were you in the restaurant? How did you get here?'

"I could get no answer from her on that. Nor have I been able to since. It's ruining my life. I *resent* her having put me through an hour of hell. I *resent* her making a fool of me."

Avalon said, "Is the marriage breaking up as a result? Surely, you need not allow one incident—"

"No, it's not breaking up. In fact, she's been sweet as apple pie ever since that evening. She hasn't pulled a single witch trick, but it bothers the dickens out of me. I brood about it. I *dream* about it. It's given her a kind of—superiority—"

Rubin said, "She's got the upper hand now, you mean."

"Yes," said Anderssen, violently. "She's made a fool of me and gotten away with it. I *know* she's not a witch. I *know* there are no such things as witches. But I don't know how she did it, and I've got this sneaking suspicion she's liable to do it again, and it keeps me—it keeps me—*under*."

Anderssen then shook his head and said, in a more composed way, "It's such a silly thing, but it's poisoning my life."

Again there was silence about the table, and then Avalon said, "Mr. Anderssen, we of the Black Widowers are firm disbelievers in the supernatural. Are you telling us the truth about the incident?"

Anderssen said, fiercely, "I assure you I have told you the truth. If you have a Bible here, I'll swear on it. Or, which is better as far as I am concerned, I'll give you my word as an honest man that everything I've told you is as completely true as my memory and my human fallibility will allow."

Avalon nodded. "I accept your word without reservation."

Gonzalo said, in an aggrieved way, "You might have told me, John. As I said, I saw Helen two days ago, and nothing seemed wrong to me. I had no idea—Maybe it's not too late for us to help."

"How?" said Anderssen. "How could you help?"

Gonzalo said, "We might discuss the matter. Some of us may have some ideas."

Rubin said, "I have one, and, I think, a very logical one. I begin by agreeing with Anderssen and everyone else here that there is no witchcraft and that, therefore, Mrs. Anderssen is no witch. I think she went into the restaurant and somehow managed to evade her husband's eyes. Then when he was busy in the kitchen or at the registration desk, she left the restaurant and the hotel quickly, took a taxi, went home, and then waited for him. Now she won't admit what it is she has done in order to stay one-up in this needless marriage combat. My own feeling is that a marriage is useless if—"

"Never mind the homilies," said Anderssen, the shortness of his temper fuse showing. "Of *course* that's what happened. I don't need you to explain it to me. But you skip over the hard part. You say she went into the restaurant and 'somehow managed to evade her husband's eyes.' Would you please tell me just how she managed that trick?"

"Very well," said Rubin. "I will. You came in, looked right and left, and were at once certain she wasn't there. Why? Because you were looking for an unmistakable redhead.—Have you ever heard of a wig, Mr. Anderssen?"

"A *wig?* You mean she put on a *wig?*"

"Why not? If she appeared to have brown hair, your eyes would pass right over her. In fact, I suspect that her red hair is so much the most important thing you see in her that if she were wearing a brown wig and had taken a seat at one of the tables, you could have been staring right at her face without recognizing it."

Anderssen said, "I insist I would have recognized her even so, but that point is of no importance. The important thing is that Helen has never owned a wig. For her to use one is unthinkable. She is as aware of her red hair as everyone else is, and she is vain about it, and wouldn't dream of hiding it. Such vanity is natural. I'm sure everyone here is vain about his intelligence."

Rubin said, "I grant you. Intelligence is something to be

vain about. Yet, if it served some purpose that seemed important to me, I would pretend to be an idiot for a few minutes, or even considerably longer. I think your wife would have been willing to slip on a brown wig just long enough to escape your eye. Vanity is never an absolute in anyone who isn't an outright fool."

Anderssen said, "I know her better than you do, and I say she wouldn't wear a wig. Besides, I told you this was a month ago. It was the height of summer and it was a hot evening. All Helen was wearing was a summer dress with only summer underwear beneath, and she had a light shawl to put on against the air conditioning. She was holding a small pocketbook, just large enough to contain some money and her makeup. There was nowhere she could have hidden a wig. She had no wig with her. Why should she have brought one with her, anyway? I can't and won't believe that she was deliberately planning to have a fight, and to trick me in this way in order to achieve a long-term upper hand. She's a creature of impulse, I tell you, and is incapable of making plans of that kind. I *know* her."

Trumbull said, "Conceding her vanity and impulsiveness, what about her dignity? Would she have been willing to duck under one of the tables and let the tablecloth hide her?"

"The tablecloths did not come down to the ground. I would have seen her.——I tell you I've gone back to the restaurant and studied it in cold blood. There is *nowhere* she could have hidden. I was even desperate enough to wonder if she could have worked her way up the chimney, but the fireplace isn't real and isn't attached to one."

Drake said, "Anyone have any other ideas? I don't."

There was silence.

Drake turned half about in his chair. "Do you have anything to volunteer, Henry?"

Henry said, with a small smile, "Well, Dr. Drake, I have a certain reluctance to spoil Mrs. Anderssen's fun."

"Spoil her fun?" said Anderssen in astonishment. "Are you telling me, waiter, that you know what happened?"

Henry said, "I know what might easily have happened, sir, that would account for the disappearance without the need for any sort of witchcraft and I assume, therefore, that that was, indeed, what happened."

"What was it, then?"

"Let me be certain I understand one point. When you asked the people in the restaurant if they had seen a redheaded woman enter, the man on the couch turned around and shook his head in the negative. Is that right?"

"Yes, he did. I remember it well. He was the only one who really responded."

"But you said the fireplace was at the wall opposite the door into the restaurant and that the couch faced it, so that the man had his back to you. He had to turn around to look at you. That means his back was also to the door, and he was reading a magazine. Of all the people there, he was least likely to see someone enter the door, yet he was the one person to take the trouble to indicate he had seen no one. Why should he have?"

"What has all that got to do with it, waiter?" said Anderssen.

"Call him Henry," muttered Gonzalo.

Henry said, "I would suggest that Mrs. Anderssen hurried in and took her seat on the couch, an ordinary and perfectly natural action that would have attracted no attention from a group of people engaged in dining and in conversation, even despite her red hair."

"But I would have seen her as soon as I came in," said Anderssen. "The back of the couch only reaches a person's shoulders and Helen is a tall woman. Her hair would have blazed out at me."

"On a chair," said Henry, "it is difficult to do anything but sit. On a couch, however, one can lie down."

Anderssen said, "There was a man already sitting on the couch."

"Even so," said Henry. "Your wife, acting on impulse, as you say she is apt to do, reclined. Suppose you were on a couch, and an attractive redhead, with a fine figure, dressed in a skimpy summer costume, suddenly stretched out and placed her head in your lap; and that, as she did so, she raised her finger imploringly to her mouth, pleading for silence. It seems to me there would be very few men who wouldn't oblige a lady under those circumstances."

Anderssen's lips tightened. "Well—"

"You said the man was holding his magazine high, as though he were nearsighted, but might that not be because he was holding it high enough to avoid the woman's head in his lap? And then, in his eagerness to oblige a lady, would he not turn his head and unnecessarily emphasize that he hadn't seen her?"

Anderssen rose. "Right! I'll go home right now and have it out with her."

"If I may suggest, sir," said Henry. "I would not do that."

"I sure will. Why not?"

"In the interest of family harmony, it might be well if you would let her have her victory. I imagine she rather regrets it and is not likely to repeat it. You said she has been very well behaved this last month. Isn't it enough that you know in your heart how it was done so that you needn't feel defeated yourself? It would be her victory without your defeat and you would have the best of both worlds."

Slowly, Anderssen sat down and, amid a light patter of applause from the Black Widowers, said, "You may be right, Henry."

"I think I am," said Henry.

Afterword

Actually, I dreamed this one.

I don't often remember my dreams since, actually, I attach no importance to them whatever. (In this, I differ from my dear wife, Janet, who is a psychiatrist and psychoanalyst, and considers them to be important guides to what makes a person tick. She may be right, of course.)

Anyway, even when I do remember my dreams, they seem remarkably uninteresting since they almost never contain any element of fantasy or imagination. It's as though I use up the entire supply in my writing business, leaving nothing over for dreams.

In one dream, however, I followed someone into a dining room and found he had unaccountably disappeared. I was quite astonished, for, as I said, even in my dreams I don't usually defy the laws of nature. A search through the room finally located the person I was looking for in the place where the heroine of the preceding story had hidden.

I stared at him and said (so help me), "What a terrific idea for a Black Widowers story."

Fortunately I woke at that moment and, for once, the dream was fresh in my mind. Thereupon I stored the notion in my waking memory and on the next occasion, I wrote the story and it appeared in the October 1984 issue of *EQMM*.

I can't help but think that if I could dream all my gimmicks, life would be a lot easier.

The Wrong House

The guest at the monthly banquet of the Black Widowers frowned at the routine question asked him by that best of all waiters, Henry.

"No," he said, vehemently. "Nothing! Nothing!—No, not even ginger ale. I'll just have a glass of water, if you don't mind."

He turned away, disturbed. He had been introduced as Christopher Levan. He was a bit below average height, slim, and well-dressed. His skull was mostly bald but was so well-shaped that the condition seemed attractive rather than otherwise.

He was talking to Mario Gonzalo and returned to the thread of his conversation with an apparent effort, saying, "The art of cartooning seems simple. I have seen books that show you how to draw familiar shapes and forms, starting with an oval, let us say, then modifying it in successive stages till it becomes Popeye or Snoopy or Dick Tracy. And yet how does one decide what oval to make and what modifications to add in the first place? Besides, it is not easy to copy. No matter how simple the steps seem to be, when I try to follow them, the end result is distorted and amateurish."

Gonzalo looked, with a certain complacency, at the cartoon he had just drawn of the guest, and said, "You have to allow for a kind of inborn talent and for years of experience, Mr. Levan."

"I suppose so, and yet you didn't draw any oval with modifications. You simply drew that head freehand as quickly as you could and without any effort as far as I could tell.—Except that somehow my head looks shiny. Is it?"

"Not particularly. That's just cartoonist's license."

"Except that," said Emmanuel Rubin, drawing near with a drink in his hand, "if licenses were required for cartooning, Mario would never qualify. Some may have talent, but Mario gets by with effrontery."

Gonzalo grinned. "He means chutzpah. Manny knows about that. He writes stories which he actually submits to editors."

"And sells," said Rubin.

"An indication of occasional editorial desperation."

Levan smiled. "When I hear two people spar like that, I am certain that there is actually a profound affection between them."

"Oh, God," said Rubin, visibly revolted. His sparse beard bristled and his eyes, magnified through the thick lenses of his glasses, glared.

"You've hit it, Mr. Levan," said Gonzalo. "Manny would give me the shirt off his back if no one were looking. The only thing he wouldn't give me is a kind word."

Geoffrey Avalon, the host of this banquet, called out, "Are you getting tangled up in some nonsense between Manny and Mario, Chris?"

"Voluntarily, Jeff," said Levan. "I like these bouts with pillows and padded bats."

"It gets wearisome," said Avalon, staring down from his seventy-four-inch height, "past the fifty-seven thousandth time.—But come and sit down, Chris. We are having nothing less good than lobster tonight."

It is not to be denied that an elaborate lobster dinner tends to inhibit conversation a bit. The cracking of shells takes considerable concentration and the dipping into drawn butter is not a matter to be carried through casually. The period between the Portuguese fish chowder and the *coupe aux marrons* was largely silent, therefore, as far as the human voice was concerned, though the nutcracking play kept the table at a low growl.

"I despise lobster salad," said Roger Halsted over the coffee. "It's like eating seedless watermelon cut into cubes. The worth of the prize is directly proportional to the pains taken to win it."

Levan said, "I suppose, then, you would be very much against interest-free loans," and he chuckled with a sated air.

"Well," said James Drake, in his hoarsely muted voice, "I imagine even Roger would consider that as carrying a principle too far."

Thomas Trumbull fixed Levan with a glowering eye. "That's a banker's joke. Are you a banker?"

"One moment, Tom," said Avalon. "You're beginning to grill and the grilling session has not yet been opened."

"Well, then, open it, Jeff. We're on our coffee, and Henry is going to come around with the brandy in a millisecond." Trumbull looked at his watch. "And the lobster has delayed us, so let's go."

"I was about to begin," said Avalon, with dignity. He tapped his glass three or four times. "Tom, since you are so anxious, won't you begin the grilling."

"Certainly," said Trumbull. "Mr. Levan, are you a banker?"

"That is not the traditional opener," said Gonzalo.

Trumbull said, "Who asked you? What you're thinking of is traditional; it's not mandatory.—Mr. Levan, are you a banker?"

"Yes, I am. At least, I'm the vice president of a bank."

"Hah," said Trumbull. "*Now* I'll ask you the traditional opener. Mr. Levan, how do you justify your existence?"

Levan's smile became a beam. "Easiest thing in the world. The human body is completely dependent on blood circulation, which is driven by the heart. The world economy is completely dependent on money circulation, which is driven by the banks. I do my bit."

"Are the banks motivated in this by a desire for the good of the world or for the profits of their owners?"

Levan said, "Socialist claptrap, if you don't mind my saying so. You imply that the two motives are mutually exclusive, and that is not so. The heart drives the blood into the aorta and the first arteries to branch off are the coronaries, which feed what? The heart! In short, the heart's first care is for the heart, and that is as it should be, for without the heart all else fails. Let the coronaries get choked up and you'll find yourself agreeing with the heart, and wishing it were anything else that was on short rations."

"Not the brain," said Drake. "Sooner the heart. Better die of a heart attack than live on in senility."

Levan thought a bit. "That's hard to disagree with, but we may treat and reverse senility a lot sooner than we are likely to be able to treat and reverse death."

Gonzalo, frowning, said, "Come on, what's this subject we've latched on to? And on a full stomach, too. Hey, Tom, may I ask a question?"

Trumbull said, "All right. Subject changed. Ask a question, Mario, but don't make it a dumb one."

Gonzalo said, "Mr. Levan, are you a member of Alcoholics Anonymous?"

There was a sudden silence about the table and then Trumbull, face twisted in anger, growled, "I *said,* don't make it—"

"It's a legitimate question," insisted Gonzalo, raising his voice, "and the rules of the game are that the guest must answer."

Levan, not smiling, and looking grim rather than embarrassed, said, "I'll answer the question. I am *not* a member of Alcoholics Anonymous, and I am not an alcoholic."

"Are you a teetotaler, then?"

For some reason, Levan seemed to find more difficulty answering that. "Well, no. I drink on occasion—a bit. Not much."

Gonzalo leaned back in his chair and frowned.

Avalon said, "May we change the subject once again and try to find something more civilized to discuss?"

"No, wait a while," said Gonzalo. "There's something funny here and I'm not through. Mr. Levan, you refused a drink. I was talking to you at the time. I watched you."

"Yes, I did," said Levan. "What's wrong with that?"

"Nothing," said Gonzalo, "but you refused it angrily.—Henry!"

"Yes, Mr. Gonzalo," said Henry at once, momentarily suspending his brandy-pouring operation.

"Wasn't there something funny about Mr. Levan's refusal?"

"Mr. Levan was a bit forceful, I believe. I would not undertake to say that it was 'funny.'"

"Why was it forceful, do you think?"

"There could be—"

Drake interrupted. "This is the damndest grilling session I can remember. Bad taste all around. Whom are we grilling, anyway? Mr. Levan or Henry?"

"I agree," said Rubin, nodding his head vigorously. "Come on, Jeff, you're the host. Make a ruling and get us on track."

Avalon stared at his water glass, then said, "Gentlemen, Christopher Levan is a vice president of the largest bank in Merion. In fact, he is my personal banker, and I know him socially. I have seen him drink in moderation but I have never seen him drunk. I did not hear him refuse a drink, but somehow I'm curious. Chris, *did* you refuse a drink forcefully? If so, why?"

Levan frowned, and said, "I'm on the edge of resenting this."

"Please don't, Chris," said Avalon. "I explained the rules when you accepted my invitation, and I gave you a chance to back out. Nothing said here goes beyond the walls. Even if you were to tell us you were absconding with bank funds, we would be unable to tell anyone that—though I'm sure we would all urge you quite forcibly to abandon your intention."

"I am not an absconder, and I resent being forced to make that statement. I don't take this kindly of you, Jeff."

"This *has* gone far enough," said Halsted. "Let's end the session."

"Wait," said Gonzalo, stubbornly, "I want an answer to my question."

"I *told* you," said Levan. "I merely refused—"

"Not my question to you, Mr. Levan. My question to Henry. Henry, *why* did Mr. Levan refuse the drink so vehemently? If you don't answer, this session might end prematurely, and that would be the first time it did so, at least during *my* membership in the club."

Henry said, "I can only guess, sir, from what little knowledge of human nature I have. It may be that Mr. Levan, although ordinarily a moderate drinker, refused a drink this time, because in the near past he had suffered keen embarrassment or humiliation through drink, and, for a time at least, would rather not drink again."

Levan had whitened distinctly. *"How did you know that, waiter?"*

Gonzalo grinned with proprietary pride. "His name is Henry, Mr. Levan. He's an artist, too. The rest of us draw the ovals, and he adds the modifications and produces the final picture.

The mood of the table had changed subtly. Even Trumbull seemed to soften, and there was an almost wheedling quality to his voice. "Mr. Levan, if something has happened that has left a lasting effect, it might help you to talk about it."

Levan looked about the table. Every eye was fixed on him. He said in half a mutter, "The waiter—Henry—is quite right. I made a total fool of myself and, right now, I firmly intend never to drink again. Jeff told you he's never seen me drunk. Well, he never has, but he's not always around. Once in a long while I do manage to get high. Nothing in particular ever came of it until two weeks ago, and then—it hardly bears thinking of."

He frowned in thought, and said, "It might help if I *did* tell you. You might be able to suggest something I can do. So far, the only one I've told is my wife."

"I imagine she's furious," said Halsted.

"No, she's not. My first wife would have been. She *was* a teetotaler, but she's dead now, rest her soul. My children would have been sardonically amused, I think, but they're in college, both of them. My present wife, my second, is a worldly woman, though, who is not easily shaken by such things. She has a career of her own; in real estate, I believe. She has grown children, too. We married for companionship—and out of affection—but not in order to impose on each other. The world doesn't crash about her ears if I get drunk. She just gives me good practical advice and that ends it."

"But what happened?" asked Avalon.

"Well—I live on a rather exclusive street—four houses. They're very nice houses, not extraordinarily large, but well-designed and comfortable: three bedrooms, a television room, three baths, finished cellar, finished attic, all-electric (which is expensive), backyards stretching to the creek, ample space between the houses, too. All four were put up by one contractor at one time about a dozen years ago. They're all identical in appearance and plan, and they were sold on ironclad condition that they be kept identical. We can't paint our house another color, or put on aluminun siding, or add a sun porch unless all four house owners agree to do the same. Well, you can't get agreement ever, as you can well imagine, so there have been no changes."

"Is that legal?" asked Halsted.

"I don't know," said Levan, "but we all agreed."

"Can you make changes inside?" asked Gonzalo.

"Of course. We don't have standardized furniture or wallpaper or anything like that. The agreement concerns only the appearance from the outside. The houses are called the Four Sisters. Right, Jeff?"

Avalon nodded.

Levan went on. "Anyway, I was out for the evening. I

192

had warned Emma—my wife—that I might not be back till three in the morning. I didn't seriously intend to stay out that late, but I felt I might, because—well, it was one of those college reunions and at fifty-five, there's this wild urge for *one* evening to be twenty-two again. It never really works, I suppose.

"I even thought I could carry my liquor, but by midnight I was pretty well smashed. I didn't think I was, but I must have been, because I can't carry my liquor well, and because several of the others tried to persuade me to go home. I didn't want to and I seem to remember offering to knock one of them down." He rubbed his eyes fiercely, as though trying to wipe out the mental image.

Drake said, dryly, "Not the thing for a bank vice president?"

"We're human, too," said Levan, wearily, "but it doesn't help the image.—Anyway, in the end, two or three of them helped me out to a car and drove me out to Merion. When they found the street in question, I insisted they let me out on the corner. You see I didn't want to wake the neighbors. It was a noisy car, or I thought it was.

"They did let me out on the corner; they were glad to get rid of me, I imagine. I realized I wasn't going to get anywhere much trying to fumble my key into the lock. Besides I knew a better trick. There's a side door that I was pretty sure would be open. There's no crime in our section to speak of—no burglaries—and the side door is never closed during the day. Half the time, it's not closed at night, either.

"So I made my way to it. I felt my way along the side of the house and found the door. It was open, as I thought it would be. I tiptoed in as quietly as I could, considering my condition, and closed it behind me just as quietly. I was in a small anteroom mostly used for hanging up clothes, keeping umbrellas and rubbers, and so on. I just made my way around the umbrella stand and sank into a chair.

"By that time, I was feeling rather dizzy and very tired. The dark was soothing, and I liked the feel of the soft old padding under me. I think I would have gone to sleep right then, and might not have been found by Emma until morning, except that I became woozily aware of a dim light under the door that led to the kitchen.

"Was Emma awake? Was she having a midnight snack? I was too far gone to try to reason anything out, but it seemed to me that my only chance of not embarrassing her, and myself, was to walk in casually and pretend I was sober. I was drunk enough to think I could do that.

"I got up very carefully, made my way to the door with some difficulty, flung it open, and said, in a loud, cherry voice, 'I'm home, dear, I'm home.'

"I must have filled the air with an alcoholic fragrance that explained my condition exactly, even if my behavior had been perfectly sober, which I'm sure it wasn't.

"However, it was all for nothing, because Emma wasn't there. There were two *men* there. Somehow I knew at once they weren't burglars. They *belonged* there. Drunk as I was, I could tell that. And I knew—my God, I *knew* that I was in the wrong house. I had been too drunk to get to the right one.

"And there on the table was a large suitcase, open, and stuffed with hundred-dollar bills. Some of the stacks were on the table, and I stared at them with a vague astonishment.

"I don't know how I could tell, gentlemen. Modern techniques can produce some damned good imitations, but I've been a banker for thirty years. I don't have to look at bills to know they're counterfeit. I can smell counterfeit, feel it, just know it by the radiations. I might be too drunk to tell my house from another house, but as long as I am conscious at all, I am not too drunk to tell a real hundred-dollar bill from a fake one.

"I had interrupted two crooks, that's what it amounted to. They had neglected to lock the side door or just didn't know it was open, and I knew that I was in a dangerous situation."

Levan shook his head, then went on. "They might have

killed me, if I had been sober, even though they would then have had all the trouble of having to get rid of the body and of perhaps rousing police activity in an undesirable way. But I was drunk, and clearly on the point of collapse. I even think I heard someone say in a kind of hoarse whisper, "He's dead drunk. Just put him outside." It might even have been a woman's voice, but I was too far gone to tell. In fact, I don't remember anything else for a while. I *did* collapse.

"The next thing I knew I was feeling a lamppost and trying to get up. Then I realized I *wasn't* trying to get up. Someone was trying to lift me. *Then* I realized it was Emma, in a bathrobe. She had found me.

"She got me into the house somehow. Fortunately, there was no one else about. There was no indication before or since that anyone had seen me lying in the gutter, or seen Emma having to drag me home.—Remember your promise of confidentiality, gentlemen. And I hope that includes the waiter."

Avalon said, emphatically, "It does, Chris."

"She managed to get me undressed," said Levan, "and washed, and put me to bed without asking me any questions, at least as far as I can remember. She's a terrific woman. I woke in the morning with, as you might suspect, a king-sized headache, and a sense of relief that it was Sunday morning and that I was not expected to be at work.

"After breakfast, which was just a soft-boiled egg for me, and several quarts of orange juice, it seemed, Emma finally asked me what had happened. 'Nothing much,' I said. 'I must have had a little too much to drink, and they brought me home and left me at the corner and I didn't quite make it to the house.' I smiled weakly, hoping she would find the understatement amusing, and let it go at that.

"But Emma just looked at me thoughtfully—she's a very practical woman, you know, and wasn't going to act tragic over my being drunk for the first and only time in her acquaintanceship with me—and said, 'A funny thing happened.'

" 'What?' I asked.

" 'Someone called me,' she said. 'It was after midnight. Someone called and said, "Your husband is outside drunk or hurt. You'd better go and get him." I thought it was some practical joke, or a ruse to get me to open the door. Still I thought if it was true and you were in trouble, I would have to risk it. I took your banker-of-the-year award with me, just in case I had to use it to hit somebody, went out in the street, and found you.—Now who could have called me? They didn't say who they were.'

"She stared at me, frowning, puzzled, and my memory stirred. My face must have given me away at once, because Emma—who's a penetrating woman—said at once, 'What happened last night? What are you remembering?'

"So I told her and when I had finished she looked at me with a troubled expression, and said, 'That's impossible. There can't be any counterfeiting in this block.'

" 'Yes,' I said, 'I'm sure there is. Or at least someone in one of the other three houses is involved in it, even if the counterfeiting isn't actually taking place on the premises.'

" 'Well, which house were you in?' she wanted to know. But how could I tell? I didn't know.

" 'Which house did you find me outside?' I asked.

" '*Our* house,' she said.

" 'Well, then, they just took me outside and put me in front of our house. That means they knew which house I belonged to. It's one of our neighbors.'

" 'It can't be,' she kept repeating.

"But that's the way it is, just the same. I haven't the faintest idea which wrong house I'd gotten into, and I don't know who is involved in counterfeiting. And I can't report it."

"Why not?" asked Gonzalo.

"Because I would have to explain that I was falling-down drunk. How else could I account for the fuzziness of the information?" said Levan. "I don't want to do that. I don't want to look like a fool or a drunken idiot and, frankly, I don't want to lose my job. The story would be bound to get out and it wouldn't look good at the bank.

"Besides, what would the police do? Search all three houses? They would find nothing, and three householders, two of whom would be completely innocent, would be outraged. We would have to sell our house and leave. Life would become unbearable, otherwise.

"Emma pointed all this out carefully. In fact, she said, there would be a strong presumption that I had fantasied it all; that I was having d.t.'s. I'd be ruined. Emma's a bright woman, and persuasive.

"Yet it eats at me. Counterfeiting! That's the banker's nightmare; it's *the* crime. I had stumbled onto something that might be big and I could do nothing about it.—I haven't touched a drink since, and I don't intend ever to, and that's why I was a bit vehement when Henry asked me, for the second time, if I would have one."

There was a silence about the table for a time, and then Avalon, drumming his fingers lightly on the tablecloth, said, "I know where you live, Chris, but I don't know your neighbors. Who are they? What do they do?"

Levan shrugged. "All well on in years. All in their fifties and beyond. Not a small child on the street. And all beyond suspicion, damn them.—Let's see, if you're facing the front of the four houses, the one on the left holds the Nash couple. He's an insurance agent, and she's arthritic; a nice lady, but a terrible bore. She's the kind you say hello to when you pass her, but keep on walking. The merest hesitation would be fatal.

"The second house holds the Johnstones. He's in his seventies and she's perhaps two or three years younger. He's retired and they're supposed to be quite wealthy, but they don't bank in our bank and I have no personal knowledge of the matter. They sort of shuttle between Maine in the summer and Florida in the winter, but they have a bachelor son, about forty, who stays in the house year-round and is not employed.

"The third house is ours, and the fourth belongs to two

sisters, one a Mrs. Widner and the other a Mrs. Chambers. Both are widows and they seem to cling to each other for warmth. They're in their fifties and very wide awake. I'm astonished they weren't aware of my being picked up at the lamppost. They're light sleepers and have a sixth sense for local catastrophe.

"Across the street, there are no houses but only a large lawn and a stand of trees belonging to the Presbyterian Church which is a distance off.—That's it."

He looked about helplessly, and Rubin cleared his throat. "If we go by probabilities, the obvious choice is the bachelor son. He has the house to himself for a couple of months at a time and has nothing to do but work at his counterfeiting, with or without the knowledge of his parents. If the Johnstones are mysteriously wealthy, that may be why. I'm astonished you overlook this."

"You wouldn't be if you knew the boy," said Levan. "Even though he's middle-aged, it's hard to think of him as a man. He's boyish in appearance and attitude, and without being actually retarded in any way, is clearly unequipped to make his way in the world."

"He's capable enough," said Rubin, "to take care of the house for a couple of months at a time."

"He's not retarded, " repeated Levan, impatiently. "He's emotionally immature, that's all. Naive. And good-hearted in the extreme. It's impossible to think of him being involved in crime."

Rubin said, "It might be that he's acting. Perhaps he's clever enough to appear incredibly naive so as to hide the fact that, actually, he is a criminal."

Levan pondered. "I just can't believe that. No one could be *that* good an actor."

"If he *were* innocent and childlike," said Rubin, "it might make it all the easier for him to be used by criminals. He might be an unwitting pawn."

"That doesn't make sense to me. They couldn't trust him; he'd give it away."

"Well," said Rubin, "however much you doubt it, that

seems to me to be the most reasonable possibility, and if you want to do a little investigating on your own, you had better take a closer look at young Johnstone." He sat back and folded his arms.

Halsted said, "What about the two men with the suitcase? Had you ever seen them before?"

Levan said, "I wasn't at my best, of course, but at the time it seemed to me they were strangers. They were certainly not members of any of the households.

Halsted said, "If they were outside associates of the counterfeiting ring, we might be reasonably sure that the two widows weren't involved. They'd be reluctant to have men in the house, it seems to me."

"I'm not sure about that," said Levan. "They're feisty ladies and they're not old maids. Men are no new experience to them. Still, I agree; I don't see them as gun molls, so to speak."

"And yet," said Drake, thoughtfully, "there may have been at least one woman present. Didn't you say, Mr. Levan, that someone said, 'He's dead drunk. Just put him outside,' and that it was a woman?"

Levan said, "It was a whisper, and I couldn't tell for sure. It might have been a woman, but it might have been a man, too. And even if it were a woman, it might have been another outsider."

Drake said, "I should think someone who belonged there would have to be on the spot. The house wouldn't be abandoned to outsiders, and there's at least one woman in each house."

"Not really," said Halsted. "Not in the Johnstone house, since the old folks should be away in Maine now. If we eliminate the widows, then that leaves the house on the left corner, the Nash house. Then, if Mr. Levan were let off on the corner, and was so under the weather he had difficulty walking, it would be likely that he would go into the first house he came to and that would be the Nashes', wouldn't it?"

Levan nodded. "Yes, it would, but I can't remember that

that's what I did.—So what's the use? However much we argue and reason, I have nothing with which to go to the police. It's just guesswork."

Trumbull said, "Surely these people don't live in their houses by themselves. Don't they have servants?"

Levan said, "The widows have a live-in woman-of-all-work."

"Ah," said Trumbull.

"But that doesn't strike me as significant. It just means three women in the house instead of two; a third widow, as a matter of fact, and quite downtrodden by the sisters. She has no more brains than is necessary to do the housework, from what little I know of her. She's impossible as a criminal conspirator."

"I think you're entirely too ready to dismiss people as impossible," said Trumbull. "Any other servants?"

Levan said, "The Nashes have a cook, who comes in for the day. The Johnstones have a handyman who works mainly in the yards, and helps the rest of us when he has time. Emma and I don't have any servants in the house. Emma is strong and efficient and she dragoons me into helping her—which is only right, I suppose. She doesn't believe in servants. She says they destroy privacy and never do things right anyway, and I agree with her. Still, I do wish we could have someone to do the vacuuming besides myself."

Trumbull said, with a trace of impatience, "Well, the vacuuming is not an issue. What about the Nash cook and the Johnstone handyman?"

"The cook has five children at home, with the oldest in charge, according to the Nashes, and if she has spare time for criminality I think she should get a medal. The handyman is so deeply religious that it is ludicrous to think of him as breaking the commandment against theft."

"Sanctimoniousness can easily be assumed as a cloak," said Trumbull.

"I see no signs of it in this case."

"You don't suspect him?"

Levan shook his head.

"Do you suspect anyone?"

Levan shook his head.

Gonzalo said, suddenly, "What about whoever it was who called your wife to tell her you were outside in the gutter? Did she recognize the voice?"

Levan shook his head emphatically. "She couldn't have. It was just a whisper."

"Is that just your judgment, or does she say so?"

"She would have told me at once if she had recognized it."

"Was it the same whisper you heard in the house?"

Levan said, impatiently, "She heard one and I heard the other. How can we compare?"

"Was the voice your wife heard that of a woman?"

"Emma never said. I doubt that she could tell. She said she thought it might be a way of getting her to open the door, so maybe it seemed to her to be a man. I don't know."

Gonzalo seemed annoyed, and said rather sharply, "Maybe there's no one to suspect. You may think you can sense counterfeit money, but how do you know you can do so when you're totally sozzled? It could be you saw real money and there's no counterfeiting going on at all."

"No," said Levan, emphatically, "and even if that were so, what would two strangers be doing with a suitcase of hundred-dollar bills? New ones. I could smell the ink. Even if it weren't counterfeiting, there would have to be some sort of crime."

Gonzalo said, "Maybe the whole thing—"

He let it trail off, and Levan said, flushing a little, "—is a pink elephant? You think I imagined it all?"

"Isn't that possible? If there's no one to suspect, if no one could be involved, maybe nothing really happened."

"No," said Levan. "I know what I saw."

"Well, what did you see?" said Drake suddenly, peering at Levan through the smoke of his cigarette. "You were in the kitchen. You saw the wallpaper, if any, the color scheme, the fixtures. The kitchen details aren't identical, are they? You can walk into each house and then identify which kitchen you were in, can't you?"

Levan flushed, "I wish I could. The truth is, I saw nothing. There were just the two men, the suitcase on the table, and the money. It occupied all my attention, and I can't even really describe the suitcase." He added, defensively, "I was not myself. I was—was—And besides, after fifteen or thirty seconds, I had passed out. I just don't know where I was."

Avalon, looking troubled, said, "What are you doing about it, Chris? Are you doing any investigating on your own? That might be dangerous, you know."

"I know," said Levan, "and I'm not an investigator. Emma, who has more common sense in her left thumb than I have in my whole body, said that if I tried to do any questioning or poking about for clues, I would not only make a fool of myself, but I might get into trouble with the police. She said I had better just alert the bank to be on the lookout for bogus hundred-dollar bills and investigate those, when they came in, by the usual methods. Of course, no hundred-dollar bills are coming in. I don't suppose the counterfeiters will pass them in this area."

Gonzalo said, discontentedly, "Then we haven't gotten anywhere and that's frustrating.—Henry, can you add anything to all this?"

Henry, who was standing at the sideboard, said, "There is a question I might ask, if permitted."

"Go ahead," said Levan at once.

"Mr. Levan, you said, earlier, that your wife has a career of her own in real estate, but you said, 'I believe.' Aren't you sure?"

Levan looked startled, then laughed. "Well, we married five years ago, when we had each been single for quite a while, and were each used to independence. We try to interfere with each other as little as possible. Actually, I'm sure she *is* engaged in real estate, but I don't ask questions and she doesn't. It's one of these modern marriages; worlds different from my first."

Henry nodded and was silent.

"Well," said Gonzalo, impatiently. "What do you have in mind, Henry? Don't hang back."

Henry looked disturbed. "Mr. Levan," he said, softly, "when you entered the house by the side door and closed it behind you, you were then in the dark, I believe."

"I certainly was, Henry."

"You circled an umbrella stand. How did you know it was an umbrella stand?"

"After I sat down, I happened to feel it. If it wasn't an umbrella stand, it was something just like it."

Henry nodded. "But you circled it before you felt it, and you dropped into a chair in the dark with relief, and enjoyed feeling the soft padding, you said."

"Yes."

"Mr. Levan," said Henry. "The houses were alike in every particular on the outside, but were free to vary on the inside, you said, and presumably they all did so vary. Yet in your not-quite-sober state, you managed to dodge the umbrella stand and drop into a chair. You did not bump into one or miss the other. You did not have the slightest idea you were in the wrong house at the time, did you?"

"No, I didn't," said Levan, looking alarmed. "It was only when I opened the kitchen door and saw the men—"

"Exactly, sir. You expected to find the arrangement of objects as it was in your own house, and you found that to be so. When you sat in the chair, which you must have thought was your own, you felt nothing to disabuse yourself of the notion."

"Oh, my God," said Levan.

"Mr. Levan," said Henry, "I think you must have been in your own house after all. Drunk as you were, you found your way home."

"Oh, my God," said Levan, again.

"You were not expected till much later, so you caught your wife by surprise. In your modern marriage, you clearly didn't know enough about her. Yet she did show affection for you. She did not allow you to be harmed. She had you carried out, and then came to get you with an invented story about a phone call. By then the men and the suitcase had gone and since then she has worked very hard to keep you from telling the story to the police or doing anything about it.—I'm afraid that's the only explanation that fits what you have told us."

For a moment, there was an absolute silence over the horrified group.

Levan said, in a small voice, "But what do I do?"

And Henry said, sorrowfully, "I don't know, Mr. Levan.—But I wish you had not refused that drink."

Afterword

By the time I had sold the preceding story, I found that I had ten stories toward a new Black Widowers collection, and of those ten, only one, "The Driver," had failed to sell.

As it happened, in my first Black Widowers collection, *Tales of the Black Widowers,* I had nine stories that had appeared in print and three stories that had not. Those stories that had not previously been published were involuntarily in that condition. I would gladly have stuck Fred with them if I had been able to.

Once the book appeared, however, it seemed to me that it had worked out properly. Many of those who bought the book might well have been *EQMM* subscribers and would have read each of the Black Widowers when it appeared in the magazine. Even allowing that their tolerance and kind hearts would allow them to read each again with pleasure, it did seem the decent thing to give them three stories they couldn't possibly have read before.

In the collections that followed the first, my record was better, and in each case (including this one) I reached the number-ten mark with only one failure to sell. In each case, therefore, I wrote two more stories that I did not submit anywhere, but saved for the collection.

And so it is now. The story you have just read, "The Wrong House," and the one that follows, "The Intrusion," were each written specifically for this collection, and have not appeared elsewhere.

The Intrusion

From the expression on the face of Mario Gonzalo, it might seem that there was something singularly unsatisfactory about this particular banquet of the Black Widowers.

There was nothing apparent to account for that. The dinner, which revolved about a main course of roast duck, smothered in dark cherries and underpinned by wild rice, with the skin delightfully crisp and the meat tender and moist, was perfection. The sausage in pasta that had preceded and the generous chocolate parfait that had succeeded represented the calories-be-damned attitude of Roger Halsted, who was hosting the evening. Now the Black Widowers sat over their brandy, grilling their guest, with all in a state of satisfactory repletion.

The weather outside was delightful, and the guest was an intelligent and articulate person whose personality fit the general aura of the society. Even the terrible-tempered Thomas Trumbull was agreeable and the argumentative Emmanuel Rubin disputed nothing in any voice that was a decibel louder than that of ordinary conversation.

The guest's name was Haskell Pritchard and he was a civil servant. It had already been established that he was in charge of solid waste disposal and some traces of merriment at the start over his perhaps having to drive a garbage truck vanished under the undoubted seriousness of the problem.

"The fact is," Pritchard had said, "that we are running out of places to put the waste and we're going to need some innovative ideas on the matter."

Rubin said, a bit sardonically, "The waste, sir, was once

raw material, and that raw material came from somewhere, certainly not from within this city. Wherever it came from it left a hole, whether you call that hole a mine or a quarry or whatever. Why not put the waste back in the hole it came from?"

"Actually," said Pritchard, "this has been thought of. There are indeed abandoned mines, quarries and other such things in the countryside and there have been attempts to negotiate their use as dumps. However, it can't be done. People are willing to sell raw materials but are not willing to accept the residue after the consumer is done with it—even if we pay both times, once for taking and once for returning."

Geoffrey Avalon said, "It's a common sociological phenomenon. Everyone is in favor of cracking down on crime and sending criminals to jail, but nobody wants to spend money on building more jails to hold those criminals and, even more so, nobody wants any new jail built in his neighborhood."

Halsted said, "I don't see the relevance of that, Jeff."

"Don't you?" Avalon's eyebrows rose. "I should think it was obvious. I am speaking of the general ability of the public to recognize a problem and to want to solve it, but to balk at any personal inconvenience involved in a solution. Might I also say that it is delightful, after a good dinner, to be discussing, in a more or less detached manner, problems that affect the public weal, with no personal puzzle involved. I take it, Mr. Pritchard, that your work, or your life, for that matter, does not at the moment involve some conundrum that is robbing you of sleep and peace of mind?"

Pritchard looked surprised. "I can't think of anything, Mr. Avalon. Ought I to have come here with something of the sort, Roger?"

"Not at all, Haskell," said Halsted. "It's just that sometimes we *are* faced with a riddle, but I find it relaxing not to have one."

"I don't," said Gonzalo, with energy, revealing his

reason for dissatisfaction, "and I hope I never do. I think all of you are getting too old, and I also think that if Mr. Pritchard thinks hard he can come up with *something* interesting."

Halsted bridled at once, and said, with the soft stutter that invaded his voice whenever he was indignant or excited, "If you're trying to say, Mario, that my guest is dull—"

James Drake interposed. "Come on, Roger. Mario just wants a puzzle.—But think a moment, Mario; shouldn't Henry have a rest at a banquet now and then?"

"Sure," said Mario, "and just serve the dishes and take away the empty plates and get us water and drinks and anything else we ask for. He's having a great rest."

Henry, that perfection of a waiter, without whom the Black Widowers were unthinkable, stood by the sideboard, and, at Gonzalo's words, a small smile played briefly over his unlined, sixtyish face.

Avalon said, "Suppose we have a vote on the matter, with the host's permission. I move we be permitted, now and then, to have a banquet in which there is nothing more than civilized conversation."

Halsted said, "All in favor of Jeff's motion—"

And it was even as the hands began to go up (minus Gonzalo's) that there came about something that marked an utterly unprecedented event in the history of the banquets of the Black Widowers. There was a violent intrusion of an uninvited person into their midst.

There was, to begin with, the sound of a scuffle on the stairs, some vague shouting, a muffled cry of "Please, mister, please—"

The Black Widowers froze—astonished—and then a young man broke into the room.

He was slightly disheveled, and he was breathing hard. He looked from face to face and behind him a waiter said, "I couldn't stop him, gentlemen. Shall I call the police?"

"No," said Halsted, who, as host, automatically took the initiative. "We'll handle it.—What do you want, young man?"

The intruder said, "Are you guys the Black Widowers?"

Halsted said, "This is a private party. Please leave."

The intruder raised a hand, placatingly. "I'll leave in a minute. I ain't here to eat nothing. But is this the place where the Black Widowers meet and are you the guys?"

Avalon, his voice as baritone as he could make it, said, "We are the Black Widowers, sir. What is it you want?"

"Well, you help guys, don't you?"

"No, we do not. As you have been told, this is a private meeting and we have no other purpose but to meet."

The intruder looked baffled. "They told me you guys figure out things. I have a problem." Suddenly, he did not look in the least formidable. He was of medium height, with thick dark hair, dark eyes, and dark eyebrows, and he was rather handsome. He seemed to be in his mid-twenties and, beneath a rather theatrical affectation of toughness, there was a touch of loss and confusion. He said, "They told me you could help me—with my problem."

His shirt collar was open and his Adam's apple, quite visible, moved up and down. He said, "I could pay—something."

Gonzalo said, joyously, "What's your problem?"

Trumbull snarled, *"Mario."* He turned to the intruder. "What's your name?"

"Frank Russo," said the intruder, defiantly, as though expecting someone to object to the designation.

"And where did you hear we solve problems?"

Russo said, "I just heard. It don't matter where, does it? Other guys who eat with you talk, and it goes from one to another. So I asked and found out you eat here at the Milano, a good *paesano* restaurant—if you got the dough for it—and you were gonna be there tonight, and I thought, what the hell, if you help other people, maybe you can help me."

Rubin, looking combative, said, "Yes, but just who told you where and when we would be meeting?"

Russo said, "If you don't like people should talk about you, then I'm telling you *I* won't. The way you're gonna know I won't is I ain't gonna talk about the guy who told me about you."

Drake muttered, "That sounds fair enough to me."

"Now if you don't want to help me," said Russo, "I'll leave. After that, though, if I hear people say you help out, I'll deny it."

There was silence at that, and then Russo said, with an authentic note of pleading in his voice, "Can I at least *tell* you what's bugging me?"

Halsted said, "What's the consensus? Anyone in favor of listening to Russo raise his hand." He raised his, and Gonzalo's hand shot up vigorously.

Drake said, "Well, listening can't hurt," and raised his.

Halsted waited, but the hands of Avalon, Trumbull, and Rubin remained resolutely down. Halsted said, "Three to three. I'm sorry, Haskell, I can see that you're itching to raise your hand, but you're not a Widower.—Henry, would you break the tie?"

Henry said, "Well, Mr. Halsted, if you insist, then my own feeling is that when the Widowers are evenly balanced on some point, the preference should be given to the merciful. It is hard to turn away someone in trouble." And he raised his hand.

Halsted said, "Good. Could you bring a chair, Henry, and put it near the door for the young man?—Sit down, Russo."

Russo sat down, put his hands on his knees, and looked about anxiously. Now that he had made his point, he seemed to be uneasy at the surroundings he found himself in.

Halsted said, "Haskell, we're going to have to interrupt your grilling to take care of Mr. Russo, if we can. I hope you don't mind."

"On the contrary," said Pritchard. "I wanted to vote in favor of the young man, as you suspected, and I'm glad the waiter tipped the vote in his favor, though I thought only members could vote."

"Henry *is* a member.—And now, Jim, would you do the honors?"

Drake stubbed out his cigarette. "Young man," he said, "ordinarily, I'd begin by asking you to justify your existence, but you are not a guest of ours and that question therefore doesn't apply. You can just tell us what your problem is, but I must warn you, that any of us can interrupt at any time to ask a question, and that Henry, our waiter, can do so, too. In return, you must answer all questions truthfully and fully, and you must understand that we cannot guarantee that we'll be able to help you."

"Okay, that suits me. I'm gonna tell you the story, but you gotta promise it don't go outside this room."

Drake said, "I assure you that nothing that goes on in this room is ever spoken of by the Black Widowers outside, although it does seem that at least one of our guests did not adhere to this rule."

"Okay, then." Russo closed his eyes a moment as though deciding where to begin. Then he said, firmly, "I got a sister who just turned eighteen."

"What's her name?" said Gonzalo.

"I'm gonna tell you," said Russo, "even if you didn't ask because that's part of the problem. Her name is Susan. All her life I called her Suzy, but she's got it in her mind she wants to be called Susan and that's what I call her now.

"She's my kid sister. I'm twenty-four and I been taking care of her for six years now—ever since our ma died."

"Have you got a job?" asked Avalon.

"Course I got a job," said Russo, indignantly. "What kind of a question is that? How could I be taking care of her without a job. I been driving a truck for a brewery since I was fifteen and two years ago I got a supervising job. I ain't rich, but I make decent money and I can pay you guys— some."

Avalon looked uncomfortable. "There is no question of payment, sir. Just go on with your story. Is your father also dead?"

Russo said, "I don't know where my father is. I don't

care, either. He's gone." His arm made a final, dismissive gesture. "*I* take care of Susan.—The thing is Susan ain't—bright."

Drake said, "Do you mean she's retarded?"

"She's not mental. Don't think *that*. She's just not bright. People could take advantage of her and there ain't much she could do in the way of a job."

"With special educational care—" began Avalon.

Russo's face twisted. "What's the use of saying that? I ain't got money for that."

Avalon reddened and muttered, "There's the sociological problem again. People recognize the need and say they want a solution, but if it's a question of public funds, the taxpayer buttons his pocket."

Russo said, "She cooks. She takes care of the place. She can go shopping, and the guys around the neighborhood know about her and they make sure nothing happens to her. Any of them step out of line, he'll be taken care of."

His fist clenched and a steely look came into his eyes. "They're all careful, you bet, but it's something I've been getting more and more worried about. She's the best-natured kid in the world, always willing to help, always smiling. She takes care of herself real good, and the thing is, she's getting to be very nice-looking. It's something to worry about, you know what I mean?"

Drake said, "We know what you mean. Does she like men?"

"Sure she does. She likes everybody, but she don't know about that sort of thing. She don't read and nobody talks dirty to her, you can bet on that. But these days, you gotta be careful about what movies she sees; it's getting so, you even gotta be careful about television, you know what I mean? Besides, any guy wants something, she'd go along, she's so good-natured, you know what I mean?"

Drake said, "Do you have a girlfriend of your own?"

Russo said, quickly, "What's that supposed to mean? You think I'm queer?"

"I'm asking if you have a girlfriend of your own?"

"Course I do."

"Does she know about Susan?"

"Course she does. And when we get hitched, she knows we gotta continue taking care of Susan. And she's willing. She sits with her evenings when I gotta be away. Like now."

Avalon cleared his throat and said, as delicately as he could, "Have you ever thought that, with an operation, she might be—"

Russo clearly had thought of that, for he did not allow the sentence to be finished. "We ain't gonna cut her up."

Gonzalo said, "Have you talked to your priest?"

Russo said, "Nah. I know what he'll say. He'll just say to keep on doing what we're doing and to trust in God."

Gonzalo said, "She might make a good nun."

"No, she don't have the call. And I'm not gonna be making her a nun just to get rid of her. I don't wanna get rid of her, see."

Rubin said, "Do you expect she'll get married some day?"

Russo said, defiantly, "Could be. She'd make a good wife; a lot better wife than most I see around. She's good-natured, hardworking, clean." He hesitated. "Course, whoever marries her's gotta understand she's not—smart, and he'd have to take care of her because anyone could take advantage of her, if you know what I mean. And he'd have to take that into account if anyone does, and not take it out on her."

"What if she has children?"

"What if she does? She'd take good care of them. And they wouldn't have to be like her. I'm not. My ma wasn't."

Trumbull suddenly clanged his spoon against his water glass. There was silence and Trumbull said, "Gentlemen, this is all very well, but Mr. Russo is wasting our time. What is his problem? There's nothing we can do about his sister, if that's his problem. If he's come to ask us for advice about what to do with her now that she's eighteen, it seems to me that what I would say would be the same as the priest might say, to keep on doing what he's doing and trust in God.—I move we end this matter now."

"Hey, hold on," said Russo, anxiously. "I ain't told you my problem yet. All this stuff so far is just to explain."

Halsted said, "Well, then, Mr. Russo, I think we understand about your sister. Would you tell us your problem now?"

Russo cleared his throat and there was a moment of silence as he seemed once again to be choosing among alternate beginnings.

He said, "Two weeks ago, on the tenth, my sister was picked up."

"By the police?" asked Gonzalo.

"No, by some guy. No one from the neighborhood. I don't know who the guy ws. I was at work, of course, and Susan, she went out to do some shopping. She got strict instructions never to talk to anybody she don't know. Never. But I guess she musta this time. I did a lot of asking around in the neighborhood these last two weeks. Everybody knows Susan and they were all upset, and from what one guy says and what another guy says, what it looks like is that she was talking to some tall, skinny guy, good-looking kind of, but no one can swear to exactly what he looked like, except maybe he had blond hair. I said how come they let something like that go on—her talking to a strange guy. They all said they thought it was some friend because they figured Susan wouldn't talk to a stranger.

"He took her off in an automobile and when I got home from work, she was still gone, and I can tell you I went crazy. I ran all around the neighborhood and I had all the guys going all over." He shook his head. "I don't know what I would of done, if she hadn't come home."

Trumbull said, "Then she *did* come home?"

"Just about when it was getting dark. Whoever it was, he had put her on a commuter train and she got off at the right station, thank goodness, and she knew enough to take a taxi. She had money. She still had her train-ticket stub and I think she came from Larchmont in Westchester."

"Was she all right?" asked Gonzalo.

Russo nodded his head. "She wasn't hurt. I sort of managed not to say anything at the time, but the next day I stayed home from work, making out I was sick, and I got her to tell me everything that happened. I *had* to know.

"Well, she met this guy and he talked to her, and he got around her, you know. She said he was very handsome and talked nice and bought her an ice-cream soda, and asked if she wanted a drive in his car and it was a very pretty car. Well, she couldn't resist; she's always agreeable to everything anyway. I figure he's one of these guys from somewhere fancy who comes into a poor neighborhood to pick up something easy for cheap. This time he picked up something easy for nothing—except an ice-cream soda."

Avalon began, "Did he—"

Russo cut him off at once. "Yeah. He did."

"How do you know?"

"Because Susan told me. She didn't know what it was all about, and she told me. The dirty—" He checked himself, then said, furiously, "He *had* to know she didn't know what it was all about. He *had* to know she wasn't—smart. It was like taking advantage of a little kid."

Avalon began. "If she had had the proper instruction—" caught Russo's furious eye, halted, and looked the other way.

Rubin said, "How did your sister feel about it?"

"She thought it was great. That's the worst part. She'll want to do it again. She'll *suggest* it to guys."

"No," said Rubin, "that's not the worst part. Is she pregnant?"

"Watch your language," said Russo, tightly.

Rubin raised his eyebrows. "Let me rephrase that. Is she in the family way?"

"No, thank God. She isn't. She had her—time—since then. She's all right that way."

Trumbull said, "Well, then, Mr. Russo, what's your problem?"

Russo said, "I want to find the guy."

Avalon said, "Why?"

"I want to teach him a lesson."

Avalon shook his head. "If you're thinking of killing him, we can't be a party to that. As it happens, your sister is over eighteen, and she was not taken over a state line. She was not hurt, or impreg— or put in a family way. She went along willingly and had a good time, and he can always claim he had no idea she was retar— not responsible. I don't think he can be charged with kidnapping. She was returned promptly and there were no ransom demands. In fact, I don't think he can easily be charged with any crime at all."

Russo said, "That's why I'm not going to the police. I couldn't anyway, even if I could nail him with a crime. I can't let people know what happened to Susan. It would be a disgrace to her and to me. And if the guys know she's not a—not a—you know what I mean, they won't have no respect for her. They might figure, well, as long as it's gone, what's one more.

"So I gotta find him. I ain't gonna kill him, but I just want to explain to him that it wasn't nice what he did, and since I probably ain't got his education and I can't explain it in fancy words, I'd like to use a different kind of language. Listen, he's liable to do this to other people's sisters or daughters and maybe, just maybe, if I rearrange his face a little so it ain't so pretty, it won't be so easy for him next time."

Avalon said, "I sympathize with your point of view. I think the man is a cad and it might do him a little good to pay for his intrusion on your life and your sister's—but I fail to see how we can help you find him."

Russo said, "Actually, Susan remembered some things."

"As, for instance."

"She said the guy kept saying, 'Don't worry. Don't worry.' *Course* he would, the dirty bastard. There was nothing for *him* to worry about. He could see she was a nice clean girl and wouldn't give *him* anything; though with his kind of life, he could have given something to *her,* and I don't mean a baby."

Avalon said, "Yes, we understand, but what was it Susan remembered?"

"Well, he said, 'Don't worry. Don't worry,' and then he said, 'See, this is my house, and see what it's called?'"

"What the house is *called?*" asked Gonzalo.

"Yeah. One of those fancy places they have in the suburbs with a name, I guess. You know, a hunk of wood on the lawn with a name on it. That's the kind of guy he is, fancy job, fancy house, fancy family, and when the fancy wife and kids go off to some fancy resort or something, he stays home and goes tomcatting around."

Trumbull said, with visibly mounting impatience, "What was the name of the house?"

"Susan said the house was named for *her*. She said this guy even thought she was a saint."

"What!"

"She said the house was called 'Saint Susan.'"

Halsted said, "Are you sure? Could Susan read that?"

"She can read some, but actually, she said he read it to her. That makes me think maybe it was in fancy writing because one word Susan can make out easy in print is her own name. She says he read the name and it made her a saint. She knows what saints are, so she loved it. She thought he named the house just for her." Russo shook his head sadly. "It's the sort of thing she would think."

Halsted said, "I never heard of a Saint Susan. Is there one?"

"I wouldn't swear there wasn't," said Rubin, "but I never heard of one, either. Did you, Jeff?"

Avalon shook his head.

Gonzalo said, "Why shouldn't a house be called Saint Susan, even if there aren't any on the list? Maybe it was a reference to his wife or his mother."

"You don't go around calling your wife or mother a saint on a board on the lawn," said Rubin.

"It takes all kinds," said Gonzalo.

"There's one more point," said Russo. "He told Susan that the reason he named his house 'Saint Susan' was because of his own name. It wasn't his wife or mother, you see, but his own name. Of course, that tickled Susan, too. It meant the house was named for him *and* for her.—From Susan's reactions to all this and from everything else she must have said, that bum *must* have known she wasn't a— a—whole person. He *had* to know he was doing something terrible. There's just no excuse for him."

Halsted said, "I agree, but is there anything else? Is it just that the house is 'Saint Susan' and that it's from his name? What *is* his name?"

Russo shook his head. "I don't know. Susan can't remember. Susan never remembers names. She knows I'm Frank, but she calls everyone else 'Johnny.' She don't remember the guy's name. Maybe he never told her for all I know."

"That's it, then? Nothing else?"

Russo shook his head again. "That's it. So what do I do? How do I find this guy?"

Gonzalo said, "I'm afraid your sister must have it all wrong. 'Saint Susan' seems silly, and it can't have a connection with the guy. He's not named Susan, I'm sure.— Unless there's a man's name that sounds like Susan."

Drake said, "Sampson? Simpson?"

Gonzalo said, "Saint Sampson? Saint Simpson? Those are worse than Saint Susan."

Pritchard raised his hand. "Gentlemen! Pardon me."

"Yes, Haskell," said Halsted.

"I know I'm not a member of the Black Widowers and can't vote. But can I participate in this discussion?"

"Oh, sure. There was no intention of excluding you."

Pritchard said, "Might Susan not be this fellow's last name? If he lives in Larchmont, you could look up people with that last name in the phone book."

Russo looked disappointed. "I thought of that myself, and I looked up the Larchmont phone book. No last-name Susans there. Course, I could try other towns. He coulda driven Susan to the Larchmont station from some other town."

"Well, let's see now," said Rubin. "Can there be a little more subtlety to it? Susan is a very common name. In fact, I have seen statements that at the present time it is the most common of all feminine names, commoner even than Mary. It dates back to the popular apocryphal book Susanna and the Elders, which was eventually stuck on to the Book of Daniel."

He smirked a bit through his sparse beard and said, "I'm sorry if I sound a bit pedantic. Generally, I leave that sort of thing to you, Jeff, but 'Susanna and the Elders' is generally considered to be the first detective story in Western literature and so it interests me professionally."

Trumbull said, "And does this have any point besides the fact that it interests you?"

"Yes, it does, because Susanna is the English form of the Hebrew name Shoshannah, which happens to mean 'lily.'"

Gonzalo said, "And you claim this guy's name is Lily?"

"His last name," said Rubin coldly, "might be Lily, or Lilly with two l's. Why not?"

Avalon said, "It might be, and if Mr. Russo is fully determined to follow every lead, I suppose he might follow that one. However, I cannot imagine anyone but the most devoted pedant—such as the one you all insist on labelling me as—would, if he wanted to name the house for himself, do so by way of the Hebrew version of the name, just in order to end up with 'Saint Susan.' Surely he might as well name it 'Saint Lily' and have done with it."

"Well," said Halsted, "has anyone else got any ideas?"

There was silence around the table, and Halsted said, "I am sorry, Mr. Russo, but the information you have given us simply isn't enough. Perhaps you had better take the attitude that your sister has not really been harmed and decide that though the incident was deplorable, there is nothing to do now but forget it."

"No," said Russo, stubbornly. "I can't forget it. I'll have to keep looking.—If it takes all my life," he added melodramatically.

He rose. "I'm sorry you can't help me. I'm sorry I busted into your dinner."

"Wait a while," said Gonzalo. "What is this? No one has asked Henry yet."

Halsted said, "I asked if anyone else had any ideas. That includes Henry, doesn't it?—Henry, do I have to ask you specifically?"

Henry looked apologetic. "It is difficult for me, Mr. Halsted, to think of myself as a Black Widower."

"That's very irritating, Henry," said Halsted. "There's not a banquet that passes that we don't tell you that you're a Black Widower."

"And the best one of all," muttered Trumbull.

"So *do* you have a suggestion to make?" asked Halsted.

Henry said, "Not exactly just yet, but I have a question to ask."

"Then go ahead and ask it."

And Russo said, "Well, go ahead, waiter. If you're one of the bunch, go and ask."

"Mr. Russo," said Henry, "you said that your sister doesn't remember names. If you were to suggest a specific name to her, do you suppose she would remember whether that name was that of the man who had carried her off?"

Russo hesitated. "I don't know. You say any name to her, and she might say, 'Yeah, that's the name,' just to be agreeable, you know."

"But suppose I give you three names and you try all three and she picks out one of them and says that's the one and not the other two. Would that be reliable?"

"It might be," said Russo, doubtfully. "I never tried anything like that."

"Can you reach your sister by telephone, Mr. Russo?"

"Yeah. Sure. She's at home right now, with my girl-friend."

"Then call her and ask her if the man's name was Bill. Then ask her if the man's name was Joe. And then ask her if the man's name was Fred."

Russo looked toward the others. Halsted said, "There's a phone over there by the cloakroom." He held up a dime.

Russo said, "I got a dime, thank you." He put it into the slot and dialled. "Hello, Josephine, it's Frank. Listen, is Susan sleeping?—Can you get her to the telephone?—Well, I know, but it's important. Tell her she'll make me happy if she comes to the telephone and it'll only take a minute and then she can go back to the program. Okay?" He waited, and said, "She's watching television.—Hello, Susan, you okay? Yeah, this is Frank. I got to ask you a question. Do you remember the guy who took you for a ride in his car.— Yes, yes, that guy, but don't tell me what he did. I know. I know.—Okay, listen, Susan doll, this guy, was his name Bill?"·

He put his hand over the mouthpiece and said in a hoarse whisper to the Black Widowers generally, "She says maybe. You can't tell from that."

"Try Joe," said Henry in a low voice.

"Susan," said Russo into the phone. "Maybe it was Joe. Do you think it was Joe, honey?"

Again his hand went over the mouthpiece and he shook his head. "She says maybe. She'll say that to anything I try."

Henry said, "Now try Fred."

"Susan," said Russo. "What about Fred? Could it have been Fred?"

There was a pause and then he stared wildly over his shoulder at the Black Widowers. "She's screaming, 'It's Freddie. It's Freddie. That's his name.'" He held the telephone receiver in their direction and the sound of girlish squealing was clear.

"Thanks, Susan," Russo said into the mouthpiece. "You're a good girl. Now go and watch television.—Yes, I'll be home soon."

He hung up the phone and said, "It's Fred all right. That was no 'Maybe' just to be nice. That was jumping up and down. How did you know?"

Henry smiled faintly. "It was just a guess. You see, there

was an eighteenth-century Prussian monarch, named Frederick the Great—"

At this, Avalon started suddenly and said, "Good God, Henry, why do these things occur to you, when I miss them completely."

"I am sure, Mr. Avalon, that given another few minutes of thought, it would have occurred to you, too."

"Hold on," said Russo, frowning, "what *is* all this? What's this Frederick the Great got to do with anything?"

"Well," said Henry, "Frederick was a hardworking monarch who built a small castle in a rural setting to which he could retire once in a while and be relatively free of the cares of the state. It was rather like an American President taking off for Camp David for the weekend. At this castle, Frederick would get together with scholars and writers and indulge in intellectual conversations. He called this castle 'Without Care' or Without Worry.' I thought of that when you described how that man told your sister not to worry and then pointed out the name of his house as though there were a connection."

Russo said, a look of honest bewilderment on his face, "He called his house 'Don't Worry'?"

"Not quite. Frederick the Great, although he ruled a German kingdom, spoke French, and he called his castle by the French phrase meaning 'without care.' He called it *Sans Souci*. I imagine that this man who carried off your sister is named Frederick and that he has had enough of an education to have heard of *Sans Souci* and had the affectation to copy the great Frederick in this respect. I am sure, Mr. Russo, that if you go to Larchmont or the neighboring towns and check the city or town directories for a house by that name owned by someone whose first name is Frederick, you will find it."

Russo said, "Is this real? *San Soo-see?* I never heard of it. But sure, Susan would think it was Saint Suzie. And even if she wants to be called Susan, all her life she's been called Suzie and she would get the two mixed up, and say it was Saint Susan." He looked up grimly, and rubbed his right fist into the palm of his left hand. "I think I'm gonna find this guy."

"You may indeed so," said Henry, "but if you do, may I make a suggestion?"

"Sure."

"We of the Black Widowers can't encourage violence. If it should be that this Frederick is a married man with a respectable position in the community, I would merely discuss the matter with his wife. You will avoid what might be a serious brush with the law, and I think the results would then be far more unpleasant to the man than a bruised face would be."

Russo thought awhile. "Maybe." And he left.

Avalon said, "That was a cruel suggestion, Henry."

"The man had performed a cruel deed," said Henry.

Afterword

Here is another case in which (as in "The Good Samaritan") I have managed to bend the usual formula without doing irrevocable harm to it. After all, by now the Black Widowers have solved no fewer than forty-seven problems and it is not in the least implausible that the word might have gotten out, and that, therefore, something would happen as it did in this story—an intrusion.

And so I say farewell once again, and very reluctantly. There are few stories I write that I enjoy as much as I enjoy my Black Widowers, and having written forty-eight of them altogether has not in the least diminished my pleasure or worn out their welcome to my typing fingers. I can't guarantee that this is true of my readers, but I certainly hope it is.

About the Author

Isaac Asimov is the author of over 300 books on subjects ranging from the Bible to astronomy, math, and Shakespeare. He is the author of I, ROBOT, THE FOUNDATION TRILOGY, FOUNDATION'S EDGE, and, most recently, the bestseller ROBOTS OF DAWN. His previous mystery books include ASIMOV'S MYSTERIES, CASEBOOK OF THE BLACK WIDOWERS, MORE TALES OF THE BLACK WIDOWERS, MURDER AT THE ABA, TALES OF THE BLACK WIDOWERS, THE UNION CLUB MYSTERIES, and A WHIFF OF DEATH.

By the year 2000, 2 out of 3 Americans could be illiterate.

It's true.

Today, 75 million adults...about one American in three, can't read adequately. And by the year 2000, U.S. News & World Report envisions an America with a literacy rate of only 30%.

Before that America comes to be, you can stop it...by joining the fight against illiteracy today.

Call the Coalition for Literacy at toll-free **1-800-228-8813** and volunteer.

**Volunteer
Against Illiteracy.
The only degree you need
is a degree of caring.**

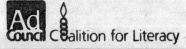

Ad Council   Coalition for Literacy

LV-2